GUERRILLA TACTICS

BOOK 4

ALASKAN SECURITY-TEAM ROGUE

Jemma WESTBROOK

CHAPTER 1

"YOU THINK BOBBY was our only issue?" Dutch sat in one of the chairs crammed into Shawn's small office.

"He was close with Micah." The line of Seth's mouth was grim, pressed thin as he shifted in his seat, eyeing the closed door.

Shawn jotted the information onto a notepad. "Anyone else?"

Seth's eyes dropped to the ground. "No."

The lead for Alpha was clearly struggling with the events of the past twenty-four hours. Made sense considering one of his men was working with the enemy and willing to sacrifice a woman they all loved for his own benefit.

Seth turned toward Dutch. "How's Harlow doing?"

"Her head hurts, but Eli says she'll be fine." Dutch's words were clipped and he didn't look Seth's way.

"That's good." Seth straightened, the line of his jaw setting. "I'll talk to Roman this morning. See if he's picked up anything I missed."

"Do that and get with me as soon as possible." Shawn leaned back, rocking in his chair, trying to work out a little of the aggravation crawling across his skin, making him need to move. "Anyone else have any great ideas about what in the hell we should do about this?"

Gentry, the team lead for Beta raked one hand through his long dark hair. "I don't know how in the hell you think we're going to infiltrate Shadow."

"No one said anything about infiltrating Shadow." Shawn took a slow breath. One of a million he'd taken in the past few days. "This isn't an us against them thing."

"You sure about that?" Dutch was understandably touchy this morning. He was on his way to rip Pierce a new asshole when Shawn caught him and convinced him there was a better, more organized way to handle whatever was going on.

But the first step was finding out what the actual fuck that was.

"I'm sure that going against Shadow won't work out well for any of us." Shawn looked around the men crowding his office. "Without Shadow we're fucked."

"We might be fucked *with* them." Gentry tipped his head toward Dutch. "Shadow might be the reason for what happened last night."

It was a point Shawn couldn't argue. He'd seen the footage team Intel found of Shadow passing Howard Richards over to an unknown group of men. "If Shadow goes down then our whole world comes to a stop. No more get-out-of-jail-free cards. No more body erasing. No more high-level intel. It's all gone." He stared the men down. "So we need to find a way to make sure that's not what happens."

The room was quiet as the gravity of their situation settled around the space.

If Shadow was in bed with the group trying to take down Alaskan Security then they were all fucked.

Or dead.

Dutch stood. "I'm done with this." He turned, pushing his way past the men seated beside and behind him. "I'm going to check on Harlow."

Shawn dipped his head in a nod. "Let me know if there's anything I can do."

Dutch didn't respond, which wasn't surprising. He'd been less than agreeable to keeping their cards close for now.

When the door closed Seth moved in to sit in Dutch's vacated chair. "I feel like shit."

"You couldn't have known." Gentry was obviously feeling more forgiving than Shawn was this morning.

"You need to do an in-depth audit of every man remaining on your team." Shawn pulled up

7

the roster for Alpha, scanning the list of names. "Vet them all. Have Intel run them all. Anything strange comes up, cut them loose."

"Are you doing the same?" Seth eyed Shawn over the paper.

Shawn held his gaze. "I'm not the one who missed the fact that one of his men was trying to take the company down from the inside out."

"Fuck you." Seth's nostrils flared. "You think I don't feel bad enough about what happened?"

"You should feel fucking bad." Shawn fought to keep his voice calm. "Harlow could have been the one headed to the morgue instead of that piece of shit you were in charge of."

Gentry leaned back in his seat. "Come on, man. Cut him a break."

"Cut him a break?" Shawn almost laughed. "You two want to be treated seriously around here but you're asking for a fucking break right now?" He shoved up from his seat. "You think I get a goddamned break when one of my men fucks up?" Shawn leveled his gaze at Seth. "Because I don't."

Seth and Gentry were in a whole new world right now. One with stakes so high they clearly couldn't even see them.

"Go audit your men and come back to me with any potential issues. I'm not risking another life because you think you need a fucking break." Shawn rounded his desk and yanked open the door, holding it wide as he waited for Gentry and Seth to leave.

He was exhausted. Frustrated.

Sick over what might have happened last night to a woman he cared about and was supposed to help protect. He and the rest of Alaskan Security had let Harlow down twice now. Allowing it to happen again wasn't an option, even if meant he had to pull the place apart at the seams.

Shawn started to close his door, needing to find a little quiet before he completely lost his mind.

The door bounced back at him, forcing Shawn to take two steps back to avoid getting hit in the face by the edge.

"I need to talk to you." Heidi marched right in, not waiting for an invitation.

Which wasn't surprising. The woman took what she wanted, when she wanted it. Without reasons.

Without excuses.

"I don't have time to talk to you." He stood by the door, holding it open, hoping Heidi might get the hint.

Knowing it wouldn't matter if she did.

"Of course you do, Shawn." Heidi went around his desk and sat in the large chair he spent too many hours occupying. She wiggled around, eyes widening as she spun it a little in one direction, then the other. "This is nice." Suddenly she dropped forward, head between her knees, bent completely in half.

"What in the hell are you doing?" He forced his gaze away from the position she was in, thighs easily folded to her sides.

Her blonde head bobbed up, blue eyes meeting his. "I'm looking to see what the brand is

9

so I can order one for myself." Her gaze barely dragged over his face. "What's a matter?" She slowly lifted her upper body to a sit before standing. "Didn't realize a thick girl could be so flexible?"

He did realize that, actually.

Knew damn well just how bendable lush curves like Heidi's could be.

"What did you need to talk to me about, Rucker?"

Her brown brows lifted toward the blonde of her hairline. "Oh. Now we're back to last names again?"

"We've always been at last names." Shawn tried to avoid her eyes as she came closer; the slow sway of her full hips tempting him in a way he struggled to resist.

It was par for the course with this woman. Everything involving her was a struggle.

"I don't think so, Shawn." Heidi stopped right in front of him, her ample tits almost brushing against his chest as she breathed. "We started off with first names, remember?"

"That was before I knew how big of a pain in the ass you were." He'd gone to pick her up in Ohio when Harlow was in desperate need of another capable hacker.

It was a mistake.

He should have sent someone else.

Someone who could handle her particular brand of sexual napalm without risking blowing up the whole world.

Her hands came to rest on his chest, fingers splayed wide across the knit fabric of his Alaskan-Security-issued thermal. "I might be a pain in the ass, but I'm a fun pain in the ass." Her head tipped toward his, the pillowy line of her full lips hovering so close he could almost taste them. "Would you like to have fun with me, Shawn?"

"Go back to work, Rucker." Fun was the last thing he would have if he gave in to the woman doing her damndest to break him apart.

He hoped the rejection might work, even though history gave him no reason to believe that.

Heidi was one of the rare women who could read a man like a book. The newest addition to team Intel knew damn well he wanted her, and wasn't afraid to keep pointing it out, even when he swore she was wrong.

The lips he'd imagined curving against every part of his body eased into a smile. One shoulder lifted and fell. "Have it your way then."

He almost let out the breath burning in his lungs. Almost relaxed, knowing she was on her way back to work and far away from him.

But instead of leaving, Heidi pushed up on her toes, shoving those perfectly rounded tits right into him as her lips brushed against his ear. "I didn't expect you to be the kind of man who's scared of a woman who knows what she wants." Heidi inhaled long and soft before lowering to the flats of her feet and backing away. She brushed away a bit of fuzz clinging to his navy shirt. "I'll see you later, scaredy-cat."

That painfully perfect sway of her hips continued to torture him as she walked down the hall, away from his office, on her way back to the large room Intel occupied.

"What did Ms. Rucker need?"

Pierce's voice knocked Shawn out of the stupor Heidi always threw him into. "Uh." He glanced back up to make sure she was out of earshot. "She wants me to order her a new office chair."

Pierce tipped his head in a sharp nod. "Order enough for the entire team." His line of sight followed the path Heidi just traced, eyes lingering on the closed door. "The best you can find."

"Best is relative." Shawn turned to go back into his office.

"Then find out what they want and order it." Pierce hadn't moved from his spot; his attention was still focused on the door to Intel's room.

"I'm not a fucking office manager." He didn't usually give the owner of Alaskan Security shit. They'd known each other long enough Shawn understood Pierce and his usually-noble reasons for the things he did.

But this Shadow thing had Shawn fucked up. Made him question the lengths Pierce was willing to go to make Alaskan Security what he wanted it to be.

"Very well." Pierce straightened the lapels of his jacket and squared his shoulders. "I'm not above doing it myself." His back was straight as a board as he marched down the hall.

It would be worth the show to stay and watch, but chances were good Pierce's visit would end with the entirety of Intel emptying into the hall, chasing the owner of Alaskan Security with any weapon they could find.

And it would send Heidi right back his way.

It'd taken everything he had to resist the most recent offer. Another one so soon after it, especially when he could use the release, would be a disaster.

Not because he didn't want her.

He did.

More than he should.

Which was why he had to find a way to keep shutting Heidi down until she got the point.

He was not the kind of man she should be chasing. Any dalliance they had would end horribly, with her seeing him for what he was.

Shawn closed the door to his office and started pulling names and basic documentation on the members of Alpha and Beta, starting with Micah. He'd seen Micah with Bobby more than a few times, and if Micah was involved then he'd be lucky if he made it out of Alaska and back to the life he came from.

The light knock at his door sent his head into his hand. "What?"

The door opened a small bit, just enough for Mona to poke her head in. "I'm sorry. Am I interrupting you?"

His shoulders relaxed at the sight of Eva's best friend. "Not at all." Shawn shoved his work to one side. "How are you doing?"

Mona saved Harlow's life. Took any lingering suspicions anyone might still have and sent them flying at the speed of a well-placed bullet.

And it made him feel guilty as hell for being one of those who'd had the lingering suspicions up until then.

"I'm okay." Mona didn't make a move to come in, instead staying exactly where she was.

Very unlike another woman he knew.

"Come in." Shawn motioned to one of the chairs left from his earlier meeting.

Mona's eyes bounced to the chairs before coming back to his. "Thanks." She slipped into the office, silently closing the door behind her before easing into one of the seats. "Heidi says you can order us new chairs."

"Heidi says that?" He tipped his head. "Not Pierce?"

Mona's chin lifted. "I don't care what Pierce says."

"I'm sure he'll love that." Shawn rested his elbows on his desk, trying his best to look relaxed and approachable. Mona was nothing like Heidi, and he didn't want her to think his bad mood had anything to do with her. "What kind of chair would you like to have?"

"I really liked the chair I had at Investigative Resources." Mona's mouth moved into a pondering line. "I can't remember what it was, though." Her pale brows lifted. "I could call the office manager we had and see if she remembers."

"See if she wants a job while you're at it." He'd been at Alaskan Security since its inception. Back then everyone carried multiple loads. It's how Dutch ended up being in charge of the technical needs for all four teams.

But now the company was so big that even without the added burden of the newest threat to their livelihood, he was drowning in added tasks. Like ordering the groceries for the break room and the kitchen of the rooming house.

"Does Alaskan Security need an office manager?" Mona perked up a little.

"Alaskan Security could use a lot of things." Shawn grabbed a pen, intending to jot down Mona's need for a chair on his constantly-growing list of things to do.

"I wasn't involved in what happened."

His pen hovered over the paper, the strength in her tone surprising him.

Shawn lifted his eyes to hers. "I know that."

"Do you?" Mona's attention on him didn't flinch. "Because I'm pretty sure you believed I was guilty."

Shawn sat up a little straighter. Maybe he'd underestimated the tiny blonde Pierce had a soft spot for. "That is true. I did think there was a chance you might have been the person feeding information outside Alaskan Security."

Mona's jaw tightened just a little. "Well I wasn't."

"I'm sorry I suspected you." He didn't have anything else to offer her, but the apology was sincere. One more thing to beat himself up over.

"It's fine." Mona's gaze finally dropped, dipping to the hands clasped in her lap. "I'll call Elise and see if she remembers what chair I used before."

"Let me know and I'll order it for you."

"Thank you." Mona stood, her posture perfect as she turned to go to the door. She paused, turning to face him. "I'm supposed to tell you Heidi says hi."

Of course she did.

Because why wouldn't Heidi find one more way to torment him.

To drive him slowly crazy.

Shawn dropped his eyes, dragging the papers across his desk without offering a response. Hopefully Mona passed it along.

Mona stepped out of the door, her soft voice carrying surprisingly well as she walked away.

"Heidi, you're right. He's scared of you."

CHAPTER 2

"WHAT'S WRONG WITH you?" Eva eyed Heidi from where she stood beside Mona's desk.

"Same thing that's always wrong." Heidi stomped across the large room to fall into her uncomfortable chair. "Shawn."

"What's Captain Uptight done now?"

Heidi snorted. "I like that. I think that's what I'll start calling him."

"Make sure you do it to his face." Eva glanced toward the door as Pierce strode through looking like someone shoved a stick right up his ass. "What do you want?"

The owner of Alaskan Security stood even straighter. "It has come to my attention that you would like new chairs. I'm here to find out what you want and to make sure you get it."

Heidi sat silently at her desk. She hadn't been here as long as her two former bosses. That meant Pierce was their problem right now. It was probably the best thing that could happen to him anyway, considering she had nothing nice to say to the man who dragged her here knowing full well one of his teams wasn't playing by the rules.

And if he didn't know then that was a big fucking problem too.

"We're fine." Eva's response was short but definitely not sweet.

Which made Heidi smile.

"Ms. Ayers." Pierce's dark blue eyes moved to Mona. "Is there anything I can do for you?"

Mona held his gaze. "I think you've done more than enough."

Heidi could almost feel the sting as Mona's comment slapped across Pierce's skin.

It was amazing.

She'd known Mona long enough to be impressed as hell at how her former boss was handling herself right now. For years she'd watched Mona try to placate everyone around her, always at her own expense.

Looks like Alaska was bringing out the best in Mona.

"Very well." Pierce tipped his head. "If I can be of any service, please let me know."

None of the women said anything; they all just stared at him.

Finally, Pierce got the picture and turned, his back just as straight going as it was coming.

Heidi leaned to watch him walk down the hall, past Shawn's closed office door and toward the rooming building. "You sure you don't want Pierce to service you, Mona?"

Mona snorted. "I don't know that he can handle servicing me." Her eyes jumped up, wide as they bounced from Eva to Heidi, her skin flushing a bright red. "Did I say that out loud?"

Heidi's head fell back as she laughed. "I think I like the new improved Mona."

Mona blinked a few times. "I don't know how to take that."

"As a compliment." Heidi took one more peek down the hall toward Shawn's office. He'd closed it the second she walked away, thinking it would shut her out.

Wrong.

Heidi turned to Eva and Mona, wiggling around in the horribly uncomfortable chair someone with significantly less ass must have ordered. "Shawn said he could order us chairs."

Eva's brow lifted. "Was that before or after you boned him on his desk?"

Heidi groaned, slumping down in her chair. "I freaking wish." She sucked down a big gulp of the ice water always on her desk. "That man is playing hard to get."

"Maybe he's not playing." Eva shrugged. "Maybe he's just not into you."

"That doesn't even make any sense." Heidi pointed both index fingers at her tits. "Have ya seen my boobs?"

Eva's gaze lowered. "More times than I can count."

"Then you know darn well he's definitely into me." She'd seen the way Shawn looked at her when he thought no one was paying attention. Caught more than a few of his lingering gazes.

"Maybe he doesn't mix work and sex." Mona offered up the most logical explanation. One Heidi had already thought of.

"I should go ask him." She started to stand up from her seat.

"Nope." Eva held one hand up. "Not until we get our chairs."

Heidi turned to her own hatefully uncomfortable seat. The things were probably crafted by the devil himself. "Fine."

"I'll go talk to him." Eva stepped out from behind her desk just as Mona leapt from her chair.

"I'll go." She squared her shoulders in an exaggerated move. "I have something I want to discuss with him anyway."

Heidi shot her a grin and a wink. "Go get him, tiger."

Maybe letting Mona have at him would be more fun anyway. Her former boss had this amazing way of making you feel like complete shit without meaning to.

Hopefully she used that ability on Shawn.

Heidi watched Mona as she went down the hall, tentatively knocking on Shawn's door before peeking her head in. "Damn she's polite."

"Maybe you should try it." Eva wiggled her brows. "That whole catch more flies with honey thing."

"You know that's a lie the patriarchy started to make women more agreeable." Heidi leveled her gaze back to where Eva still stood. "And I'm telling Shawn you called him a fly." She went back to watching Mona as she gracefully slipped through the tiny opening in the door, disappearing into Shawn's office. "And it's not like I'm asking him to be my boyfriend. I'm strictly interested in his bedroom abilities."

"Maybe they suck." Eva turned from where she'd come to watch Mona, heading back to her own desk. "Maybe he's awful at the sex."

Heidi rolled her eyes Eva's way.

That comment didn't even warrant an argument.

The man was too focused. Too obsessed with completing every job assigned to him.

Too much of a perfectionist.

He would definitely approach sex the same way.

It's why her search for a fun partner started and ended with him.

Unfortunately, Shawn was turning out to be much harder to get than she was used to.

Potentially impossible if Eva's suspicion was correct.

What a bummer that would be.

"What about Zeke?"

Heidi's head snapped Eva's way. "Shadow's lead?"

21

Eva shrugged. "Why not?"

"Uh, because his team is one giant douchebag." She'd watched Shadow hand creepy Howard right over to God only knows who.

"I thought you were just looking to get off." Eva eyed her. "Does it really matter what else he does?"

"Eh." Heidi turned back to her computer. "Maybe. I dunno."

Zeke was ginormous. Probably had a big giant wiener too. She tipped her head Eva's way. "You think his dick is too big to do anything with?"

Eva didn't look up from the file in front of her. "Only one way to find out."

"Not if I can get into his medical records." Heidi pulled up the Alaskan Security interface.

"Heidi."

She kept moving through the screens, logging into the secure server.

A stack of sticky notes bounced off the side of her head.

"You can't look at his medical records." Eva used her feet to scoot her rollered chair Heidi's way.

"I'm pretty sure I can." Heidi picked up the stack of pink papers Eva threw her way. "I'm keeping these."

"I know you *can* look at his medical records." Eva snatched her Post-it's back. "I'm saying you shouldn't."

Heidi dropped her hands from the keyboard. "You're right." She grabbed the sleeve of mini doughnuts from the pile of stuff on her desk. "I doubt there's anything in there about his dick size." She opened the plastic wrapper, pulling out a circle of powdery cake just as Mona started back their way, head held high.

Heidi smiled. "Mona looks like she just ripped someone a new asshole."

"She's been doing a lot better." Eva rolled back to her desk. "I'm super proud of her."

"Me too." Heidi was used to being the loudest in every room. The least interested in what anyone else in that same room thought of her. It's why she loved working at Investigative Resources. Eva was a lot like her, and generally didn't balk at the things she said or did like most people.

Unless it involved medical records apparently.

"Shawn says he will order us whatever chairs we want." Mona walked straight to her desk, carefully sitting in her seat before leaning forward to put her head between her knees.

"You did good, Monster." Heidi spun to Eva, pointing at her. "That's what we're calling her from now on."

Mona's head lifted. "Please tell me you're joking."

Heidi shook her head. "Not even a little." She sucked down a little more of the icy water that kept her hydrated and happy. "Come on. Let's go see how Harlow is." Heidi stood up, stainless steel cup in hand.

"Good idea." Eva picked up her own drink and waited while Mona took a few more deep breaths before straightening.

23

"Come on, Monster. You can do it." Heidi waved them toward the door.

"I did do it." Mona tucked her swingy blonde bob behind one ear. "I told Shawn I knew he was one of the ones who thought I was the mole."

Heidi bobbed her head in a nod, walking to Mona with one hand up in the air. "Nice."

Mona slapped her hand in a sturdy high-five. "I only almost puked on his floor once."

"I'm really proud you didn't, but I would have loved to see the look on his face if you did." Heidi could only imagine the panic Shawn would go into at the sight of vomit disturbing the perfect order of his life.

"Maybe he doesn't want to have sex with you because you clearly enjoy torturing him." Eva lifted her brows, giving Heidi a pointed stare.

"Ugh." Heidi dropped her head back. "Fine. I'll try to be nicer to him."

"I'm just saying maybe he wants to be with a woman who doesn't do her best to drive him absolutely crazy."

"I don't want to be with him." Heidi lifted both hands, making a circle with the fingers on one and poking her other pointer through it. "I want to be *with* him."

"Yeah. I got that." Eva tipped her head. "Maybe that's not his jam."

"It's all men's jam." It was a fact she'd used to her benefit many times. Men were always down to fuck. It meant her effort into the arrangement was minimal, leaving plenty of time for more interesting things.

24

Like learning to hack.

It was time well-spent. Certainly was doing more for her than any penis ever did.

Not that they weren't useful in their own way. They just didn't pay off financially the way other things did.

Not that she'd discovered anyway.

Shawn's door was closed as they went past. The itch to knock on it just to interrupt whatever he was doing gnawed at her.

"Don't do it." Eva stepped between her and the door. "I think you need to make him miss your presence."

"Pretty sure that's not what will happen." Heidi hefted out a sigh. "You're probably right. I should leave Captain Uptight alone."

Eva dropped one arm around Mona's shoulder and one arm over Heidi's. "Look at us. We're all growing."

"I don't like it." Heidi shoved her lower lip out in a pout. "Growing sucks."

Mona nodded. "Agreed."

The outdoor barricades were still up as they went through the walkway, the large panels blocking out the view of the property surrounding Alaskan Security's main campus.

According to Harlow there were a few satellite offices scattered across the country that served as home bases for when the teams were on location, which hopefully would be happening again soon.

"Are we going to get to travel with the teams when they go out on location?" Heidi went straight to the kitchen of the rooming house, popping the top of her cup and shoving it against the ice dispenser.

"I don't think so." Mona leaned against the counter. "I think we are always here."

"That sounds boring as hell." Heidi switched the dispenser to water and filled her stainless-steel jug.

"You think this place is boring?" Eva snorted. "I'm not sure I want to be with you when you find something exciting."

Heidi shrugged. "It's not boring." She pressed the lid back into place. "I just didn't realize it was going to be all Alaska, all the time."

"Alaska is actually pretty nice." Eva's eyes moved to the row of windows lining the sitting area of the space. The wood blinds covering them were closed tight, blocking out the view. "When you can go outside and enjoy it."

"You got to enjoy it for all of what," Heidi tried to remember just how long Eva was here before the shit hit the fan, "like five minutes?"

"It was more than that." Eva huffed out a sigh. "Not much though." She backed toward the hall. "Come on. Let's go see if Harlow needs anything."

The women grouped around Harlow's door. Heidi reached out and rapped on the metal plane.

They waited.

Nothing.

"She's not in her room." Dutch came down the hall, a white paper bag in one hand and a drink carrier with four frosty iced coffees shoved into the cardboard holders. "She's in mine." He led the way to his room, swiping his badge across the sensor before opening the door with the hand holding the bag. "Your friends came to check on you, Mowry." Dutch walked in, going straight to the bed where Harlow was propped against the headboard, computer perched on her lap.

She smiled at them. "Thank God."

"I don't get a thank God?" Dutch leaned down to press a kiss to her forehead. "I brought donuts and coffee."

Harlow barely pressed her smile down. "You're awful needy, Pretty Boy."

Dutch tipped her on the chin before backing away. "Don't let her work too hard." He pulled the door open, his eyes lingering on the woman stretched out on his bed, wearing a pair of snowflake pajama pants that were about two sizes too big for her petite frame. "I'll be up in Brock's room if you need anything."

Harlow nodded, her expression soft. "Okay."

Heidi was already on the bed before the door latched. "He brought you four coffees?"

Harlow pulled one free of its holder and passed it Heidi's way. "I'm guessing he knew you'd be here sooner rather than later." She freed the next one and handed it to Eva before offering the other cup to Mona. "He's just trying to lure you in here so I won't get out of bed."

"You think he'll bring us lunch too?" Heidi pulled the bag open and peeked in. "Are these cider donuts?" She reached in. "Holy shit. They're still warm."

Harlow grabbed the cinnamon-scented breakfast treat away. "I get the first one." She held the bag Mona's way. "Mona gets the second."

"What's a girl gotta do to get the first donut?" Heidi snagged one as soon as Mona's hand was clear.

"Shoot a guy." Mona took a bite of her breakfast as the three women turned her way. "What?"

"You're just handling it really well." Eva's eyes swept Mona from head to toe. "You really doing okay?"

Mona's narrow shoulders lifted. "Zeke said if I pulled my gun I had to be willing to use it." Her blue eyes went to Harlow. "I was willing to use it I guess."

Heidi sucked down a mouthful of the frozen coffee Dutch brought. She pointed at Eva. "Do you have a gun too?"

Eva shook her head.

Heidi leaned to Harlow. "I'm guessing you don't have one either or you would have shot that dick yourself."

"Pierce said I should carry one, but they make me nervous."

Heidi settled back, leaning into the headboard as she studied Mona. "Did you just ask Zeke to get you a gun?"

Mona's eyes went wide. "No." She gently sat on the bed beside Harlow's feet. "Pierce suggested it."

"Pierce wanted you to be armed?" Eva came to dig into the bag, grabbing a donut.

Mona's head dipped in a nod. "After he was shot in the walkway."

Heidi sipped at her coffee, eyes moving around the room.

Coming to Alaska was a risk. She knew some shit was going down.

Didn't expect to be in direct danger, though.

"You want a gun?" Heidi directed the question at Eva.

Eva pursed her lips, shifting them from one side to the other. "I think I do."

"Zeke is a really good teacher." Mona sat a little straighter. "He explained everything and made sure I was comfortable with it."

Eva's brows lifted, her eyes on Heidi. "That is good to hear. Isn't it, Heidi?"

"Eh." Heidi shrugged it off. "He'll do in a pinch."

"This is actually a really good idea." Harlow nodded as she spoke. "You guys can snoop around Shadow. See if you can find anything out."

Eva pointed Harlow's way. "Also a good idea." She turned to Heidi. "I vote Heidi is the one who asks him to help us. She's the most likely to get us what we want."

Mona deflated a little. "Why Heidi?"

Eva's pointing finger leveled right at Heidi's chest. "Boobs." She grinned Heidi's way. "It's recently been pointed out to me that they make her irresistible."

Heidi scrunched her face up at Eva. "Kiss my ass, Tatum."

CHAPTER 3

"I THINK WE NEED to confront them." Dutch sat in one of the armchairs in Brock's room. The bag of donuts he brought up sat in the center of the coffee table, the scent of sweet spice tempting Shawn almost as much as the woman one floor below.

"I'm not sure we'll get anywhere." Shawn forced his gaze away from the bag, turning his attention to the men around him. They were his closest friends. The men who walked headfirst into danger beside him. "Zeke doesn't say anything he doesn't intend to."

The team lead of Shadow was about as abrasive as it got. Probably had to be, considering the nature of his team.

"His fucking men handed Richards over on a silver damn platter." Brock leaned forward, wiping both hands down his face. "Eva is scared to death."

Shawn lifted a brow. "Eva is scared?"

"You know what I mean." Brock paused a second. "She's nervous."

"That sounds more on point." Shawn didn't know Eva well, but from what he'd seen on the footage from the night she, Mona, and Harlow were taken, Eva wasn't the kind of woman to cower in fear. "Maybe we go to Pierce. See what he has to say about it."

"You don't think he already knows?" Wade sat on one of the stools lining the small counter in the suite. Parker was balanced on one of his father's knees, smashing a donut across the granite surface.

"I want to think he doesn't know." Shawn shook his head. "But that in itself is a problem. If Shadow is running wild then he will have to do something about it, and I'm not sure we can survive as we are without Shadow's connections."

It was the biggest sticking point of the whole situation. If it was Alpha or Beta it would be a simple solution. Cutting them loose wouldn't really harm Alaskan Security. They might lose a few clients while they rebuilt, but that was currently happening anyway.

"Seth and Gentry are chomping at the bit to get back out in the field." Shawn hoped the other leads would have had some insight to offer him this morning. A more definite idea of who else might be involved.

And who might not.

But it seemed like neither man really had a handle on their team members which was one more problem to be dealt with. Until now it didn't matter so much, but times changed and they changed fast.

"Everyone wants Alpha and Beta out in the field. This place is packed." Brock crossed his arms, sinking down in his seat. "I can't wait to get the hell out of here for a while."

"Everyone wants the hell out of here for a while." Dutch glanced Shawn's way. "Except you."

Shawn gave a little shrug. "Where am I going to go?"

His dad was gone. Any friends he might have had from before had moved on. Built lives filled with wives and kids.

Everything he had was here.

"Maybe you should try to get a hobby." Dutch held both hands up. "Maybe something to do besides work and go to the gym."

"You want me to get a hobby?" Shawn almost laughed. "What in the hell kind of hobby do you see me doing?"

"I don't fucking know." Dutch grabbed another donut. "But you need some sort of outlet." He tipped the donut Shawn's way. "Especially since you decided not to let Heidi have her way with you."

Even a full floor away the woman still found a way to worm into his mind. "She's not what I'm looking for."

"Oh, now you're looking?" Dutch bit off a chunk of donut.

"She's just not a good fit for me." Shawn tried to backtrack. "If I was interested in finding a woman, she wouldn't be it."

"Suit yourself." Dutch dusted the sugar off his fingers. "Not so sure she believes what you're saying, though."

"Doesn't matter what she believes." Shawn stood up, ready to cut this conversation short. If they weren't going to help him figure out what in the hell to do about the bullshit infiltrating Alaskan Security then he was done.

Especially if Heidi was part of the discussion.

She was the last thing he wanted to think about.

See.

Touch.

"I'm going back to work." Shawn walked out of the suite and made his way back to the main hall where his office was. Seth had taken over Harlow's old office with Gentry filling the room between them. Seth was sitting at his desk, a stack of files at one corner. "You got all the information for Intel to get started?"

Seth nodded to the files. "I pulled all their files. I'll take 'em down in a minute." He eyed Shawn. "Unless you don't want to wait that long."

"Do you have something more pressing to handle?" Shawn crossed his arms. The leads for Alpha and Beta weren't used to dealing with the same stakes Shadow and Rogue dealt with on a daily basis. If one of their men fucked up someone got into the wrong car at an event. A fan might manage to get a finger on some celebrity's arm.

No one died.

Seth's gaze slowly lifted to his. "Actually, I do." He straightened in his seat. "I've got to explain to a terrified woman why we can't be there to make sure the lunatic who broke into her house won't get in again." His eyes narrowed on Shawn. "I know you think what we do is bullshit, but it's just as fucking big of a deal as what you do."

Shawn stared Seth down. He and the team lead for Alpha had their differences, but the thought of a client being left high and dry didn't sit well. "Talk to Pierce. Tell him what's going on. He'll find a way to send someone to her." Shawn grabbed the files, backing toward the door. He pointed a finger at Seth. "But you better be confident as hell in whoever you assign to the job."

He didn't wait for Seth to come back at him with another excuse for why his men were just as trustworthy as everyone else's.

The door to Intel's room was open wide. He walked right in, keeping his eyes at the center where Eva was seated. "I've got the files for Alpha for you to start on." He dropped them on her desk, the sight of Heidi's empty desk catching in his peripheral vision. "I'll have Beta's as soon as I can get them."

"Fantastic." Eva took half the stack and passed it to Mona. "We'll get through these as fast as we can manage."

"Don't have to be fast. Just have to be thorough." Shawn turned, ready to get the hell out of the room before the tornado returned.

"You think any of these guys are involved?" Eva lifted the cover on the first file, her eyes dropping to the documents inside.

"I hope to hell they're not." He couldn't begin to guess what might happen to a man caught in that situation.

"We looked into Bobby." Mona grabbed a file from her desk and held it out to him. "Researched all his findable connections. Bank accounts. Everything."

Shawn took the file from her. "Find anything interesting?"

"Howard sent him a big pile of money after Shadow handed him over." Mona folded her hands on the desk in front of her and leaned into them. "It seems like Howard might be the one controlling the payouts."

Shawn flipped open the folder and scanned the top sheet inside. "Cell records?"

Mona nodded, her expression serious. She was still pissed he suspected her, which was fine. He had bigger shit to worry about and unlike Pierce, he was fine with Mona being mad at him.

Shawn held the folder up. "Mind if I borrow this?"

"As long as you bring it back." Eva's gaze locked onto him. "We want to keep this information locked down until we know more of what's going on with Shadow."

"I'm working on that." Shawn went back toward the door, watching the clock.

"So are we."

He turned, catching Eva's smile as he walked out.

They were up to something. Probably nothing good either.

Shawn dropped the file off on his desk before making a stop in Pierce's office. The owner of Alaskan Security was at his desk, computer out, brows wound tightly together.

Any other time Shawn would ask what was wrong, but right now he wasn't sure where Pierce stood. If his friend was withholding information about Shadow, even after what happened with Harlow, then what ever was going on outside Alaskan Security would be the least of his worries. "I just dropped Seth's files off to the girls."

Pierce straightened, his attention focusing on Shawn. "Why did he not drop them off?"

"Apparently he's having an issue with a client his team was working with before the all-back was instituted."

Pierce made the decision to bring anyone in the field to headquarters until whatever this was could be resolved. Unfortunately, it wasn't turning out to be the simple solution everyone assumed it would be at the beginning.

"What type of issue?" Pierce leaned back in his chair. He looked about as calm and relaxed as a man could look, but Shawn had known him long enough to know there was plenty going on under the smooth surface.

That water was churning.

Shawn shrugged. "You'll have to ask him."

He didn't give a rat's ass about what Alpha and Beta did, and right now he didn't have time to pretend he did.

"I will do that." Pierce lifted his brows. "Anything else?"

There was so much more he wanted to discuss with Pierce, but not yet. Not until he knew more about Shadow and whatever it was they were doing. "Nope."

"Very well."

Shawn was at the door when Pierce asked one more question.

"Did you get Ms. Ayers' chair ordered?"

He turned. "I thought you were going to handle that yourself." He couldn't resist the dig.

Pierce always got what he wanted when it came to women. Always had. It was nice to see him struggling for once.

"Ms. Ayers didn't seem very interested in my help."

"Smart girl." Shawn smiled as he left. At least he wasn't the only one suffering because of the new team.

He walked down the hall toward the main entry. It was time to figure out what in the hell was going on.

Shadow was scheduled to be in the training wing of the third building, working with a thinned-down batch of Alpha, trying to get a few ready for covert operations.

Shawn passed through the bricked-in walkway that led to the least fancy portion of headquarters. It's where Eli's clinic was located, along with the bunk rooms that were meant to be temporary overflow but now served as more long-term housing for most of Alpha and Beta. A completely outfitted gym and a large open training area rounded out the building.

The lights were dim in the training area when Shawn walked in. The space was filled with a random assortment of items. Cars. Large cardboard boxes that sat at least eight feet high and ten feet wide. Camouflage netting hung from everything, adding an additional layer of mess for the men to learn to silently move through.

He couldn't see Zeke, but the lead for Shadow's voice carried through the raftered room.

Along with a feminine one.

A familiar feminine one.

"You are so funny." Heidi's tone was light and lyrical.

Flirtatious.

Shawn moved closer, using the congestion to his advantage, taking careful steps to avoid making any sort of sound that might alert Zeke to his presence. "You're sure Pierce signed off on this?" Zeke sounded how he always did.

Like an asshole.

"After what happened with Harlow, he really wants all of us to be able to protect ourselves." Heidi still sounded relaxed and unfazed by Zeke's suspicions that she was lying to him.

Which she was.

"I mean, I wish we could have someone to keep us safe all the time, but that's not really possible, is it?"

Shawn held his body tight as he slowly leaned to gain a thin line of sight around the corner of one of the boxes. Heidi stood close to Zeke, her full lips pursed in the kind of pout most men couldn't look away from. One hand came to rest on Zeke's arm. "We just want to be safe, Zeke." She stepped a little closer. "Would you help us feel safe?"

Zeke stared down at her with a look that would wither most women. Not this one. Heidi was unflappable.

He knew. He'd tried to intimidate her more than a few times.

She never backed down. She might step away. Regroup. But she always came back.

Only now it appeared she'd moved on. Decided to believe the lies he fed her.

Tried to digest himself.

Shawn turned from the sight of Heidi touching Zeke, giving the lead of Shadow the same lingering looks he ran from.

And he was running from it again now.

This time Shawn wasn't as careful as he moved through the training area. His steps weren't as silent. His breathing wasn't as controlled.

Because he was pissed. Frustrated.

Jealous.

He didn't stop until he was back in his office, falling into the chair and catching his head in his hands.

"What's a matter, Captain Uptight?"

Heidi's voice had his head snapping up. Shawn shoved one hand at the open doorway. "Get out."

Heidi's lips barely lifted at the corners. "I don't think I will." She stepped farther into his office, closing the door behind her. "I think I might stay for a minute."

"I'm not fucking playing with you right now, Heidi." He stood up, ready to do whatever it took to get this woman far away from him.

Before she saw him for what he was.

Her eyes narrowed on him. "No one's playing, Shawn." She stood tall, head up, shoulders straight. "I'm a grown woman. I don't pretend to be something I'm not, and I sure as hell don't play games."

"Oh really?" He moved closer to her, the bite of jealousy stinging more with each passing second. "Then what in the hell would you call that bullshit with Zeke?"

She didn't flinch at the venom in his tone. "Strategizing."

"Good for you, then." He knew Heidi was the worst thing for him from the second she stepped on that damn plane. Knew this woman would kill him if he let her. "I'm glad you found someone interested in strategizing."

One brown brow lifted slowly up her forehead. "Is that a little bit of jealousy I sense, Captain?"

"Don't call me that." He'd made it this far by never answering any of her problematic questions. Hopefully it could carry him through the final stretch. "You know what? How about you just don't fucking call me anything."

Heidi's head tipped just a little. "I think I'll call you what I want to call you, *Captain*." Heidi dragged the last word out, coming a little closer as she said it.

He'd tried avoiding her. Tried being an asshole. Tried being a complete dick.

But none of it was working.

"Say you don't want me, Shawn." Heidi reached out to flatten down the shoulder seam of his shirt in a touch that would be easy to let become familiar. "Say you don't want me in your bed and I'll leave you alone." Her eyes lifted to meet his. "But you should know that if you aren't interested, I *will* move on."

Shawn glared down at her. The woman who was a terrible fit for him. The woman who tempted him in ways no one had before, making him want to believe he was something he wasn't.

But today proved exactly what he was.

A jealous motherfucker who had no business being with someone like her.

But hell if he could stand the thought of Zeke having her. Holding her.

Spreading those soft thighs so he could seat himself between them.

Shawn grabbed her face with one hand, shoving Heidi back against the wood panel of the door she should never have closed.

"Like fucking hell you will."

CHAPTER 4

SHE WAS JUST looking for a button to push. Something that might tempt Shawn into admitting what she knew was true.

But right now it seemed like what she pressed was more of a self-destruct button.

And considering it resulted in his hard body finally being pressed to hers, she might just have to push that bastard again.

"What the fuck were you doing with Zeke?" His lips hovered just over hers. The hand on her face was firm but surprisingly gentle. It didn't squeeze. Didn't pinch. Just braced. Forced her eyes to stay on his.

"You saw what I was doing. You were there." It was obvious as hell when Shawn came into the room. Something changed while she was talking to Zeke. The air became heavier. The room almost got quieter. "You didn't think I would know, but I did." She sucked in a breath as Shawn pressed into her harder. "I knew you were there. Watching me."

"Why were you there?" Shawn's words sent the warmth of his breath skating across her skin. "What do you want from him?"

"Worried I want the same thing from him that I want from you?" She'd been poking at him for days, thinking Shawn was one more harmless man intimidated by her forward ways.

Scared of a woman who knew what she wanted and wasn't afraid to ask for it.

Now it didn't seem like that was the case at all.

"I'm worried you don't know what in the hell you're playing with."

"Are you talking about Zeke?" She pushed against him. "Or are you talking about yourself?"

His nostrils flared.

Heidi tipped her head, smiling just a little. "That's what I thought."

The width of his body still held her in place, every ridge and plane of his muscular frame pressing into hers, proving Shawn damn well wanted her as much as she wanted him.

"Why do you pretend you don't want me, Shawn?" Heidi tipped her head toward him, trying to tempt him into kissing her.

Normally she was fine with making the first move, but so far Shawn had been less than eager to consider any sort of physical interaction. While it was clear his body was on board, she didn't want to use that against him.

"Because I'm the last man you should ever consider fucking, Rucker." His voice was a little rough. A little edgy. "We aren't a good fit."

"See, that's where I think you're wrong." She slowly lifted her hands, which so far had remained pressed against the door at her back, and rested them against his chest. "I think we would be a very good fit."

He wasn't like most of the men she propositioned.

Hell, Shawn might not be like most men period, based on her current situation.

His eyes barely flicked to where she touched him. "I don't fucking share." He shook his head. "Not ever."

"Is that what you're worried about?" Why were men so freaking presumptuous? "I don't go around fucking everyone if that's what you think."

"That's not what I—"

"You know what?" Heidi used her palms to shove against him. Shawn's body easily moved off hers. "Never mind. If you're going to be a dick about it then I—"

"You jumped from me to Zeke when I wouldn't give you what you wanted. What am I supposed to think?"

She scoffed, working her jaw from side to side. "First of all, I didn't *jump to Zeke*." Heidi grabbed his face the way he'd held hers seconds ago and used the hold to shove him backward. "Second of all, you should be flattered that I would even be willing to grace you with my pussy." She slammed into him as his back hit the wall opposite the door.

"Third, you're supposed to realize, and be thrilled, that I'm a progressive enough woman to not only acknowledge that I have sexual needs, but that I even for a second thought you could fulfill them." Her eyes skimmed his face, chin lifting. "I'm not so convinced you have that ability anymore."

"That ability—" Shawn grabbed her hips in a firm grip, using the hold and the element of surprise to roll them down the wall. Their bodies bumped into a small table holding a printer, knocking it off and sending the machine crashing to the floor.

But Shawn didn't even glance that way.

Didn't even blink.

His eyes stayed locked on her. "You listen to me—"

"I don't listen to anyone, least of all you, Captain." He was starting to piss her off a little now. She could handle strong men. Preferred them actually. But this one was a different sort of breed of strong, and it bordered assholery.

"That's fucking clear as hell." He pointed in her face. "Stay the fuck away from Zeke."

"I don't think I will." She smirked up at him. "I think I'll hang out with Zeke every day if I want."

Shawn's lips curled into a scowl. "Zeke isn't the kind of man you should be fucking with."

"I thought you weren't the kind of man I should be fucking with." Heidi lifted her brows, lowering her lids in exaggerated blinks. "Which is it, Shawn?" She knew what he was doing.

What this was.

"Or is it one of those *you don't want me, but you also don't want anyone else to have me* sort of situations?" Heidi expected him to be silent. Give her an unstated admission.

"You come in here," Shawn's dark gaze raked down the front of her body, "knowing how fucking irresistible you are, and then you torment me." He paused, holding her gaze. "You tease me, knowing damn well what will happen." His eyes dropped to her mouth.

"What will happen?" This morning she had a pretty good idea how the day would go, but it looked like she was wrong.

Never in a million years would that idea have included being pressed against the wall in Shawn's office, getting stared down by a man who appeared to be as angry as he was turned on.

Shawn stayed silent.

"Whatever." Heidi pushed him off her for the second time. "I'm over this. I'll find what I want somewhere else."

Shawn's body bumped into hers from behind, this time pressing her front to the door. "What is it you want, Heidi?" One hand slid across her stomach, moving over her belly button. "You just want to get off, is that it?"

The press of his rigid dick against her backside made her gasp. "You act like that's too much to ask."

"I don't think you really understand what you're asking me for." The tips of his fingers tickled along the skin between the waistband of her pants and the hem of her shirt. "It's not as simple as it sounds."

"It is for men who know what a clitoris is." Heidi curved her spine, pressing her ass harder into his cock.

Shawn growled in her ear. "I can promise you I know what a clitoris is, Kitten."

"Kitten." She worked her hips a little, grinding into him. "Is that because I scratch?"

"It's because I know I can make you fucking purr." The hand on her belly tucked into the waistband of her pants. "Isn't that what you want, Heidi? For me to make you come and send you on your way?"

"Don't make it sound like such a sacrifice." Heidi gasped as his hand teased the lips of her pussy.

"Say it or it doesn't happen, Kitten. You have to ask for what you want." The gravely grind of Shawn's words was doing as much for her as the way he held her against the door was.

"I feel like that's what I've been doing, Captain." She turned her head, peeking at him over one shoulder. "I've asked nicely dozens of times."

"Dozens?" His hand pressed deeper, the pads of his fingers skating over her heated flesh. "Have you been keeping track?"

"I have if you're going to be paying up." Heidi's eyes rolled closed as his touch barely brushed her clit. "Are you going to do this or not?"

"You still haven't asked." His teeth caught the lobe of her ear, tongue flicking the spot as his not-enough touch continued teasing her.

"Get me off, Shawn."

He let out a low hum. "Say it again."

Her eyes snapped open, ready to lay into him for being an asshole, but before she could say anything he spread her pussy lips wide, using a finger to slide down the center, stroking right against her clit. Her legs wobbled a little, threatening to give under the sudden focus of his attention.

Shawn pushed against her. "Say it again, Kitten."

She whimpered as his fingers continued rubbing against her.

Shawn's lips moved against her ear. "Say it or I stop."

"Make me come." No way was she risking him stopping.

"Who?" He flattened his fingers, moving them side to side. "Who's making you come, Heidi?"

"Shawn." She bit her lip as her orgasm built, climbing faster and faster with each glide of his hand.

"Spread your legs." He wrapped one arm around her waist, pulling her tight to him. His touch disappeared for a second, the back of his hand stretching the crotch of her panties away from her body. "Now." He slapped her with a sharp smack.

Heidi sucked in a breath at the erotically stimulating sting that seemed to send rippling aftershocks straight to her core. "What the fuck was that?"

Did he really just hit her in the pussy?

And was she actually hoping to God he did it again?

Yes. To both.

"Still think I can't satisfy you, Kitten?" Shawn barely waited a heartbeat before his hand connected with her again. "Answer me."

The sound that came out of her on that second slap was inhuman. Like nothing she'd ever heard before, let alone from her own mouth. "Maybe you can do it."

He chuckled, low and a little ragged as the hand banded around her middle shoved up her shirt to yank down the cup of her bra. "Maybe I should just send you on your way then." He pinched her nipple, twisting it between his fingers, just to the point before pain. "Let you suffer for doubting me."

"I'd finish myself."

Another slap, this one harder than the ones before. It was perfectly placed, the stinging strike hitting right against her clit. Her legs shook as she teetered on the edge of an orgasm.

Shawn pressed into her harder, his hips thrusting the ridge of his dick along the crack of her ass. "Like hell you will." He rolled the nipple still caught between his fingers. "From now on every time you come belongs to me, you understand me, Kitten?" One single finger flicked against her clit. "You want to get off then you come to me."

"Those are your terms?" She blinked, trying to find some clarity around the aching need clouding her mind. "All or nothing?"

"Only me or none of me." The finger rubbing her clit pressed a little harder. "That's the deal."

She tried to work her body against his hand, the need to come making her feel a little desperate.

Shawn slapped her again, dragging out another needy grunt she didn't mean to make. "What's your answer, Kitten?"

"What if I want it in the middle of the night?" Certainly he didn't mean what he said. There had to be some sort of wiggle room.

She was after easy breezy casual sex, but what Shawn was proposing felt more…

Intense.

"Then you come to my room and I give you what you want." His touch gentled against her, barely brushing when she wanted more of what he gave before. "There's no limits here, Kitten. If this is what you want then I'm at your disposal." Shawn's lips brushed her ear. "But only me. No one else touches you, are we clear?"

No man ever asked to be the only one to touch her. Probably because she made it clear they might not be the only one she touched.

The proposition was unexpected.

But also a little arousing.

And isn't that what this was all about? "Fine."

Shawn's satisfied growl came the second before another smack to her clit, this one forcing her to reach back to loop one arm around his neck in an attempt to stay upright.

"Who gives you what you want, Kitten?" The next smack came right after the last, its accuracy as perfect as its force.

"You do." She would tell him anything he wanted to hear at this point. Whatever kept his hand doing what it was.

"Who's the only man who touches you?"

"You are." Heidi whimpered as another blessed slap sent her cunt clenching.

"Who makes you come, Heidi?" The hits were coming in rapid succession now, the continuous stimulation taking her over the edge almost instantly.

"You do-o-o." She bit her lip to clamp down on the wail trying to slip free as her body jerked, fighting against the tight hold Shawn had on her. His fingers pressed against her, rubbing as she came, dragging out the climax so long she lost the ability to think.

Or see.

Or hear.

Shawn's lips moved along the back of her neck, nipping as he worked his way to a spot just below the neckline of her soft cotton shirt. His mouth locked onto her skin, sucking hard enough to bring on a stinging burn that shot straight to where his hand continued to work her clit with a solid pressure.

"Holy shit, Shawn." Heidi blinked, trying to find the focus he stole. "What the fuck was that?"

His hand eased up the curve of her belly, sliding free of her pants as the other righted the cup of her bra. Without a word the weight of his body left hers. The arm around her waist pulled her from the door.

Then he opened it and gently directed her out.

52

She blinked at him. "What are you doing?"

"You need to go back to work. You've got shit to do."

"Now? You want me to go back to work right now?" She could barely put one foot in front of the other, let alone work her way into a high-security system.

Shawn smirked at her. "You should be fine. I might not even be able to satisfy you, remember?" He grabbed the door, starting to swing it closed. "Go back to work, Rucker." Just before the door closed in her face Shawn slipped the fingers he'd had on her pussy between his lips, his eyes locked onto hers as the steel panel clicked shut.

"Everything okay?" Mona stood just outside the bathroom, eyes moving from the closed door to where Heidi stood gaping at it. "You look pissed."

Was she?

Heidi pressed one hand to her head. "Maybe."

Maybe not?

Mona walked toward her, headed in the direction of their shared work space. "Did you talk to Zeke?"

"Oh." Heidi glanced toward the door to Shawn's office. "Yeah. He said he'd do it."

Mona smiled a little. "Good." She tucked her hair behind one ear. "I don't really want to be the only one of us with a gun."

"Yeah. That'll probably be a good thing." Heidi worked to get her feet moving as Mona reached her side.

Mona's smile slipped as they walked down the hall. "You sure you're okay?"

"Uh-huh. Yup." Heidi snuck a peek down at her clothes, double-checking that her knit joggers and shirt were where they were supposed to be.

Everything was perfectly in place. Didn't look like they'd recently been shoved in all directions by a man's hands.

Her pussy clenched and her throat worked on an involuntary swallow.

She might have bitten off more than she could chew with this one. Shawn was definitely nothing like anyone she'd ever pursued before him.

He and those men might not even reside on the same planet.

Eva glanced up from her desk as she and Mona walked in the room. "Thank God you're back." She picked up a stack of files and held them out. "Gentry just dropped these off for us to go through."

Heidi took the pile of information on the men of Beta team. "Do we have all of them now?"

"We have all of Alpha and Beta." Eva's cheeks puffed out on an exhale as she scanned her desk. "I'm guessing we won't get Shadow. I'm not sure about Rogue."

"Did you ask Brock?" Heidi's brain was slowly coming back around, thank goodness.

If Shawn could break her brain she'd be screwed.

The whole company would.

Because chances were good she'd still go back for more of whatever it was he was serving up.

She sat down at her desk, holding the files with one hand as she shifted the other piles around, trying to make a spot.

"You want me to help you clean up your desk?" Mona was already on her feet, intending to head over to help.

"Nope." Heidi managed to get a square just big enough to fit the stack cleared. "I'm good." She flipped the cover on the first file and opened her computer as Brock, Wade, and Dutch walked into the room.

Brock's face was serious. "I think we need to talk."

CHAPTER 5

"IS THERE SOMETHING wrong?" Pierce held open the door to Shawn's office, one brow lifted in question.

"Besides the fact that one of our men tried to kill Mowry and he might not have been working alone?" Shawn grabbed the mouse of his computer and pretended like he was working. "No. Nothing's wrong." He glanced Pierce's way when the owner of Alaskan Security didn't respond. "You need something?"

"Have we delivered all the files to Intel?"

"You'll have to ask Gentry."

Pierce opened the door fully, standing straight. "Have I done something to upset you?"

"I've got a lot to get done and you're eating up my time."

Pierce tipped his head a little. "I apologize. I assumed you had time to spare considering how long Ms. Rucker was in your office."

He'd hoped no one noticed Heidi's visit to his office. "You know damn well Ms. Rucker likes being a pain in my ass."

"I know Ms. Rucker's interest is in a very specific part of your body." Pierce stepped into the office. "I don't believe your ass is it." He slowly lowered into one of the chairs across from Shawn's desk. "I hope you intend to tread lightly if a situation arises between you two."

"I don't intend to tread at all."

"Isn't it too late for that?" Pierce crossed his legs, settling one ankle on his knee. He picked at a bit of something stuck to the hem of his pants. "Is she aware of your history?"

"My history is no one's business."

Pierce's gaze lifted to level on Shawn. "I feel like I should tell you I have no intention of losing Ms. Rucker as an employee."

Shawn's brows lifted in surprise. "What's that supposed to mean?"

"It means what it means." Pierce stood from the chair. "Ms. Rucker is a huge asset. One we desperately need right now. I will not tolerate anything that could put her position here at risk."

"You don't have anything to worry about." Shawn kept his tone dry.

Unaffected.

He didn't want to think about what just happened in his office, let alone have Pierce realize the mistake.

And that's what it was.

A mistake.

A big fucking one.

"Happy to hear that." Pierce backed into the hall. "I have scheduled an all-call meeting for this afternoon. I will see you there."

Shawn turned back to his computer, focusing on the nothing there. "Have I missed one yet?"

He watched Pierce stare him down in his peripheral vision, pretending to be engrossed in his computer until his friend and boss finally walked away. Shawn waited a minute longer before leaning back in his chair and wiping both hands down his face.

The scent of Heidi still clung to his skin, digging the regret filling his gut even deeper.

What the fuck was wrong with him?

He knew she was not a woman he should ever consider touching, let alone actually doing it.

And he'd done so much more than touch her.

He'd fucked up in every possible way. Put the extent of his issues on full display for her to see.

Hopefully it was enough to make her avoid him forever. It was the only way he'd survive the mess he'd started.

The fucked-up situation he'd created.

Shawn leaned to grab his ever-ready gym bag from the corner of his office before leaving in search of the physical exertion he needed. Craved like a drug.

The gym was full when he got there. Having all of Alpha and Beta on campus with nothing to do meant the space was rarely unoccupied during the day, so he usually tried to make his visits at night. But today he needed an outlet and he needed it now.

Shawn quickly changed in the locker room and immediately went to the treadmill, setting the pace at a punishing level. It's what he deserved for what he'd done.

Five miles in his lungs burned and his legs ached, but he continued on, trying to force out the memory of Heidi pressed against the wall, her soft body wet and willing under his hands.

"Hey." Gentry slapped his towel across Shawn's face. "You're not the only one here, man."

Shawn slapped the panel, shutting the machine down. He glared at Beta's lead. "You get your files to Intel?"

"Sure did." Gentry slung the towel in his hand over one shoulder as Shawn stepped off the treadmill. "Was hoping to see the new chick, but she wasn't there when I dropped them off." He twisted at the waist, rotating from side to side. "You know anything about her?"

The familiar burn of jealousy crept across Shawn's skin. He gritted his teeth against the sensation. "Nope."

Shawn turned and went straight back to the locker room, feeling fucking worse than when he started. He showered before redressing. As he tugged his shirt over his head the sweet, barely floral scent of Heidi tickled his nose.

"Jesus Christ." He ripped the shirt back off, stuffing it into his bag along with the sweat-soaked workout gear. He grabbed the handles and stalked out into the hall, shirtless and agitated. His half-nakedness garnered a few odd looks as he passed through the enclosed walkway leading to the main building. The entry was empty as he made his way toward the rooming building. The glassed-in walkway leading to the third building was now hidden behind barricades meant to keep prying eyes from finding a good target.

Again.

Shawn yanked open the door at the end of the walkway and turned to go down the first-floor hall.

"Oh." Bess jumped back, pulling Parker close to her chest as she went. "Holy cow, Shawn. You scared me." Her nose lifted on one side. "Where's your shirt?"

"Got something on it." He tried to skirt past Wade's girlfriend. "I came to get another one."

Bess stepped along with him. "Can I ask you a question?"

He took a breath, trying to calm the prickle of frustration biting at his skin. "Sure."

She glanced from side to side before stepping a little closer. "Do you think Shadow is behind all this?"

That was the million-dollar question. Maybe literally at this point. Alaskan Security was all but shut down. No money coming in. No teams going out.

"I wish I knew."

Bess nodded a little. "Me too." She rocked Parker from side to side.

Shawn's gaze dipped to the little boy held tight in his momma's arms.

"The girls said it was okay if I brought him with me." Bess sounded a little defensive.

"That's good." Shawn reached up to tickle Parker on the belly. "It's hard to be a working mother."

Bess's eyes came to rest on his face. "It's not as hard as it used to be."

"Good."

Bess was a single mom for over a year before she found the man who unknowingly knocked her up. While Wade probably wasn't what she was expecting, and his profession landed Bess in the middle of the mess they were struggling to end, it also brought her endless childcare and countless men willing to put their lives on the line to protect her and her son.

Him being one of them.

"Well, I'll let you go get your shirt." Bess stepped back. "I'll see you later."

Shawn watched her go into the tunnel, moving in close enough he could be sure she made it to the other end safely. As soon as she was out of sight he went to his room, switched out the clothes in his gym bag and pulled on a new shirt. One that didn't smell like the woman who brought out the worst in him.

The man he had no clue how to stop being.

By the time he was finished Shawn had to rush to make it back to his office, grabbing the clipboard he used to stay as organized as possible before hurrying to the large hall where all-team meetings were held. Most of the staff was already milling around the large space. Members of Alpha and Beta grabbed coffee at the station in the back while Shadow sat in the same corner they always occupied, silently watching everyone around them.

Rogue was near the front of the room, each man lined down the first two rows of chairs on the left side. Shawn sat in his place at the wide table spanning the front wall of the hall, facing the team seating. He kept his eyes down as Intel came through the open doors.

He couldn't look at Heidi right now. Just knowing she was in the same room made him jumpy and on edge.

Pierce strode in behind Intel, immediately going to his place at the table and sitting. Seth and Gentry filed in next, each one sitting at opposite ends of the table with Pierce, Shawn, and Zeke's empty chair between them. Zeke was the last man through the door. His eyes came straight to Shawn as he walked along the side aisle.

Shawn stared him down, the ugly jealousy he couldn't seem to fight rearing its head even before Zeke smirked at him.

It took everything in him to stay seated, to stay under control.

He held Zeke's gaze without blinking until the bigger man finally took his place on the other side of Pierce. When Shawn finally looked away his attention stumbled, snagging on a set of wide smoky blue eyes. Heidi's gaze snapped to Zeke before coming back to him, barely narrowing as it moved over him.

"Find your seat so we can begin." Pierce focused on the men still loitering. "We have many issues to discuss." He barely waited until the final man was in his chair before continuing on. "As most of you know, there was an incident here last night." His head slowly moved along with his gaze, resting on one man after the next as he spoke. "One of our team turned, choosing his own financial gain over the safety and well-being of another member of Alaskan Security." He paused for a second, continuing to scan the faces in the room. "I am here to tell you that I will not tolerate any behavior that puts a member of my company at risk." Pierce's eyes lingered as they moved across where Shadow sat. "If I discover anyone else attempting to exploit their position here in a similar manner I will have no problem taking extreme action."

Heidi lifted one hand, her eyes shifting to Shawn before quickly going back to Pierce. "What kind of action are we talking?"

Pierce's jaw clenched. "That is not something I'm interested in disclosing at this time."

Heidi nodded like she understood perfectly. She turned to where Eva and Mona sat beside her, swiping one finger across her neck as her face twisted, the tip of her tongue peeking out the corner of her mouth.

Shawn stared at that tiny bit of pink.

He hadn't even fucking kissed her. Just fed his own overwhelming need to lay down boundaries and rules he had no right to inflict on her.

"No one said anything about..." Pierce shifted in his seat. He pointed one finger at Heidi, moving it around. "Whatever that was."

"It was dead." Heidi repeated the move, this time with a gagging sound effect followed by a more dramatic false expiration. "See? Dead."

"No one said anything about making anyone dead." Pierce's tone rose a little.

"That's what will happen though, right?" Heidi looked at the men around her. "That's what he means, right?"

"Enough." The sharpness in Pierce's voice sent Shawn's head snapping his way.

"Talk to her like that again," he leaned close to Pierce, keeping his voice low, "and you and I will have a problem."

Pierce didn't look Shawn's way, but his posture stiffened just enough for it to be clear the threat was heard loud and clear. The owner of Alaskan Security took a long, slow breath. "If you would like to discuss this matter further, Ms. Rucker, then you are welcome to do so in my office after we are finished here."

That wasn't any better.

Heidi could hold her own with Pierce, he didn't doubt her for a minute, but still.

"If you and the rest of your team have questions for me then I encourage the four of you to come together."

Shawn relaxed just a little, finally turning his glare from Pierce. He purposefully avoided looking in Heidi's direction. He could feel her gaze on him and he didn't want to see what lingered there.

Probably regret. Rightfully so.

He was not the man she thought he was. Not by a long shot.

"I don't believe we have anything we would like to discuss with you." Mona's head sat at an angle, her ice blue eyes trained on Pierce.

"Very well." Pierce's head dipped as his eyes went to the agenda in front of him. "In that case I think it's time to get on with it."

The rest of the meeting involved briefing the teams on the events of the past twenty-four hours, as well as informing the men that they were currently being reviewed by Intel.

"If anyone has an issue with this review process then you are welcome to part ways with Alaskan Security." Pierce scanned the room, pausing for a second.

Being an open book was something most of the men were used to. Many had backgrounds in military or law enforcement and this was par for the course.

Pierce turned to Zeke. "This includes your team."

Zeke's brows barely twitched. It was more of a reaction than normal from the lead of Shadow. "I don't think so."

"It's a non-negotiable." Pierce didn't flinch as Zeke's already hard expression turned to steel.

"Good luck with that."

"We can handle it." Eva crossed her arms, her own expression nearly as intimidating as the one Zeke wore.

Zeke snorted out a scoff, his lips staying completely flat and humorless as he looked toward Intel. "Then you'll have to find someone else to get you the toys you want." His head tipped Pierce's way. "But I'm sure boss man won't mind helping you out since he knows all about it."

"I have no problem ensuring the members of Intel feel as safe as possible." Pierce's shoulders seemed to relax just a little as he focused on the women. "I will be happy to assist you myself. We can schedule a meeting to discuss your needs this evening."

Zeke's lips pressed tight together.

Shadow had done pretty much whatever they wanted since the inception of Alaskan Security. They'd worked as almost their own entity and it showed.

But that was true of all the teams to some extent. Alpha and Beta were usually out in the field, spread across the country. Only Rogue was consistently in Alaska, using it as a way to protect their questionable clientele.

One they may or may not go back to servicing when this was all over.

"It is important that we all find a way to come together at this point." Pierce stood from his chair, rebuttoning the jacket of his suit as he moved. "I have done a less-than-satisfactory job of instilling the sense of camaraderie I envisioned at the inception of this company and it shows. I want to rectify that now. Until further notice there are no more individual teams. We will be acting as a single All-Team. Our divisions weaken us and that is being used against us."

Shawn turned to where Gentry sat at his side. The Beta's lead looked as shocked as he was.

"What?" Zeke was on his feet in an instant. "Not fucking happening." He pointed at Pierce. "I've humored your bullshit since this started. Trained these half-assed teams." One hand swung Mona's way. "Hell, your lady's a better shot than most of them."

"Oh. No." Mona looked around the room, turning a little in her seat. "I'm not his lady." Her eyes darted to Pierce for a second before dropping to the ground in front of her.

The public rejection almost made Shawn feel bad for his friend.

Almost.

But given the potential bullshit happening with Shadow, he just couldn't pull up the sympathy.

Pierce stood perfectly still, his eyes resting on Mona for a heartbeat before moving away. "This meeting is over."

CHAPTER 6

"YOU ARE A savage, Mona." Heidi dropped into her uncomfortable chair but even the terrible back support couldn't dim her smile. "I am so freaking proud of you."

"I think I'm going to throw up." Mona went to her own desk, but skipped the chair and sat on the floor, immediately putting her head between her knees. "I didn't mean for it to sound like it did."

"You better have meant for it to sound like it did." Heidi kicked her empty trash can toward Eva. "Pass this to her."

"Why is your trash can empty?" Eva made a show of eyeing Heidi's messy desk. "Has anyone ever explained what these are used for?"

"Right now it's going to catch Mona's barf." She scrunched up her face at Eva. "And then you'll both be super glad I'm a messy bitch."

"I think I'm okay." Mona leaned her head back to rest it on the seat of her chair.

"You don't look okay." Mona was always pale, but right now she was completely white. "You look like you're going to pass out."

"I've had a rough couple of days." Mona pressed one finger between her brows. "I can't believe I said that the way I did."

"Why? *Are* you his lady?" Heidi grabbed a bag of sour-sugar-covered gummies and went to sit on the floor beside Mona.

"No."

Heidi held out the open bag, shaking it when Mona didn't immediately take one. "Do you want to be his lady?"

Mona shook her head. "No."

"Then why does it matter?" Heidi popped one of the candies in her mouth.

"Because he's the owner of the company and I made him look bad?" Mona finally reached in and retrieved a single gummy, her pale brows coming together in question.

"How does not wanting to date your boss make him look bad?" Eva came to sit on Mona's desk. "Why does society believe that a woman not wanting a man is something *she* should feel bad about?" She reached down to grab a handful of candy. "It's misogynistic bullshit."

Mona straightened. "It is, isn't it?"

"Fuck the patriarchy." Heidi grinned as Mona finally chewed her candy.

"Indeed."

Pierce's voice sent Heidi peeking over the desk Eva sat on. "Can we help you?"

"I am here to discuss your desire to be trained in weaponry."

Heidi lifted one brow at Pierce. If she didn't know better she'd think he sounded a little offended. "Zeke was going to do it until you pissed him off."

"I am unconcerned with Zeke's current state of mind." Pierce took a few ambling strides their way. "What I am concerned with is your safety and well-being."

Eva turned Pierce's way, swinging her legs around the corner of the desk as she went. "That's awful nice of you." The sarcasm in her words was unmissable.

"It's not about being nice, Ms. Tatum. It's about protecting a valuable asset."

"So we're assets now?" Heidi glanced Mona's way.

"Of course." Pierce held his perfectly straight stance as the women glared. "There is no way this company would survive all that's happening without this team."

"I feel like you're buttering us up for something." Heidi stood up from where she'd been sitting behind Mona's desk. "What do you want?"

"I want Shadow investigated." He slowly walked to Heidi's desk. "I want to know everything about their activities as a team."

"Shouldn't you already know that? You're the boss." Eva's eyes were narrow as she watched Pierce study the contents of Heidi's desk.

"I should." He lifted his brows at the mess before turning back their way. "The fact that I don't is troublesome."

"To say the least." Mona stood beside Heidi, a little of the color coming back in her cheeks.

"Yes, Ms. Ayers. To say the least." Pierce was quiet for a minute. "Investigating Shadow will need to be handled carefully. The entities they regularly interact with are possibly problematic."

"You mean the government?"

Pierce's eyes immediately came to Heidi. "That is one of them, yes." He tucked one hand in the pocket of his pants. "It is imperative this is an unseen operation. There can be no evidence it has even happened."

Eva and Mona both turned to Heidi.

She'd been digging into places she wasn't supposed to be for years. Just to see if she could. This was no different.

Technically.

"What happens if someone finds out?" She'd been in government systems before. The hacking world was a small one and she'd been around for a long time, learning the ropes in chat room challenges and underground competitions.

"The risk to everyone here is substantial." Pierce focused completely on Heidi. "You asked earlier what would happen to anyone found to be working against us." He stepped closer. "I can promise you it will be significantly less horrific than what will happen if it's discovered I've attempted to gain access to locations I do not have clearance for."

Eva's brows came together. "Now wait one fucking minute." She shook her head. "You can't expect Heidi to put her ass on the line for—"

"This is my ass on the line." Pierce's voice was louder and sharper than Heidi had heard it before. "I am the only one who will be at risk if this mission is discovered."

Mission.

It sounded so important. So different from the bullshit she'd been doing for the past few years.

Not that her job at Investigative Technologies wasn't important to someone.

It just wasn't her. She loved working there, but it wasn't really a challenge.

"I'll do it." Heidi nodded her head along with the verbal agreement. "I can do it without getting caught."

Pierce's gaze leveled on her. "Are you positive?"

"Very." Heidi glanced to the door as Harlow came through with Dutch hot on her heels. "Especially if Harlow helps."

"Harlow is only here to get her—" Dutch's lips tipped to a frown as Harlow sat down at her desk. "Damn it, Mowry."

Harlow's blue eyes went wide. "What? I said I needed something."

Dutch held one finger up. "One thing. You said you needed to get one thing and then you would go back and lay down."

"The thing I needed was to get some work done." Harlow turned in her seat until her face was directed Pierce's way. "What am I helping Heidi do?"

"Pierce wants us to investigate Shadow." Heidi glanced Dutch's way. They'd already decided on their own to investigate Shadow last night after Harlow came to Eva and Brock's room.

Dutch wasn't thrilled about it then and clearly his opinion of things hadn't changed.

His eyes narrowed on Pierce. "Do you know how fucking dangerous that is?"

Pierce held his perfect posture. "I think you know I do."

The men stared each other down.

"Jesus Christ." Heidi leaned toward Eva. "Are they always like this around here?"

"Pretty much." She glanced Heidi's way. "Brock and Shawn got in a fight the night we were all kidnapped."

"Brock and Shawn?" Heidi pressed her lips together as she considered the matchup. "Who won?"

"I did." Brock came into the room, his attention immediately going to Dutch and Pierce. "What's up?"

"Pierce wants Intel to investigate Shadow." Dutch didn't look away from Pierce.

Brock's brows lifted. "He does?" His eyes moved to where Eva sat at Heidi's side. "That's interesting."

"Not sure how you think we're going to do it with all of you standing around here staring at each other." Heidi went to her desk and sat in her chair. "So you should probably get the hell out."

"I work here, Rucker." Dutch sat in the chair at his desk. "I'm part of Intel, remember?"

"Not a very useful part." She shrugged at him. "No offense."

"Just because my talents aren't of any value to you doesn't mean they aren't still amazing." Dutch's gaze slid to Harlow.

Yesterday the comment would have made her feel stabby with pent-up sexual frustration.

Not so much right now.

"Gross." Mona wrinkled her nose Dutch's way.

"Can everyone either leave or become useful?" Harlow waved one hand around as the other worked across the keyboard of her laptop. "I have things to do and in case you didn't remember I have a headache."

"My apologies, Ms. Mowry." Pierce dipped his head at Harlow. "If there is anything I can do to assist you please don't hesitate to let me know."

Heidi gave Pierce a thumbs up. "Will do, boss man."

Pierce blinked at her for a second. "Okay then."

She could add Pierce to the list of men who weren't sure how to handle her personality.

Most men were actually on that list.

Not all. Anymore.

Brock went to Eva's desk and had a quiet conversation with her before leaving to go down the hall and duck into Shawn's office.

The same office she'd visited not long ago.

And was very interested in visiting again.

Harlow glanced toward the door. Dutch immediately got up and closed it.

"So here's how I think we need to handle this." Harlow's voice wasn't as strong as normal. She took a sip of water from the bottle Dutch set on her desk. "Heidi and I will look into Shadow. I'm guessing it will get pretty deep pretty fast with them, so I think it's best that she and I handle it." Harlow's mouth clamped shut as the door opened.

Bess peeked her head inside.

Heidi waved her in. "Close the door behind you."

Parker's tow-head came into view as Bess slipped through the door. "Gloria is with Wade learning gun safety." She dropped her diaper bag on the top of her desk.

"Gloria already has a gun?" Heidi looked at Dutch. "How does Gloria already have a gun?"

"Gloria came with a gun." Bess pulled a container of snacks out of the bag and handed a few to Parker before setting him down on the floor. "Apparently it's a big thing in the retirement community where she lives. They have a ladies' shooting club."

"Go Gloria." Heidi held her arms out, wiggling her fingers in an attempt to lure Parker her way so she could sniff his baby-ish smell.

"Not go Gloria." Bess set the bag on the floor before dropping into her chair. "Apparently she's a little bit of a hazard."

Parker grinned at Heidi. Probably because he already knew her desk was the best place to find sticky sweet snacks. He rushed toward her. "Too bad you didn't fly her commercial. She couldn't have brought it with her."

"Yeah. Now she doesn't want to ever fly commercial again and I'm pretty sure Rico won't make her." Bess scooted to her desk, turning to Harlow. "What are we doing?"

"We're investigating Shadow."

Bess looked from Harlow to the rest of the women. "I know. I was there when we decided that last night."

"No." Mona leaned Bessie's way. "Pierce came in and asked us to do it."

Bessie's eyes widened. "He did?" She turned to Harlow. "That's good, right?"

Harlow shrugged her shoulders. "Maybe. It could mean he's not a part of whatever is going on with Shadow." Her eyes went to the whiteboard taking up the entire side wall, skimming across the large web of names and lines covering it. "Or he might just not want us to realize he is a part of it."

"Does that seem like something Pierce would do?" Bess directed her question at Dutch.

Dutch was quiet for a minute. "I don't want to think Pierce is involved."

"That's not an answer to my question." Bess held Dutch's gaze. "You've known him a long time. Do you think Pierce would be involved in this?"

"You should ask Wade." Dutch tried again to dodge the question.

"I did."

"And what did he tell you?"

Bess crossed her arms. "I'll tell you when you tell me what you think."

Dutch's eyes narrowed at her. "I feel like this is a trick."

"He doesn't think Pierce is involved." Harlow turned when Dutch scoffed. "What? I was tired of dragging it out."

"Wade doesn't either." Bess lifted one shoulder. "I just wanted to know what you really thought."

Eva turned to Bess. "Brock said the same."

"So three men who know him well all say Pierce isn't involved." Bess grabbed a dry-erase pen from the container on her desk and went to the board. "We need to come up with a way to identify him on this so he won't know it's him." She tapped the pen against her lips as she stared at the wall.

"What if we project it on there?" Heidi tipped her head back to peer at the ceiling. "I guarantee we can get him to install a projector in here. We can hook it up to one of our computers and keep his part hidden there."

Bess pointed the tip of her marker Heidi's way. "You are really smart."

"I spent all of high school playing with computers instead of boys, so…"

Bess's brows came together.

"Don't feel bad for her." Eva leaned back in her seat. "She's made up for it."

"Don't hate the player." Heidi shot Eva a grin before turning back to the white board. "If someone wants to sweet talk Pierce into getting us a projector then I'll set up the screen we can display over the wall.

"On it." Dutch stood up and immediately left the room.

"That was easy." Heidi leaned to peek out the door as it swung shut behind him.

"I think he's going stir crazy." Harlow had both her computers sitting side-by-side. "He's used to being involved in tons of missions with Rogue and handling all the tech needs for Alpha and Beta and now everyone is grounded."

"That's got to be costing Pierce a shit-ton of money." Heidi tapped her fingers against the table. "I mean, it would make sense that he'd be willing to do whatever it takes to get back up and running, right?"

"You trying to say you don't agree with the guys?" Bess didn't even look down as she snagged a stapler away from Parker and set it out of his reach.

"I don't know, but I don't think we should assume he's innocent just yet." Heidi tucked her legs up into her chair, trying to find a comfortable position. "Maybe we should look into him too."

"It's only fair." Eva lifted her brows. "We're looking into everyone else."

Most of the men wanted to be investigated. Rogue requested it with Wade, Brock, and Dutch specifically asking them to do complete background checks on the whole team.

"I'll do it." Mona's offer sent everyone eyes her way. "I mean, I can't really help with Shadow so I might as well do Pierce, right?"

"Sure." Heidi went along with Mona's assertion that her desire to be the one looking into Pierce was strictly professional. "That would be awesome."

Harlow focused on Heidi. "You got a program that will be helpful for us?"

Heidi laughed.

Did she have a program.

"I think I've got us covered." She reached into her bag and pulled out the personal computer she built herself, along with five external hard drives.

Harlow's eyes widened. "Wow."

"This is what happens when you have an addictive personality and impulse control issues."

Drugs weren't any fun because she liked to know exactly what she was doing. Smoking meant she'd have to stand out in the snow and rain to feed her need.

But hacking. That was an obsession she could get behind.

Obviously.

Heidi shoved around the crap on her desk, making room for everything. After some maneuvering she finally had just enough space.

"You know if you cleaned that off you'd have plenty of room." Mona's eyes were stuck to the stacks of files and empty wrappers strewn around.

"Cleaning is boring." Why clean when there were so many fun things to do with your time? "I'd rather wear jeans." She glanced at Mona. "And I fucking hate jeans."

"You've never worn the baggy kind then." Harlow lifted her legs, rocking back in her seat, kicking her feet to show off the loose-fitting jeans she always wore. "Ow." One hand went to the back of her head as it bumped the chair.

"Still terrible." Heidi rested one finger on the print sensor, waiting for it to register before laying the next. After recognizing both prints, the screen unlocked, allowing her to open the browser. "I'm a joggers all day, every day sort of girl."

"That's because you have a nice butt." Mona leaned to peek at her backside. "They make mine look flat."

"Yours *is* flat." Heidi opened her private email, sitting up a little as she read the title of the top one. *Weird shit is happening.*

She clicked on the message from a coworker from Investigative Resources. "Uh-oh."

"What?" Eva scooted her way to Heidi's desk, eyes scanning the text of the email. "Uh-oh."

"I'm going to need you to stop saying *uh-oh* and just tell me what the hell is going on." Harlow glanced up as Dutch came in, passing a towel-covered ice pack she immediately held to the back of her head.

Heidi chewed her lip, rereading the message to be sure it was still the same.

She winced as she turned to Dutch and Harlow. This was not going to go over well. "Looks like someone's soliciting the people I used to work with."

CHAPTER 7

"YOU'RE GOING TO get them fucking killed."
Shawn sat across from Pierce.

"They will not be the ones to take the fall for
this should it come to that." Pierce's expression was
as unreadable as ever. His composure cool and
indifferent.

Which meant Pierce was anything but.

"You know damn well you can't be sure of
that." Shawn was already pissed at Pierce for the
way he spoke to Heidi during the all-team meeting,
and now the prick was putting her in a danger she
wouldn't even see coming. "If she or Harlow leaves
any sort of evidence then they will come for them
and do whatever it takes to shut them up."

"We don't have a choice." Pierce's voice was
a little sharper, hinting at the unrest brewing under

his pristine exterior. "Shadow has run wild for too long. I cannot allow it to continue."

"What makes you think they're running wild?" Shawn watched Pierce for any indication of what the owner of Alaskan Security might know. As far as he knew Pierce had no clue the video of Shadow passing Richards off existed.

Hopefully he didn't know the event even happened.

It was the line they were walking right now. Trying to tease out who was on the right side.

And who wasn't.

Right now no one was quite sure where Pierce stood.

Pierce tapped the tip of one finger against the pristine surface of his desk as his eyes held Shawn's. "I have reason to believe Howard Richards may not have escaped on his own."

Shawn didn't have to feign surprise. "Do you? What reason is that?"

Pierce's eyes dropped. "That's classified."

"Of course it fucking is." Shawn snorted out a bitter laugh. "Isn't that what got us here? Classified bullshit?"

Pierce raked one hand through his hair, immediately using his palm to flatten it back down. "This is different."

"It always is." Shawn stood up. "Call me when you're ready to stop being a fucking dick."

"It's an informant."

Shawn paused just inside the door. "An informant. Who?"

Pierce let out a slow breath, shaking his head. "I won't risk their safety."

"But you'll risk everyone else's?" He turned to leave. "Nice, Pierce." He made it one step out of the office before stopping dead in his tracks.

Heidi stood just outside the door, the rest of Intel right behind her. Her gaze slipped down his body before coming back to his. "Shawn."

"Rucker." He started to walk away, but Heidi's voice stopped him.

"You're probably gonna want to stay for this."

He looked down the line of women at her back. "Why?"

"Someone's offering the people who used to work for us a shitload of money to go work for them." Eva's expression was somber. "And it sounds like a few of them are considering taking it even though we warned them."

"Twenty grand is a lot of money to turn down." Heidi's eyes were still on him, but now they held curiosity as they moved around his face.

"Shit." Shawn raked one hand through the length of hair at the top of his head.

"That's what I said." Heidi tried to lean against the door jam to Pierce's office but missed and ended up staggering a few steps before straightening and propping one hand on her hip.

"You okay?"

"Fine." Heidi's cheeks barely pinked.

"Who have they contacted?" Pierce stood at the door to his office.

"At least five that we know of." Eva moved to the front of the group. "We still have a few people we're waiting to hear from."

Pierce tucked one hand in his pocket. "Are any of them the individuals we intended to bring on here?"

Eva nodded. "Three of them."

Pierce was silent for a minute before turning to Shawn. "Call Rico. Tell him to prepare for a flight to Cincinnati." He turned to the women outside his office. "Call everyone who wanted to come to Alaskan Security. I think we have no choice but to bring them here now."

"What if they decide to take the twenty grand?" Heidi crossed her arms and again tried to lean against the frame of the door, this time succeeding. "It's a lot of money."

This time Pierce didn't hesitate. "I will match the offer."

Heidi's eyes went wide. "Can you just keep hemorrhaging money like this? We don't have anyone out in the field working—"

"I have no problem spending what is needed to ensure the safety of people I've agreed to employ, Ms. Rucker." Pierce's attention snapped to Shawn. "As soon as Rico is ready, fly out."

"You're going?" Heidi's eyes were on him.

"Sounds like." Shawn pulled his phone from the holster attached to his pocket.

"How long will it take to do that?"

Shawn glanced up from the screen of his cell. The flush of Heidi's cheeks was a little deeper. "Depends on how fast your people can be ready."

"The faster they can leave, the better." Pierce's gaze was now on Eva, drifting over her shoulder to where Mona stood. "Tell them it is important they move as quickly as possible."

"We will do what we can." Eva turned. "Come on girls. We've got calls to make."

Heidi's eyes stayed on Shawn a second longer. "Enjoy your trip to Cincinnati."

"I'm sure it will be less interesting than the last one."

He knew Heidi would be an issue from the second her blue eyes landed on him. The open way she drank in every inch of his body with a heated gaze.

Avoiding her advances took every bit of willpower he had. Literally. Used it all up and left him with nothing.

Which resulted in his bad behavior this morning.

Hopefully the trip to Cincinnati would give him the time he needed to hit the reset button and put that distance back between them.

Shawn went straight to his office, leaving Heidi standing in the hall as he closed the door on her for the second time today.

It's what he had to keep doing. Close the door on her and any ideas she tried to give him about what they could have together.

It didn't matter. He wasn't in a place to offer her any sort of healthy relationship, especially considering she seemed to be entirely uninterested in a relationship at all.

He dialed Rico's number, sitting through three rings before Alaskan Security's resident pilot finally picked up. "Yello."

"We need to fly back to Cincinnati." Shawn turned to his computer and pulled up the schedule of the small private airport in Fairbanks. "Looks like we can head out in two hours if you can be ready."

"How many are we picking up?"

"Not sure yet. Waiting on a final number from Intel. I'm guessing no more than ten." Shawn fired off an email to the controller at the airport, advising them of the plans. "Meet me at the front in an hour and I'll have a final number for you."

A soft knock came at the door just as he disconnected the call.

His stomach clenched at the sound.

"What?" Shawn tried to force the aggravation he should be feeling over Heidi and the stupid mistake he made this morning into his voice.

The door slowly opened, his heart picking up speed with each tiny bit of hall that appeared.

Because he knew damn well if she came in here that chances were good he would give her anything she asked him for.

When Mona's sleek blonde hair came into view Shawn was as relieved as he was disappointed. She pressed her lips into a tight almost-smile. "We got ahold of everyone who agreed to come initially."

"How many are still willing to come?" He stood, sliding his phone back into its holster.

"Five."

Shawn paused. "Weren't there initially nine who planned to come?"

Mona nodded. "A couple got nervous and decided it wasn't something they wanted to do."

"Not a bad move on their part." Most people weren't cut out for the level they worked at here. It was better if those people weeded themselves out now, before they affiliated themselves with Alaskan Security and potentially ended up in danger because of the association. "What about the other two?"

"They took the other offer."

"Who took it?" Shawn grabbed his gym bag. It was the easiest thing to pack for a possible overnight trip since it already held the basics he needed for a shower. "One from my group and one from Eva's group." Mona backed up as he came toward the door. "The one from my team was a guy named Allen. The other was a woman named Bridget."

Shawn let out a sigh. "Hopefully they know what they're getting themselves into." He glanced at Pierce's closed door. "I wouldn't tell Pierce about Bridget."

Mona's brows went together. "Why?"

"Just trust me." Shawn forced his eyes not to trail down the hall toward Intel's office. "Send me the names of the takers so I can add them to the passenger list."

Mona nodded. "I can do that."

"Thanks." Shawn turned to walk away.

"Shawn."

He stopped, glancing Mona's way over one shoulder.

She pursed her lips before rolling them together. "Never mind."

If she thought he was the kind of person who would try to drag something out of her then Mona was about to realize she was very wrong about him.

Most women were.

Including the one he was leaving behind.

Forty-five minutes later he was packed and ready for the flight, waiting for Rico at the entrance to the main building.

Ten minutes later Rico came rushing in from the direction of the rooming building. "You said an hour, dick." He went straight to the doors leading to the parking that ran across the front of the entrance, pulling one open and holding it as Shawn passed through.

"And you're still early." He held out the fob for the black Rover they were taking.

"Because I know an hour means forty minutes to you." Rico went to the back hatch, lifting it open and tossing his own small bag inside before going to the passenger's door.

"So what you're saying is you're late." Shawn added his bag to the back before pressing the button to close the door and climbing into the driver's seat.

"I'm saying you're always fucking early." Rico pulled down the visor, flipping open the mirror to slick down his still-wet black hair. "You find out how many we're getting?"

"Sounds like only five." Shawn pulled down the main drive leading to the gates barricading the property surrounding Alaskan Security's headquarters. "A few jumped ship."

"Smart chicks." Rico snapped the visor back into place. "They should probably stay as far from this place as possible until shit gets straightened out."

"That would be great except someone else is offering them twenty grand to come work for them." Shawn tipped his head at the two members of Beta stationed at the gate as the Rover passed through. "Cash."

"Shit." Rico wiped one hand down his face. "And we still have five who turned it down?"

"Seems like." Shawn headed toward the airport. Fifteen minutes later they were parked just outside the hangar and walking to the plane. After a thorough safety check they were on their way. The flight was uneventful, with their stop for fuel adding less than half an hour to the total time.

Shawn sat in the cockpit with Rico, enjoying the first bit of peace he'd had since his last trip to Ohio. As soon as they landed he checked his emails, finding one from Mona letting him know all five of the newest additions to Intel were at the airport and ready to go. He finalized their return flight plan before following Rico out. As promised, all five of their passengers sat inside the terminal of the small private airport an hour north of Cincinnati. "You guys ready to go?" Shawn eyed the group of four women and one man. The girls all seemed a little unnerved but the guy was already on his feet with his bags in his hands.

"Is that the plane we're taking?"

Shawn glanced back at the sleek jet. "It is."

The man's head bobbed in a nod. "Awesome." His attention snapped to Shawn, right hand coming out. "I'm Alec."

"Shawn." He grabbed Alec's hand in a shake.

Rico came up, a wide smile on his face. "Are we ready ladies?"

Shawn thumbed over his shoulder at Alec as he went to grab as many of the bags as he could carry. "This one's ours too."

Rico's brows went up. "Brave dude." The pilot grabbed a couple of the larger bags and started rolling them toward the glass doors leading out onto the tarmac. "Let's get going. We might be able to get back before the sun comes up."

"It's already three in the morning." One of the women struggled with her bags, nearly dropping one. Alec stepped in to catch it before it could hit the ground.

"It's midnight in Alaska."

"Oh." She frowned. "I wasn't even thinking about that."

"Is it cold there?" Another of the women followed along, her limited bags making it easier for her to keep up with Shawn's pace.

"It's not hot." Shawn held the door open as the group made their way outside, moving slower than he'd like.

He shouldn't be in a hurry to get back to Alaska. Every second he stayed away was one more second he was away from Heidi. One more second he could use to get his shit together.

But being here reminded him of only her. The night he picked her up. The smell of her skin as they sat together in the back of the plane. It was before he knew she would push every button he tried to not have.

Before he knew she would test the decency stolen from him by a woman who claimed to be devoted.

Faithful.

The last woman out the door gave him a hesitant smile as she passed. "Thanks."

Shawn dipped his head in a nod before letting the door swing closed.

He was the last one in the plane. By the time he climbed through the door everyone was seated except for the final woman. She stood in the center of the seats, one hand on her chest.

"You okay?" Shawn stepped out of the way as Rico closed and locked the door.

"Um." The hand on her chest patted the spot a few times. "I don't love flying and I thought the plane might be a little bigger than this."

He glanced around the space, hoping someone would step up and help their coworker get more comfortable. No one was paying attention to the brunette who looked about thirty seconds from bursting into tears.

He let a silent sigh slip free. "Come on." Shawn went to the front two seats, pulling down the cover to hide the window. He tipped his head for her to sit.

She barely hesitated before hurrying to the seat. Shawn sat beside her, buckling up. He intended to ride back in the cockpit with Rico, but having one of these people freak out mid-flight was not something he wanted to deal with.

"Thank you." She held her bag on her lap, squeezing it tight as the plane started to bounce toward the runway. Her brown eyes squeezed shut as the engine revved at the end of the strip.

"What's your name?" Shawn watched as the knuckles of her hands turned white.

"Lennie."

He frowned down at the clipboard in his hands. He didn't remember—

Lenore Bates

"This is the hardest part, Lennie."

The nose of the plane lifted, sending him back against his seat as the wings caught air.

Lennie's hand slapped across the armrest, grabbing around until it found his.

Shawn almost yanked it free. There was no desire in him to touch this woman, let alone hold her hand.

But he also didn't have the desire to deal with a panicked passenger.

As the aircraft leveled out Lennie's eyes slowly opened and she exhaled, pulling her hand from his. "Thank you." She gave him a weak smile. "Sorry I just grabbed you like that."

Shawn held his clipboard with both hands. "Sorry you don't enjoy flying."

Lennie leaned her head back against the seat, closing her eyes as she seemed to finally relax a little. "It's going to be worth it." Her head rolled his way and she opened her eyes. "I need a change."

"That's what this is." Didn't get much different than moving across the country to Alaska.

"I hope so. I never take any chances. Not ever." Her lips pressed into a sad line. "But I had to move anyway. Might as well move to Alaska, right?"

"It's as good a place as any." Two weeks ago this woman might have piqued his interest. Lennie was probably pretty. Maybe even beautiful.

But she wasn't blonde. Or loud.

Or fearless and mouthy.

Lennie was the kind of woman he should pursue. The kind who would make it easier for him to act like the man he tried to be instead of the man a fractured past made him.

But there wasn't an inch of him that had any interest in her.

Because he was an idiot. One who already made the bed he was either going to have to destroy—

Or sleep in.

CHAPTER 8

"WHAT IN THE hell are you doing?"

Shawn glowered at her from the door to his room.

Heidi yawned as she sat up in his bed. "You told me to come here if I wanted—"

"You knew damn well I was gone." Shawn tossed his bag into the room, but didn't step in along with it.

"You had to come back sometime." Heidi lifted one shoulder, trying to look way more calm than she felt. It took her forever to fall asleep, excitement and fear warring over the space in her belly. "I figured I'd be here when you got back." She sat up a little taller. "Thought maybe you might have a little stress you needed to work off after all that traveling." She grabbed the covers, ready to toss them to one side.

"What are you wearing?"

The sharpness in Shawn's tone stopped her hand mid-air. "I found it on the chair." It was the shirt Shawn wore earlier today when he made it clear her ideas of who he was were way off base. Heidi snapped the covers off her lower body. "I figured you wouldn't mind." She let her knees drop open as she worked her way across the bed, hoping Shawn would notice the shirt was all she wore.

"You have no fucking idea what you're doing, Rucker."

"I have a very good idea of what I'm doing." She stepped onto the floor and walked his way. "I'm cashing in on the offer you made me."

"I shouldn't have made it." His dark eyes followed her every move as she came closer.

"Are you saying you take it back?" Heidi stood right in front of him and forced a chill, watching the pupils of his eyes dilate as they fell to her tightening nipples.

It was a trick that worked every damn time.

"I'm saying I shouldn't have made it." Shawn's gaze slowly came to meet hers. "And the best thing you can do right now is walk out of this room and never come back."

"If you don't want me all you have to do is say it, Shawn." She'd asked him a million different times in a million different ways.

That was an exaggeration, but only slightly.

Never once had Shawn been willing to simply say he didn't want her.

Because he did want her, but for some reason really thought she shouldn't want him.

Maybe he was a killer.

Oh. That's right. He was.

Maybe he broke the law.

Oh. That's right. He did.

And she wanted to bone him anyway, because lots of reasons. Quite a few of them having to do with what happened in his office yesterday.

Heidi took a breath, knowing this could be the end of the single most exciting sexual relationship she'd been in.

And the man hadn't even taken his clothes off yet.

"Tell me you aren't interested, and I will go back to my room and we can pretend like none of this ever happened."

Shawn's whole expression darkened. "Is that what you want? To pretend nothing happened?"

"Why are you acting like you're mad at me right now? Isn't that what you're telling me to do?" Heidi scoffed out a huff of irritation. "You are about the most frustrating man I've ever met."

"Good. I'm glad I'm not the only one frustrated right now." He finally took a step into the room, bumping her back with his big body. "Because you've done nothing but frustrate the hell out of me since you got on that goddamned plane."

"Well I'm sorry I'm such a pain in your ass. At least I've been straight up with you." She stabbed at him with one finger. "You can't even decide if you want to fuck around with me or not." She poked at him again just because it felt nice to take a little frustration out. "One minute you have your hand down my pants and the next you kick me out on my ass. Make up your mind, asshole."

"What did you call me?" Shawn's eye twitched just a little as he glared down at her.

Heidi stood a little taller. "I called you an asshole."

Shawn's head dipped, bringing his face closer to hers. "You should probably say it one more time so you'll remember it, Kitten, because you hit the nail on the head." He crowded her space, somehow coming closer without moving his feet. "I am all that and plenty more."

Oh she knew he was plenty more. That's why she was still here, fighting with him instead of banging on Zeke's door.

Wherever it was.

Because Shawn's plenty more was more addicting than her computer could ever be. "You've made that perfectly clear."

His dark brows raised.

Like she'd surprised him.

"What? You think I didn't notice you're as big of a pain in the ass as I am?" Heidi smirked. "Because it's pretty fucking evident."

"Then why in the hell are you here right now?" Shawn sounded almost exasperated by her pursuit.

Yet another mixed damn message. "I'm here because I was willing to agree to the terms you've suddenly decided to take back."

He stared at her silently.

Because of course he did. Giving her a straight yes or no is clearly too difficult of a thing for him to do.

Heidi took a half step toward his side, keeping her eyes on his as she went around him on her way out the door. "But I guess since the offer's off the table then I'll just have to go handle things myself."

She made it three steps.

Three heartbeats.

Half a breath.

Before Shawn's big hand clamped down on her arm, yanking her back. His shoulder pressed to the center of her stomach and a second later she was up and flying toward the bed, his hand on her back controlling the fall as she hit the mattress a second before his body hit hers. "Why do you do this to me?"

"Because you won't just tell me to leave you alone." She could barely breathe as his nose ran alongside hers. "And you won't just tell me you want me."

"I don't want to want you."

"See?" She shoved at his chest. "That's the bullshit I'm talking about."

Shawn's weight didn't budge as his lips hovered just over hers. "You're all I fucking think about."

"Then maybe you should fuck me and get it out of your system." The feel of him on her, the stiff length of his dick pressed tight to her thigh already had her aching.

"That's not how this works with me, Kitten. If I fuck you I'll want to do it again." His lips brushed against the spot just at the corner of her mouth. "And again." Another pass on the opposite corner. "And again."

"That sounds like fun too." She whimpered as his hand fisted in the back of her hair, holding her head tight as he leaned up to look down at her.

"Why won't you just leave me alone?"

It was a really good question. One she didn't actually have an answer to outside of the fact that her entire body responded to him in a way it never had for any other man. "I don't know."

His gaze moved over her face. "That's not a good answer, Rucker."

"It's the truth." She swallowed down the anticipation making her throat tight.

"The truth." Shawn's head tipped close as his lips skimmed over the skin of her jaw. "The truth is an important thing, Kitten."

"Then why don't you ever give it to me?" She blinked up at the ceiling as Shawn froze.

"I'm not sure you can handle the truth, Heidi."

"I can handle anything." She'd spent her entire life being an outcast. A little different from everyone else.

The odd one in every group she tried to be a part of.

Nothing and no one ever fit with her.

It gave her a thick skin and an early understanding of the way the world worked.

The way relationships worked.

Which is why she chose not to have them.

"Not this." Shawn's head lifted. "Not the way you think you can." He started to ease off her.

Heidi grabbed him, latching on. "Then why did you make me that offer earlier?"

Shawn's lips flattened.

"I gave you the truth." She grabbed onto the tiny handhold he'd given her and planned to dig in. "Now you give it to me."

He didn't move for at least ten seconds and she held onto him the whole time.

"I offered it to you because it's what I want."

Heidi nearly choked as her throat swallowed involuntarily. "That's really what you want?"

Shawn's eyes closed for a second before coming back to find hers. "That is a version of what I want."

"A version of—"

"What I want is more complicated than that." He tried to get up again but she held fast. "Let me go, Rucker."

"No." She held tighter, adding her legs in for good measure. "We're finally getting somewhere."

"We're not." Shawn moved across the bed, taking her clinging body with him. "Because I'm not fucking you."

She'd never worked so hard for a dick in all her life. Never had to, honestly. They were easy enough to catch. Stick your boobs out and lick your lips and the offers poured in.

"God you're frustrating." Heidi held tight as Shawn managed to stand up. She peeked down at the floor. "If you're trying to convince me to not want to have sex with you this is probably not going to help your cause any."

She was not a tiny little slip of a woman. She didn't miss a meal and frequently added in an extra one for good measure. Yet Shawn just stood up with her latched onto him like it was nothing.

"You shouldn't want to have anything with me."

"Yet here we are." Heidi's thighs burned from holding herself up in place, but she was going to get an answer from him even if it meant she couldn't walk in the morning. "Still going in the same damn circle."

"Because your stubborn ass won't just leave it alone." Shawn glanced down as her thighs started to shake. "Damn it, Heidi." He banded one arm around her waist, supporting her weight. "You're making this really fucking impossible."

"Then man up and tell me to leave." She was a little mad at the fact he thought she was the one making this fucking impossible. "Just say you don't want to do this and I'll leave." She smirked as he stared at her silently. "That's what I thought." Heidi wrapped her arms tighter around his neck. "You can't say it because it's not true."

"What I want shouldn't matter."

An odd emotion pinched her gut.

Hell, it was odd that emotion was involved here at all. Sex was just sex.

"If you want me, and I want you, then that's all that should matter." It was a simple enough thing to understand. They were two grown people who obviously found each other attractive.

Why not have sex?

"You make it sound much simpler than it is, Kitten."

Kitten.

The word snaked down her spine, making every inch of her tingle as it went. When he was trying to push her away Shawn called her Heidi or Rucker.

Or pain in the ass.

But when Shawn called her Kitten his thoughts seemed to be headed in a very different direction.

"You're the one making it difficult." Heidi used the last bit of strength in her legs to pull tighter to him.

A deep rumble moved through his chest as the move rubbed her right against the rigid line of his dick. "I disagree completely with that assessment." Shawn stepped toward the bed, dropping forward, catching their fall with one arm against the mattress. "You have made my life fucking impossible since you got on that damn plane." He walked them up the bed on his hands and knees before pulling the arm holding her in place free. "Coming in my office every fucking day." His wide body lifted up as he grabbed the hem of the shirt she wore and yanked it up, revealing her bare body. "Coming to my room and lying in my bed with no fucking panties covering your pretty pussy."

This man went from cold to hot in about two freaking seconds. It would give her whiplash if she wasn't already a puddle of anticipation completely at his mercy.

Shawn shoved the shirt up to her chin, exposing her belly and breasts to his dark gaze.

Another low growl shot straight to her core, making her breath catch and her skin pull tight on a shiver.

"Fucking perfect." Shawn's eyes snagged on her nipples as they puckered. His head dipped, mouth meeting one tip to pull it deep between his lips.

Heidi's eyes rolled closed as his body settled over hers, Shawn's teeth and tongue rolling across her ready flesh with calculated, perfectly executed precision.

It's why she wanted him. They way Shawn carried himself made it clear he excelled in everything he did.

Every activity he performed.

With him there would be no fumbling hands. No clit confusion. No being left high and dry in the climax department.

The heat of his mouth moved down her body, nipping at the soft fullness of her belly before pulling her legs wide enough his shoulders could fit between them.

And that was real freaking wide.

He didn't waste any time kissing her thighs or licking useless parts that literally did nothing.

Shawn went straight for the money shot. His tongue immediately found her clit and went to work, rubbing the spot with wide, flat strokes that sent her back bowing off the bed as she clawed at the sheets. When his fingers slid into her body she was gone, the glide of some part of him finally fucking her sending her straight over the edge. Shawn's tongue stayed on her as she came, the steady pressure dragging it out until her body went limp.

Limp enough she didn't fight when Shawn grabbed her legs, pressing them tight together and pushing her knees to her chest as his tongue slid the length of her slit, licking along her now drenched opening, his tongue dipping inside. "Your cum is so fucking sweet, Kitten."

Jesus.

What in the hell had she gotten herself into? Whatever it was, she planned on getting into it as often as possible.

Shawn slowly rocked her legs to one side, his teeth sinking into the cheek of her ass as he sucked the skin there to the point of stinging on his way to lie beside her. He collapsed onto the mattress, one arm wrapping around her waist to pull her tight to him.

"What are you doing?" She leaned to peek at where his face was planted into the center of the pillow.

"I'm going the fuck to sleep."

****

"YOUR HAIR LOOKS extra fluffy today." Mona reached out to flick a strand of Heidi's hair with one finger. "I wish my hair did that."

"You bleach it enough it would." Heidi had all of five minutes after Shawn passed out to get ready for her morning meeting with the girls. She'd wobbled to her room, pulled on some clothes, thrown a few waves in her hair, and spritzed on some body spray, hoping to cover the smell of the naughty way she spent the previous hour.

Mona's nose wrinkled. "Nope." She twisted a lock of her own hair. "This is what it looks like bleached." She tipped her head down to show the barely-there darkness of her roots. "See?"

"I didn't know you bleached your hair, Mona." Heidi assumed Mona's icy hair color was natural. It sure as hell looked like it was.

"If I don't it just looks dirty." Mona glanced up as Eva and Harlow came down the hall. "And here I figured you'd be the one who was late."

"What can I say?" Heidi shrugged her shoulders. "I was up early today." It was actually kind of nice. She had time to fill up her water. Grab a pack of trail mix for breakfast. Even chat a little with Mona about their plans for the meeting.

"Now if I can just get you to clean off your desk." Mona's lips barely lifted at the tease.

"Now you're pushing it." Heidi leaned back in her chair, shoving the extra sweatshirt she brought behind her lower back.

"That help any?" Mona watched as she poked at the makeshift pillow.

"Not really." Heidi finally gave up and pulled the shirt out, stacking it on her desk. "These chairs just suck."

"Then thank God Elise came." Eva dropped her bag next to her desk. "Hopefully she can order us some new ones since no one else seems capable of doing it."

"Pierce probably would have but Mona wouldn't let him." Heidi grinned as Bess came

108

through the door, her smile dropping almost immediately at the sight of Bessie's empty arms. "Where's my man?"

"He's with his Nene eating cinnamon rolls." Bess let out a breath. "Thank goodness, because I needed a break."

"Cinnamon rolls?" Heidi peered down into the plastic sleeve of trail mix that suddenly didn't taste as good as it sounded.

"Brock's expanding his culinary skills now that the same woman keeps showing up for breakfast every day." Eva leaned back to poke at her stomach. "I think he's hoping I'll start looking like you."

"Can't say I blame him there." Heidi picked through the peanuts to fish out a chocolate bit.

"Please tell me you do squats or something to make that thing look the way it does." Harlow pulled her computer out of her bag and set it on her desk. "Something to make it so perfectly round."

"It's genetics." Heidi wiggled her brows. "It's how my mom snagged my dad." She pointed to her derriere. "The booty."

"Ladies." Dutch came through the door, two coffee cups in his hands. He passed one to Harlow, along with a kiss to her lips. "Are we ready to go?"

"We were just waiting for you to grace us with your presence, Pretty Boy." Harlow gave Dutch a little smile as she sat in her seat. She turned to where Eva and Mona sat. "Tell me about the new additions to the team."

"Technically there's only four who will be joining Intel." Eva opened her own computer. "The fifth was our office manager."

"Whose team were they on, yours or Mona's?" Harlow jotted the information down as Eva continued to explain.

"Both. Two from mine. Two from Mona's." Eva picked up two files from her desk. "Mine are Paige and Lennie." She took the files to Harlow, passing them over.

"Mine are Alec and Willa." Mona passed her files to Bess. "Both are very skilled at digging into the business end of bad behavior."

"And your team focused on personal issues, correct?" Harlow flipped through the information on Eva's two recruits.

"Yup." Eva tipped her head toward Heidi. "This one was on my team too."

"Do you trust them to be a part of what we have going on now, or should we set them up in a separate room and give them other things to focus on?"

"I've worked with both those women for years. They routinely dealt with highly private situations and I never had an issue."

Mona nodded along with Eva. "They are all used to confidentiality."

"This is more than confidentiality, though." Harlow looked up, her eyes moving between Eva, Mona, and Heidi. "If they decide to discuss something they shouldn't then there's a very real chance they could end up in a dangerous situation."

Heidi leaned toward where Eva and Mona sat beside her. "Pierce will kill them."

Mona's attention turned her way. "Pierce will not kill them."

Heidi lifted her hands. "Fine." She leaned back in her horrible chair. "Pierce will have them killed."

CHAPTER 9

"I DIDN'T EXPECT to see you up and around so early." Brock was in the kitchen area of the rooming building when Shawn went in to grab a cup of coffee.

"I have work to do." Shawn eyed the baking dish Brock set on the counter. "We're all going to get fat sitting around and eating the bullshit you keep making."

"Some people like my bullshit." Brock grinned at him. "Particularly the ladies."

"I thought you were over the ladies." Shawn dragged out the s at the end of the word. He never understood Brock's love of one-night stands. The thought of having a woman in your bed and then wanting her gone was almost impossible for him to comprehend.

"No more ladies for me." Brock pulled back the foil covering the cinnamon rolls. "I mean Intel. Those girls can pack away some food." He leaned against the counter. "Heidi especially loves the cinnamon rolls."

"Good for Heidi." Shawn turned his attention to making his cup of coffee. Hopefully no one saw her leaving his room this morning, but knowing Heidi she probably skipped her way down the hall.

"You're smiling awful big at that coffee."

"Cause I'm fucking tired and I need the caffeine." Shawn pressed his lips into place as he tipped back the drink, letting the burn distract him from the pride trying to straighten his shoulders and puff out his chest.

He could almost guarantee she was a happy woman this morning.

Because of him. What he gave her.

"Might want to pour a second cup then, cause I heard Intel's calling a meeting to go over what they found out about all of us." Brock grabbed a bottle of water from the fridge. "And I'm sure it's going to be a shit show."

"Noted." Shawn drank down a little more coffee as Brock left. He eyed the cinnamon rolls sitting on the counter and the stack of paper plates sitting beside them. Shawn glanced around, making sure no one was looking. He quickly scooped out one of the center rolls, spooning on some more of the glaze that rolled down to the bottom of the pan, before grabbing the plate and going to his office. As he rounded the corner he caught sight of Heidi's head ducking into Pierce's office just before the door closed.

The hall was quiet. No sounds of feminine voices carrying down from the open door to Intel's office. He slowly walked past Pierce's door, listening to be sure the room at the end of the hall was empty. Shawn leaned through the doorway, scanning the space before quickly stepping in and depositing the cinnamon roll on Heidi's crap-covered desk.

He stared at the mess. It was insanity that she could even think sitting there, let alone function at the capacity they needed her to.

The trash can beside her desk was empty except for the plastic liner. Shawn glanced over his shoulder before quickly tossing anything that was clearly trash. He stacked like items before grabbing all the pens and pencils to put them in—

He squinted down at the workspace.

She needed something to hold her pencils and pens. Shawn hurried down the hall to the kitchen and grabbed one of the glass tumblers from the cabinet, dropping in the writing utensils as he walked back into the office and placed them on Heidi's somewhat more organized desk.

It was still out of control, but at least now it wasn't covered with trash and she could find something to write with. Shawn went back to his office, leaving the door open as he checked the list of emails he had from past clients hoping to secure protection he currently couldn't offer. One of them caught his eye.

Wade and Brock went to Florida right before Bess came on as a client. The client there was the daughter of a well-known player in the cartel smuggling cocaine in from South America.

Shawn scanned the email from Courtney twice to be sure he was reading what he thought he was.

No way was Pierce going to let him turn this down.

"Shit."

"What's wrong?"

Shawn glanced up. Heidi stood in the doorway to his office, propped against the jam, a plate in one hand and a fork dangling from her lips.

"Nothing."

Heidi poked her fork into the cinnamon roll on her plate. "Doesn't seem like nothing." She slowly walked into his office, sitting down in the chair as she bit off another chunk of the pastry he left for her. "Seems like you're upset."

"I'm fine." He turned away from her.

"I'll find out anyway. Might as well tell me now." Heidi leaned to peek at the screen of his computer.

Shawn leaned forward to block her view. "Aren't you supposed to be looking into the teams?"

Heidi shook her head. "No. Apparently now I'm supposed to be finding where Twatty Tod is hiding." She sighed. "And Chandler." She wrinkled her nose. "I can guarantee you that one isn't hiding out in some freaking motel..." Her eyes slid to one side. "I gotta go."

"Nice talking to you." Shawn watched as she rushed away, disappointment tugging at his gut.

And disappointment was a dangerous thing.

"Oh." Heidi's head poked in. "Don't make me hack your email. I want to know why you're upset." Her lips twisted into a wicked smile. "Maybe you can tell me tonight."

"Maybe."

She lifted her brows at him. "Back to playing hard to get? I thought we were over that hump." The plate of cinnamon roll eased into view. "Especially considering you're leaving me presents and cleaning up my messes."

Then she was gone, not even pausing to give him a chance to explain.

Not that he had an explanation.

A good one, anyway.

He was falling right back into the same pattern that ended so badly for him last time.

The need to work out made him jumpy. A nice run or good lift session would work out the frustration constantly eating at his mind.

But there wasn't any time today.

Shawn stood and went across the hall to Pierce's office, striding in and closing the door behind him. "We've got a problem."

"Christ." Pierce dropped the pen in his hand to the surface of his desk. "What now?"

"Courtney Vasquez just sent me an email." Shawn went to sit down in one of the leather chairs across from Pierce. "She's in trouble."

Pierce took a long breath. "Damn it." He leaned back in his chair. "I don't have time for this right now."

"Then I'll tell her we can't help her." It would make everyone's lives easier.

Except Courtney's.

"You know damn well we can't do that." Pierce tapped one finger on the top of his desk, staring at the spot. He was silent for a few long seconds. "I can't send men to Florida right now. They'd be sitting ducks."

"Especially if Courtney's daddy has any connection to the problems we've got going on up here." They'd dealt with highly questionable people over the years. The kind of people that could be with you as easily as they could be against you. "Maybe it's a set up."

Pierce's eyes lifted to Shawn's. "You think Vasquez might be involved in what's happening?"

"I think anything's possible at this point." Shawn raked one hand through his hair. "We could tell her that if she can get here we can protect her. See what happens."

Pierce fell silent again as he stared across the room. "Very well." He stood. "Where can we house her?"

"Let's worry about that when and if the time comes." Shawn wasn't convinced the woman wasn't just being dramatic, trying to find a way to get attention from anyone she could. Brock and Wade had a hell of a time wrangling the wild socialite during their time with her, and it wouldn't be a surprise to find out all this was just done out of boredom.

Unless it wasn't.

"I will go tell Intel we have yet another lead for them to look into."

"I can do it." Shawn was on his feet before the offer fully registered.

Pierce stood at the door. "We should both go." He turned to look down the hall. "It's probably safer than sending just one of us in anyway."

"Don't tell me you're scared of a little blonde woman, Pierce." Shawn stifled a smile. Everyone knew Pierce had his eye on a member of Intel.

Everyone except the woman in question.

"I could say the same thing to you," he turned to give Shawn a knowing glance, "couldn't I?"

They walked through the door one after the other with Pierce leading the way.

Harlow groaned. "We are never going to get all this shit done if you keep coming in here to bother us."

"I apologize for the intrusion." Pierce stood at the front of the room. "Unfortunately I do not have good news."

"Imagine that." Heidi's feet were on her desk and her computer was perched on her knees. "What now?"

"Now we have an additional lead to investigate in the search for who exactly is causing our problems." Pierce glanced to Shawn. "This morning Shawn received an email from a former client hoping to hire us again." The owner of Alaskan Security slowly stepped toward the windowed side of the room. "The client in question is the daughter of a well-connected drug smuggler located in Florida."

"And you think her daddy might be involved in what's happening?" Mona eyed Pierce as he came closer to her desk.

Pierce gave her a slow smile. "That's right, Ms. Ayers." His attention focused on the woman watching him with a wary gaze. "The timing of her request is suspicious at the very least."

"What is it at the very most?" Heidi's eyes found Shawn, hanging on his for a second before slowly moving down his frame.

"A set up." Mona answered for Pierce. She sat perfectly straight in her seat, attention fixed on Pierce. "We will need names and locations. That will make our job move faster."

"I will have them to you immediately." Pierce's tone softened. "Is there anything else I can offer you, Ms. Ayers?"

Mona held his gaze for a second longer before dropping it to the screen of her computer. "No thank you, Mr. Barrick."

Ouch. Shawn lifted his brows at the thinly-veiled rejection Mona didn't even realize she made.

"Hey, Captain."

Something bounced off the front of Shawn's shirt. He glanced down at the orange circle sitting just beside his boot before looking up at Heidi. "Did you just throw candy at me?"

She smirked. "When are you getting us new chairs?"

"Shawn doesn't have time to deal with that." Eva rocked from side to side in her seat. "I'm going to have Elise order them when she gets in this morning."

"Who is Elise?" He didn't have time to deal with piddly bullshit like ordering chairs and groceries.

But that didn't mean he wouldn't.

"She was our office manager at Investigative Resources." Eva popped the cap off a tube of chapstick and wiped it across her lips. "You picked her up last night. Did you not even introduce yourself to anyone?"

The reminder of his plane ride sent a twist of guilt through Shawn's gut. "Not everyone."

Two. He'd interacted with two of the people they picked up in Ohio. One of them ended up talking his ear off the whole plane ride.

After she held his hand.

His attention slid to Heidi, only to find her watching him with interested eyes.

"If you tell me what you want I'll get them ordered today." Shawn avoided Heidi's gaze.

"That's why it will just be easier if Elise does it. She knows what we had at IR and where to order them." Eva waved her hand Shawn's way. "It's fine. She should be in soon anyway."

"I have scheduled a meeting for this afternoon where I can touch base with the new arrivals and make sure they understand what is expected of them. As soon as we are finished I will send them your way." Pierce turned to where Dutch and Harlow sat. "If you find anything of interest before then please don't hesitate to find me."

"You're feeling awfully optimistic today." Harlow lifted her brows as she frowned at her computer screen. "Because I'm not sure we're going to find anything of interest anytime soon."

"There has to be something we're missing. Some connection that explains why this is all happening." Bess stared at the large white board Pierce installed after the women took permanent markers to the wall in an effort to untangle the mess unraveling around them. "We just have to find that one thing and the rest will make sense."

"I have no doubt you will do it. If this room can't solve it no one can."

"You don't have to butter us up, Pierce. We're already working as hard as we can on this." Harlow's eyes lifted to where Pierce stood. "You could see about putting a rush on those chairs, though, since we're having to spend a shit-ton of time on our asses." She thumbed Heidi's way. "And not all of us have the cushion that one does."

Heidi shrugged. "Can't help it." Her eyes slid to Shawn. "It's just what the good Lord gave me." She winked at him.

He forced his lips into a frown, smothering down the smile trying to push its way into being. "I've got work to do." Shawn turned to leave.

"Hey, Shawn?"

He stopped, taking a breath before turning around to face Heidi. He lifted a brow in question.

"I'll see you later."

There was no answer to give her. The best thing he could do was turn back around and go to his office, hoping to God no one knew she'd finally managed to wiggle her way into his bed.

He dropped into his chair and pulled up the office supply website he ordered from. After spending a few minutes narrowing down the best options he fired off an email to Heidi sharing the links so she could choose which one she wanted.

Three minutes later she was at his door. "An email? Really?"

"What's wrong with an email?" She wanted a chair. He wanted to be the one to provide it for her.

Heidi meandered her way into his office, closing the door before taking slow steps around the side of his desk. She rested a palm on each arm of his chair and leaned down. "You could have just shown me tonight."

"Tonight?" He was used to working for his sex. Putting in extreme time and effort to make his way into where he wanted to be.

Heidi didn't make him work for it, and damned if that didn't make him want to prove he could.

That he was willing to do whatever it took to be all she wanted.

All she needed.

Heidi's head tipped in a slow nod. "Tonight." Her eyes raked down the front of his chest. "Unless you're unavailable. In that case—"

"Why would I be unavailable, Heidi?" He studied her expression, looking for some sort of clue into what she was thinking.

Why she would think he had better things to do.

What she might think those better things were.

"I don't really know anything about you." The confession was softer than her words normally were. "Maybe you have other things going on."

"Like?" It shouldn't matter what else she thought he might have going on, but it did.

Because maybe Heidi thought the deal he made her was one-sided.

The deal he half-heartedly tried to take back out of guilt and embarrassment.

One of her shoulders lifted and dropped. "I don't know. Just other things."

"You mean other women."

Her eyes snapped to his. "That's not what I said."

"But is it what you meant?" Jealousy was the fuel that fed the fire he had no clue how to extinguish. It was an emotion he believed Heidi didn't possess.

But if she did...

Shawn reached out to grab the front of her shirt, pulling her down, catching her as she fell into him. He held her close, one arm around her waist, his hand pressed to the soft curve of her belly as the other palm cradled her head, holding her ear to his lips. "How does the thought of me touching another woman make you feel, Kitten?" Heidi gasped as his teeth caught the lobe of her ear.

"You can do whatever you want."

He nipped her skin a little harder. "That doesn't answer my question." Shawn pressed the hand on her belly higher, lifting the weight of one full breast in his palm. "What if I did to another woman the

124

things I do to you?" He thumbed her nipple through the fabric of her shirt and bra. "What if I licked another woman's pussy the way I licked yours this morning?"

She shivered, the nipple between his fingers pulling tight. He twisted the pinched tip. "Answer me."

"I'd be pissed as fuck."

The unrest he'd felt since Heidi stepped on the plane in Cincinnati stilled at the admission. "Say it again."

Heidi grabbed his face with one hand, the hold tight enough his lips parted. She leaned in close, bringing her eyes in line with his. "I'd be pissed as hell if your mouth was on another woman."

Jealousy. It was a beast he didn't mean to create and tried never to feed.

And this woman was a fucking feast.

But what if she ate at the same table?

Shawn shoved one hand into the front of her pants, immediately going under the lacey fabric of her panties to find the swollen lips of the pussy he buried his face in only hours ago. "What if I promise to only touch you, Kitten?" He shoved two fingers into her slick cunt, working the nub of her clit with his thumb. "Would that make you happy?"

Heidi's head dropped to his shoulder, her eyes rolling shut as he fucked her with his fingers. "Yes."

He pulled his fingers out, giving her a light slap. "Spread you legs so I can play with my pussy."

Her thighs immediately parted.

"That's my girl." Shawn leaned into her ear as he worked his fingers back inside her. "Who owns your pussy, Kitten?"

"You do." She whimpered as he rubbed against her wall, finding the spot that would make her toes curl.

"That's right." He moved faster, stroking her clit in time with each slide of his fingers. "Who owns your cum, Heidi?"

Her walls clenched tight as her thighs jerked. "You do." Heidi's lower lip pressed tight between her teeth as she came, one hand fisted tight in his shirt.

Her softly relaxed body went rigid at the sound of a knock on his door.

"Relax, Kitten." Shawn quickly slid her off his lap and into his chair standing to the side just as the door opened. He dropped his hands to his hips and glared at her as Pierce came into view. "You like the chair or not?"

Heidi blinked at him twice before her lips curved into an easy smile. "I really enjoy sitting in it."

Pierce's gaze moved from Heidi to rest on Shawn. "If you're done here I would appreciate both of you coming to Intel's office. There's been a development."

CHAPTER 10

HOW IN THE hell could there be a development? She'd been out of the office for less than fifteen minutes.

Heidi marched down the hall with Shawn and Pierce following behind her.

Pierce definitely knew something was up between them, but right now she didn't have the time to worry about that.

"What did you find?" Heidi stood in the middle of the room, glancing at the women working at their desks.

"What are you talking about?" Harlow's brows came together.

Heidi turned to where Pierce was walking through the door.

"I'm afraid this isn't that kind of development, Ms. Rucker." Pierce's eyes were pinched at the corners and his lips pressed into a tight line. "One of our safe houses has burnt down."

Heidi turned to fully face Pierce. "I bet I can guess which one."

None of the men seemed to think Pierce could possibly be involved in this. If she was a better woman she would have taken advantage of the private time she spent with Shawn to get his take on Pierce's possible knowledge of what Shadow was doing.

But that didn't sound as fun as what she actually did during that time, so...

Pierce's gaze sharpened on her. "Why would you think that?"

Heidi glanced over her shoulder, catching Dutch's eyes before looking to Harlow. This wasn't her fucking circus and she was already risking stepping on toes. Confronting Pierce about his possible involvement would be more than stepping on toes.

It was banging them with a hammer.

"We know about what Shadow did, Pierce." Shawn's admission surprised her, taking Heidi out of the hot seat and immediately turning Pierce's attention away.

"What are you talking about?" Pierce's head spun back and forth as he looked between Dutch and Shawn.

"We know what really happened to Richards." Shawn glanced Heidi's way before stepping closer to Pierce, putting his body between her and the owner of Alaskan Security. "We know Shadow handed him over."

"What?" Pierce's brows lowered over his dark eyes. They immediately snapped to where Dutch sat beside Harlow. "To whom?"

Dutch studied Pierce for a minute. "Are you trying to say you didn't know this happened?"

Pierce raked one hand through his hair, leaving it looking looser than normal. "If you're saying that you believe Shadow handed Howard Richards over to someone then yes, I'm saying I was unaware that could be a possibility."

"Not a possibility." Heidi pulled up the video they had of Howard and Shadow, playing it across one of the large screens on the wall behind Harlow and Dutch. "It's what happened."

Pierce watched the grainy scene she'd studied a hundred times, trying to figure out a way to determine who the other group of men were.

Pierce's expression was unreadable as he stared at the screen. When the footage was over he continued to stand still for a few seconds more before finally turning to the door. "I have calls to make."

"Wait." Heidi stood behind her desk. "What was the development you wanted to tell us about?"

"Oh." Pierce glanced to the screen. "It's irrelevant now."

"Irrelevant? How?" The more information they had the better off they'd be. Even something that seemed unimportant could be the key to cracking this whole mess of a thing open.

Pierce stood in the doorway a second longer, his eyes on her. "Howard Richards was found this morning by local law enforcement."

Heidi almost dropped into her chair. "Really?" Of all the things Pierce might say, that wasn't even on her radar. "How is that not relevant? Where is he now?"

Pierce reached up to smooth down the hair he mussed earlier. "You misunderstand, Ms. Rucker." He glanced at Shawn. "Howard Richards is dead. He was found in a snowbank just outside Fairbanks."

Heidi did drop into her chair this time. "Dead?"

She didn't like Howard. Did her best to stay away from him when they worked together.

Back when she thought his name was still Mike Nestor.

But no one she knew had ever been killed before.

"How did he die?" Eva's complexion was a little pale.

"I don't know that information." Pierce hesitated before continuing. "I would venture to guess that, officially, it will be attributed to hypothermia."

"But he didn't really freeze, did he?" The strength of Eva's voice was surprising given how white her skin was. "He was killed."

"I wish I had proof that was true, Ms. Tatum." Pierce worked his jaw from side to side. "I would say you should continue your investigation in a way that takes any possibility into consideration."

"Who did they give him to, Pierce?" Harlow clutched her ever-present coffee cup close to her chest. "Your best guess."

Pierce's eyes flicked from Dutch to Shawn before returning to Harlow. "I am concerned that we are dealing with a much bigger problem than I initially realized." Pierce turned to leave.

"That doesn't answer my question, Pierce." Harlow stood up, clearly ready to chase him down the hall if she needed to. "Who was that in the video?"

Pierce stopped, his back staying to them for a second before he finally turned around. For a split second Heidi could see the weight pressing down on him.

The responsibility Pierce shouldered.

But his polished mask slipped back into place almost instantly as he straightened, tucked one hand in his pocket and met Harlow's gaze.

"I believe who you saw in that video was GHOST."

****

HEIDI RUBBED HER temples. The past hour gave her a headache of epic proportions. One that no amount of painkillers could obliterate.

"What the fuck are we supposed to do now?" Eva had been pacing the room since Pierce and Shawn left. "I was just starting to think Howard might be a bigger deal in this than we initially thought." She whipped her arms out then dropped them down by her sides. "But now he's fucking dead."

"Maybe he was a big deal. Maybe all this will just fall apart now." Bessie's eyes followed Eva as she paced.

"Or maybe he was as big of a peon as we thought and whoever we're dealing with got tired of his shit." Harlow stared at the whiteboard that was absolutely no help right now.

"Or GHOST killed him." Mona glanced up from her computer. "Used him for whatever they needed and then got rid of him."

"But what would they need him for?" Heidi moved through the forums on one of the underground sites where she cut her hacking teeth when she was younger.

All Pierce would tell them was GHOST was a division of the CIA.

Sort of.

A division that didn't officially exist.

Heidi found the chat room she was looking for and started typing. Until they knew more about what GHOST was, they wouldn't be able to understand what might be going on.

"I wish freaking Pierce would have told us more about GHOST." Harlow huffed out a breath.

"He doesn't know any more." Heidi was confident in that. Pierce was hard to read on a lot of different levels, but he definitely wanted them to find out what in the hell was going on. His company depended on it. "He would have told us if he did."

Mona looked from Heidi to Eva.

"What?" Heidi sat up straight. "What are you thinking?"

Mona pressed her lips together, rocking in her chair for a second before her thought came tumbling out. "Wouldn't Zeke know who they are?"

Heidi chewed her lip. Mona was really getting so much better at voicing her ideas and opinions and she hated to shoot any of them down.

But even if Zeke knew he definitely would not be telling any of them. "Do you think that's information he would give anyone?"

Mona tapped her fingers against the desk. "He might accidentally give it to me."

"Accidentally?" Heidi glanced at Harlow to see if she was the only one not following Mona's train of thought on this. "How would he accidentally give it to you?"

"Well most people find me unintimidating." Mona's words moved faster. "They think I'm weak." She smiled a little bit. "I don't think he would ever guess that I'd know what was going on." Her lips spread wider. "Like how they talked about Santa's cabin in front of me."

"Holy shit, Mona." Heidi leaned back in her seat. "I think your super power is being unassuming."

Mona sat a little straighter and smiled a little brighter. "I know."

"Would you feel comfortable doing that?" Eva didn't sound as eager as Mona clearly was. "What if Zeke figures out you're trying to get information?"

Mona worked her lips to one side. "I think it's still worth the risk."

"But the risk is that you could end up frozen in a pile of snow. Eva turned to Harlow and Heidi. "Am I the only one who realizes what could happen here?"

"We have to do something." Mona glanced up as Dutch came back from his meeting with the team leads. She immediately went quiet, turning back to her work.

Dutch didn't seem to notice the change in Mona as he went to his desk, dropping a kiss on Harlow's head as he passed her.

Maybe Mona was right. Zeke might not ever see her coming. It didn't seem like many people did.

"Holy cow this room is huge."

Heidi turned to the door as a group of familiar faces filed through. "Hey." She jumped up from her seat. "Isn't it crazy how big this place is?" She and Elise were pretty good friends when they worked together at Investigative Resources, so she was thrilled when the office manager agreed to come to Alaska. "How was your flight?"

Elise's eyes widened. "I've never flown private before. It was an experience."

"It was terrifying." Lennie edged her way past Elise, giving Mona a little wave. "But on the plus side I didn't barf on poor Shawn so that was good."

Heidi's eyes immediately went to Lennie. "That is good."

Lennie was gorgeous. Dark shiny hair. A sweet face and wide eyes that made her look innocent and even more delicate than her small frame did.

Heidi pushed the odd sensation aching in her chest away. "I'm sure he would have gotten over it if you did."

"He is just the nicest guy." Lennie smiled her bright smile. "I was so scared and he held my hand while the plane took off."

Heidi's smile froze on her face, the skin of her cheeks pulling tight as she tried to keep it where it was. "That was nice of him."

"Where should we set up?" The deep voice came from the back of the group. Alec made his way to one side where he stopped to shoot Heidi a grin. "Hey, Heidsters."

Heidi gave him a quick smile. "Hey."

Alec was nice enough. Good-looking. Acceptable in bed. But right now she was struggling to find the appeal he once had.

"I think we're going to start you guys out in a separate room." Harlow stood up with Dutch following behind her. "We actually have another technical coordinator training as well, so we thought it would be a good idea to have you in the same place." Harlow led the group out of the room and two doors down to where they'd set up a smaller space where the four new members of Intel and Roman could get their feet under them.

Without coming into contact with any of the sensitive information currently being thrown around in the main office.

Eva leaned toward Heidi as the last of the group disappeared into their new workspace. "You still okay with Alec being here?"

"Fine, actually." Heidi lifted one shoulder and let it drop. "He's just a guy."

There were many of those in her past.

Not *many*-many.

Just many.

Eva's brows lifted, making her expression appear even more serious. "A guy you had a relationship with."

Heidi started laughing. "I definitely did not have a relationship with Alec." She hadn't had a relationship with anyone. They took up too much time and effort.

"Okay then." Eva turned back to her desk, grabbing the stack of Alpha's files. They'd all agreed it was the best place for the new arrivals to start. It was familiar-ish territory for them and shouldn't be too difficult of a task. She stood up. "I'll take these over and pass them out." She eyed Heidi. "Wanna come?"

"Nah." Heidi pointed to her computer screen. "I've got a thing I'm doing."

Eva's gaze moved over her desk. "Did you clean up?"

"Seems like." Heidi brushed at a few crumbs left from the cinnamon roll Shawn brought her earlier as she leaned to watch Eva go two doors down to drop off the files.

"What are you doing?" The closeness of Mona's voice made her jump.

Heidi leaned away from the tiny blonde woman standing at her side. She must have learned stealth maneuvers from Zeke too. "How did you get over here?"

"I'm telling you, no one seems to notice what I'm doing." Mona crouched down. "It's why I think I should go see what I can find out from Zeke."

"It's not a terrible idea, but you've got to come up with a good excuse for what you need from him." Heidi's eyes caught on her screen as a comment popped up on the thread she started in the chat room.

"I would like to learn some more self-defense type things."

Heidi looked Mona up and down. "Seriously?"

"No." Mona smiled. "See? I can do this."

Mona was probably right. "Eva's not going to be happy about it."

"Maybe we shouldn't tell her." Mona glanced at the door before leaning closer. "Maybe we shouldn't tell anyone."

"Except me, right?"

Both women turned to look at Bess. She smiled. "Forgot I was here, didn't you?"

Heidi pointed Bessie's way. "Maybe you should go with Mona."

"Wade would crap his pants." Bess sighed. "And with Parker I just don't have time."

"If you ever need a babysitter for a date night or something." Heidi shoved both pointers at her chest. "I would be happy to babysit."

"All those date nights we can take off campus?" Bessie wrinkled her nose. "Hopefully I can take you up on that soon."

Heidi tipped her head at Mona. "This one might make it happen."

Everyone underestimated Mona. Always had.

"I'm going to." Mona straightened.

"I believe you." Heidi scanned the lines of text coming across the screen of her computer. "Well this is interesting."

"What is it?" Bess moved closer, coming across the room to stand beside Mona. The women were silent as the comment continued populating.

Heidi's heart rate picked up speed as she read the words.

"Who is that?" Bess crouched down, her attention locked on the chat room displayed.

"A friend of mine." Heidi tipped her head side to side. "Sort of. I don't know their name or anything." The person in question used the handle *govtsnoop69*.

"Is it a man?" Mona glanced Heidi's way before turning immediately back to the information *govtsnoop69* was dishing out in giant helpings.

"I would say considering the number 69 is at the end of his handle it's safe to assume it's a man." Heidi chewed her lip as she typed out a response thanking him for his insight into what they might be dealing with.

"Does he really know what he's talking about?" Mona's eyes were wide.

Heidi gave her a little nod. "Probably." It was the point of this whole hidden corner of the digital world where wannabe virtual spies wormed into high-security places just to prove they could. "He's been at this for a long time."

Mona's fair skin went a little paler.

Heidi managed a smile in spite of the information they just learned. "Still want to go hang out with Zeke?"

CHAPTER 11

"WHAT IS THIS place?"

Heidi's voice shouldn't have surprised him.

"The men's locker room." Shawn turned to find her giving the bin of towels in the corner the side-eye.

"That's what it smells like."

"Can I help you with something?" Shawn faced her, the towel around his waist tucked tightly in place.

Heidi stared at his still-damp bare chest. "Probably."

"Eyes up here, Kitten."

Her gaze immediately snapped up. "Kitten?" Her cheeks barely flushed. "Now?"

"I'm not following."

Heidi stepped a little closer, peeking from side to side as she moved. "You only call me Kitten when…" Her brows lifted a little. "When you're not pretending you aren't interested in me."

"That's not true."

"It definitely is. I'm starting to be like Pavlov's dogs." Heidi reached out to skim one finger down the center of his chest. "I expected you to have more hair than this."

"Sorry to disappoint you." He tried to breathe as she continued to touch him, but his lungs were still burning from the run he just finished, making them uncooperative.

"You haven't disappointed me yet, Captain." Her gaze lifted to his.

Shawn tried not to focus on her comment. "What do you want, Rucker?"

Her lower lip pushed out in a pout. "Damn it." Heidi huffed out a breath. "I need to talk to you about something."

"Then talk." He stepped back, finally finding the strength to move from her touch.

"Not here." Heidi glanced around again before her eyes came back to him, head tipping as he pulled on a shirt, eyes following the drop of the hem. "Looks like you come here a lot."

"Every day." Shawn forced his shoulders not to push back at her observation.

"I was thinking about doing some squats or something." Heidi's eyes lingered over the towel still covering his lower half. "See what would happen to my ass if I worked it out a little. Maybe I'll come check the gym out sometime."

Shawn glanced up as a few members of Beta came through the door, stopping short at the sight of Heidi in the locker room.

He shoved one finger toward the door. "Get out."

Gentry's brows lifted up. "Now you want the whole locker room too?"

"I said get the fuck out." Shawn didn't look away from Beta's team lead.

Heidi's brows were the next to lift as she looked from him to Gentry. "Should I leave?"

"No." Shawn grabbed her arm, pulling her close at the thought of her going out alone into a room filled with amped-up, lonely assholes from Alpha and Beta.

Make sure no one else tried to steal her away before he even really had her.

It was a thought he never intended to have, but right now there wasn't time to dwell on it. "Come on." Shawn tried to tug her along as he made for the door.

"What?" Heidi laughed, tugging her arm back from him. "No."

"No?" The rejection stung. More than it should.

"You're wearing a towel, and as much as I like it, it's probably not something you need to be marching around the halls in." She dropped to her butt on the wood bench running in front of the wall of lockers and smiled up at him sweetly. "Go ahead and finish getting dressed. I'll wait."

"Does that mean we can come in now?" Gentry and the other three guys with him eased closer.

"No." Heidi wrinkled her nose at them. "You and your sweaty balls can wait two more minutes." She waited until they were out of sight before turning back to Shawn, her smile a little devilish. "Proceed, Captain."

"Why'd you kick them out?" He reached into his gym bag, pulling out the rest of the clothes he'd packed inside this morning before leaving his room.

"I figured you had a good reason for not wanting them in here." Heidi's eyes lingered over his chest as he unrolled his pants and socks. "Why do you pack them up like that?"

"Keeps them from getting wadded up and saves space."

She leaned to peek in the large bag. "Seems like there's plenty of space in there."

Shawn shook out his pants. He glanced at Heidi. "You closing your eyes, Kitten?"

Her lips lifted in a small smile. "I think I am." Her lids dropped, long lashes playing across her cheeks. "I want to be surprised."

He snorted out a chuckle as he stepped into his boxer briefs.

"Was that a laugh?" Heidi squinted one eye open.

"Thought you wanted to be surprised?"

Her eyes opened fully as she lifted one shoulder and let it fall. "Mostly." Her gaze lingered over his lower half. "You're a boxer-brief man then."

"Seems like."

"Good to know." Heidi held out his socks as Shawn tugged on his pants, tucking his shirt into the waistband.

"Why is that good to know?" He sat beside her and quickly put on his socks before stuffing his feet into the boots he always wore.

"I've been thinking maybe I should start returning all the favors you're giving me." Heidi's head tipped as he stood.

Shawn held his hand out to her. "Nothing I give you is a favor, Kitten." He held his breath, hand hanging in the air between them.

Heidi didn't make him wait long. Her soft palm hit his almost immediately as she used the hold for leverage to pull up from the bench. "What would you call it then?"

"A gift." Shawn grabbed his bag with his free hand.

"Then maybe I will start reciprocating the gifts you keep giving me."

Shawn paused just before the door, tugging her close with the hand she so willingly put in his. "The gift isn't for you, Kitten." His lips hovered just over hers. It would be so easy to kiss her. Know what those full lips would feel like under his.

It was the one line he'd managed not to cross. Barely.

Because kissing was different. Closer.

Holding Heidi while her mouth was under his would be something he'd never be able to come back from.

"Come on." He kept her close as they walked through the gym hand-in-hand, the eyes of every man there following her path.

Heidi stayed right at his side, closer than she had to be.

She didn't say anything until they were well down the hall connecting to the main building. "Where are we going?"

"My office." Taking her to his room right now was not an option.

Neither was anything else Heidi might have in mind. He had a meeting in fifteen minutes. One he needed to have his head on straight for.

Shawn pushed her into his office first, scanning the hall before following her inside. "What do you need to talk about?

"Oh." Heidi blinked a few times. "I almost forgot."

"You almost forgot why you came to find me?" Shawn dropped his bag into its designated spot in the corner.

"That might not have been the only reason I came to find you."

"What was the other reason?" Shawn held one of the chairs across from his desk, tipping his head to it when Heidi didn't immediately sit.

She lowered into the seat. "You just weren't in your office. I didn't know where you were."

"You need to know where I am at all times now?" He tried to sound put off by the thought.

"Why not?" Heidi's eyes were a little wide. "What if I have a question about Rogue?"

146

"Then you should probably ask Dutch considering he's in the same room as you." Shawn sat in his chair, leaning back a little hoping it made him look more relaxed than he felt.

"I guess." Heidi's lips almost pursed into a pout.

"Is that why you're here? You had a question about Rogue?" Thinking Heidi would skip the obvious availability of Dutch and take the opportunity to seek him out pleased the deep-seated part of him that yearned to be needed.

To be relied on.

To be enough for someone.

He'd tried to starve it into extinction, but this woman managed to breathe life into that withered corpse and now had it upright and running amok.

"No." Heidi glanced to the open door before leaning closer, her voice low. "Can I close the door? It's not for..." Her eyes met his as her cheeks flushed a pale pink.

But not out of embarrassment. This woman hadn't known an embarrassed day in her life. She lived proudly. Open and honestly.

So different from him.

"Whatever you need, Kitten."

Heidi shoved one finger his way. "No more of that Kitten stuff. I won't be able to act right and I have work to do."

He couldn't stop a smile from working its way onto his lips. "Whatever you need, Heidi."

She groaned as she reached out to shut the door. "Maybe it's the 'whatever you need' part that's the problem." When they were closed off

147

from the hall she scooted her chair closer. "What do you know about GHOST?"

The warmth Heidi's actions brought to his insides dissipated almost immediately. "What did you find about them?"

Pierce should never have told them his suspicions about GHOST. Not without proof.

"That they're not actually a part of the CIA. They're a part of the Secret Service."

Shawn blinked. "You found that out already?"

Heidi's head dropped toward one shoulder. "Did you already know that?"

He didn't want to give her the truth so instead stayed silent.

"Damn it, Shawn." Heidi stood up, leaning both palms against his desk as she glared at him. "How in the hell do you expect us to figure this out if you don't give us all the information?"

"Who knows you were asking around about GHOST?" Shawn raked one hand through his hair as the reality of the situation settled down around him.

And not simply the issue he was facing with Intel digging into GHOST.

"Some guy I used to chat with on a hacking site." Heidi's expression changed, irritation giving way to something surprising.

Caution.

"We have to look into them, Shawn. If GHOST is who took Howard then—"

"If GHOST is who took Howard then we have a problem." Shawn checked his watch. "Go get the rest of Intel and meet me in the blue conference room." He stood from his desk, rounding the edge to grab Heidi's face in his hands. "Bring the transcripts from the chat so I can see exactly what you said."

He expected to see fear in her eyes. At least worry. Maybe concern.

None of it was there as her eyes settled on his. "Okay."

It was an easy agreement from a woman who was never easy. At least that was what he thought.

"I'm sorry I didn't warn you about GHOST." Shawn hesitated on the reason. "I didn't think you'd get anywhere with it."

"You should have known better."

That applied to a lot of his life. "I should have."

"I'll go get them then." Heidi didn't make a move to step away.

Shawn held her face a second longer before dropping his hands and pulling the door open. "Go."

Heidi shot him a grin. "Yes, Captain."

He watched her hustle down the hall.

"Your girl can't come in the locker room like that." Gentry stood beside him, long hair still wet from the shower he must've taken after working out. "Not if you're going to ban everyone while she's in there."

"She can do whatever she wants." Shawn glanced at the lead for Beta. "And you'll fuckin' deal with it."

"Are we ready?"

Pierce's voice cut short what might have turned into an issue. The owner of Alaskan Security stood at the door to his office, gaze leveled on Shawn and Gentry.

"Yup." Shawn grabbed his clipboard.

"I'll be a minute late." Gentry stared Shawn down as he went to his own office. "Had issues getting into the locker room after my workout."

"Issues?" Pierce's brows lifted.

"Greer's woman was in there." Gentry smirked. "He was worried she'd see how big my dick was and want a piece of it."

There were only a handful of things that made Shawn lose his shit. Gentry managed to hit all of them at once.

Shawn was on him before the last word was out of his mouth, taking Beta's lead to the ground hard and fast. Unfortunately, Gentry wasn't as surprised by the move as Pierce was. Gentry was already working out of his hold before Shawn could fully grab onto him. While the lead for Beta wasn't nearly as tall or broad as Shawn, he was definitely just as strong, and possibly just as skilled of a wrestler.

After fighting for the dominant position a handful of minutes, Shawn finally managed to work Gentry into a spot he probably couldn't get out of.

"Whatcha doin'?"

He tipped his head back to find Heidi crouched right beside him, chewing on the end of a Twizzler.

Shawn immediately released Gentry. "Nothing."

Heidi's brows went up. "That seems inaccurate."

"He's being an asshole like always. That's what he's doing." Gentry stood up, straightening the fabric of his shirt.

Heidi's eyes lifted to where Gentry stood. "You know there's camera's here." Heidi pointed to one of the tiny devices tucked into the corner where the wall met the ceiling. "I can go back and see what you did." She stood. "I'm guessing maybe you were being a bit of an asshole yourself." She bit off another chunk of her candy. "Am I right?"

Gentry's hazel gaze leveled on the woman staring him down as she chomped her way through a cherry vine, not looking remotely intimidated.

He shot Shawn one last look before stalking past where Heidi stood and disappearing into his office.

Heidi's eyes dropped to Shawn. "I thought we had a meeting to go to." She passed the file in her hand off to Mona before reaching down for him. "And you're here wasting time like we don't have shit to do." Heidi grabbed his hand and started pulling. "Come on, Captain. Up off your ass."

Pierce glanced to where all of Intel stood in the hall. "I was unaware Intel was joining us for this meeting."

Heidi grabbed the file from Mona and slapped it against Pierce's chest. "We figured out who GHOST was."

Pierce's mouth flattened into a thin line. "Of course you did." He looked to Shawn before turning back to Heidi and the rest of Intel. "I suppose it's best you join our meeting then." He turned to Mona. "Ms. Ayers, if you would lead the way to the blue conference room."

Mona eyed Pierce for a second before wordlessly walking past him in the direction of the conference rooms.

Shawn motioned for Heidi to go ahead. He hung back as Harlow, Bess, and Eva passed, waiting for Dutch as Rogue's technical coordinator brought up the rear. "You couldn't give us a heads up that they were close to finding GHOST?"

"Wasn't in the room." Dutch tucked his hands in his pockets. "Took 'em all of about five minutes."

"Shit."

Pierce's swear was shocking enough to drop Shawn's mouth open.

"We've got to make sure they understand what the risks are." Pierce wiped one hand down his face. "I should have known better than to say anything before we were sure."

"I was going to mention that in our meeting." Shawn watched the last woman disappear around the corner. "Doesn't matter now."

Pierce flipped open the file Heidi shoved at him earlier, scanning the top page. "Who in the hell is *govtsnoop69*?"

"Someone Heidi knows." Shawn took the paper and scanned the rows of conversation between *govtsnoop69* and someone with the handle *beiberlover530*. "Whoever it is, they know a surprising amount for someone who's still alive."

Pierce passed the rest of the folder over. "For now."

CHAPTER 12

"SO YOU *DON'T* want us looking into GHOST?" Harlow sat in the front of the room, her brows low as she glared at Pierce. "How exactly do you think we will be able to find out what's going on if we can't look into some of the people caught in the middle of it?"

"I'm not saying you can't look into GHOST." Pierce took a slow breath. "I'm saying you have to be careful in how you go about it." He held up the print outs from the conversation Heidi had with *govtsnoop69*. "And this is not what I would consider being careful."

"Then you've never been in a chat room on a hacker site." This was starting to get frustrating.

Pierce kept changing the directions he sent her in, and now he wanted to tie her hands behind her back. "How in the hell are we supposed to find out about a government entity that supposedly doesn't exist if we can't go to the kinds of places that know about things like that?"

"I don't think you understand the potential issues that can come from a misstep, Ms. Rucker." Pierce's eye was twitching a little as he focused on her. "GHOST is exactly what it sounds like they are. They were built to be invisible." He stepped closer to where she sat at Shawn's side. "They find you in the dark and drag you down to the depths of the hidden hell they come from."

She didn't expect Pierce to be so dramatic. "That's a demon."

Pierce paused. "What?"

"If it lives in hell it's a demon." Heidi shook her head. "Not a ghost."

Pierce closed his eyes for a second. "You're still not hearing what I'm trying to explain to you."

"We definitely are hearing it, Mr. Barrick." Mona sat on Heidi's other side. "We just don't really care at this point."

Heidi turned to Mona. "Impressive, Monster."

"Thanks." Mona kept her eyes on Pierce. "Your belief that there is some magical way for us to put ourselves in more danger is, honestly, ridiculous at this point." She continued on. "I have been kidnapped, shot at, and forced to murder a man to protect my friend. I'm not sure how you could possibly think things could get worse for us."

Pierce stood still for a minute, indecision warring across his handsome features.

He took a small step toward Mona. "I understand how it could seem that way to you, Ms.

Ayers. Unfortunately, I can promise you that if GHOST decides to come for you, or anyone around you, there will be virtually nothing I can do to stop it from happening."

"We don't have a choice." Mona sat straight under Pierce's startlingly intense gaze. "It has to be done."

Pierce's shoulders barely dropped. "I will find another way."

"There isn't one." Mona stood. "I appreciate and understand your concern, but right now it's useless." She turned and walked out of the room, leaving everyone staring after her.

"She's right, Pierce." Harlow stood up. "You've got us in a shit position and we don't have a choice. We're too far in now. We can't back out." She grabbed her computer, tucking it under one arm. "We have to go forward."

Heidi watched as Eva and Bess followed Mona out of the room with Harlow bringing up the rear.

"You aren't going with your team?" Shawn's voice was low in her ear.

Heidi shook her head. "Not just yet." She turned to Pierce. "What information am I allowed to disclose?"

Pierce blinked at her, the question clearly taking him by surprise. "To who?"

"*Govtsnoop69* isn't my only contact. I have a handful more I can reach out to. People who've been hacking for longer than I've been alive and sort of took me under their wing when I was a kid." Heidi glanced to Shawn. "They could be helpful if you think it's okay."

He'd been a part of this world for longer than she had, and his knowledge was all firsthand while most of hers was hearsay from people who spent their days hiding behind a computer screen.

Like she used to do.

"Do you think they'll have information you can't get on your own?" Shawn shifted in his seat, leaning a little closer and dropping one arm around the back of her chair.

"I mean, I can probably find the same things they have, but even with both me and Harlow it will take some time." Heidi reached out to smooth down a wrinkle in his shirt. He packed them so carefully into that bag so wrinkles probably bothered him. "It will save us a lot of time if I can ask what other people have found."

"Do you trust these people?" Shawn's voice was so low she might be the only one who heard it.

"I don't distrust them." Heidi glanced at Pierce as he came closer, invading the bubble of privacy she didn't actually have. "But I can't promise they are trustworthy."

Pierce's gaze met Shawn's.

"We don't have time to waste on this, Pierce." Shawn's eyes came back her way. "I say we let her see what she can find."

Pierce studied her for a minute. "Keep transcripts of everything." He crossed his arms. "And I think you should look into the people you're speaking with."

Heidi laughed. "Yeah, no." She stood up. "That's the first rule of hack club. No one investigates anyone else in hack club." She peeked Shawn's way over her shoulder, shooting him a wink. "Come visit me later, Captain."

His lips twitched in what might have almost been a smile. "Go get to work, Rucker."

Heidi grinned the whole way back to the office.

"Got permission to do what we need to do." Heidi wiggled as she walked to her seat. "Just gotta keep transcripts."

"Good." Harlow smiled. "Especially since we were going to do it anyway."

"I will work my way through the people I know who might be able to help us." Heidi sat in her seat just as Lennie knocked against the doorframe, her smile wide as she waited.

"You don't have to knock if the door's open." Heidi tried to dig up warm feelings for the woman who technically had done nothing to her.

Except see Shawn with similar eyes.

Which made her feel oddly inclined to scratch out Lennie's.

"We finished those files." Lennie slowly walked in. "They were pretty easy. Most of the information we needed to work with was already in the system." She set the stack on Eva's desk. "There was only one that we had any sort of issues with."

Eva looked up from the stack she was already grabbing. "Really? What sort of issues?"

"We found a private Facebook account and email address that wasn't listed." Lennie grabbed the top file. "It was this guy. Micah Warner."

"Anything else?" Eva took the file and flipped it open to scan the pages. "Bank accounts? Maybe a PO box?"

"We searched for those and came up with nothing. All we could find were the Facebook account and email." Lennie smoothed down a chunk of her shiny dark hair, stroking the strands with both hands as she continued to talk. "We will keep digging, but I knew you were wanting this expedited."

"Good job." Harlow rounded her desk. "Definitely keep looking into Micah. See if you can find anything else." She passed Lennie a piece of paper. "See what you can find on these three names." She pointed to the paper after Lennie took it. "We know that one's dead. See what else you can find about them."

Lennie beamed at Harlow. "Okay. Yeah. We can do that."

Harlow's blue eyes followed Lennie as she left the room. "That one's sweet as shit isn't she?"

"She'll rot your freaking teeth." Heidi's head popped up at the snide edge her own comment carried. "That sounded really mean." She winced a little. "I didn't mean it that way." Mostly. "She is a very sweet person."

One who definitely wouldn't have tried to hold Shawn's hand if she knew—

What? If she knew what?

That Shawn was messing around with her? That they still hadn't even really kissed?

The realization that she and Shawn really didn't have anything at all made Heidi's insides sting in an annoying way.

She'd never given two shits if a man she was interacting with took the opportunity to move along to another woman. It was the nature of the beast. Casual relationships were just that.

Casual.

It meant if she got busy and didn't feel like calling a guy for a few weeks then that was fine. If she didn't want him crowding her bed and sent him on his way right after sex, then that was fine too.

But none of that felt fine right now.

Not with Shawn.

It felt…

Angry.

Heidi grabbed her ear buds, shoving one into each ear and this time turning her actual music on. She could see lips moving out of the corner of her eye, but ignored it.

She had shit to do. Important shit.

Definitely more important than worrying over what Shawn might have thought of Lennie and their plane ride from Ohio.

Heidi carefully worked her way through the chat rooms she used as a replacement for the social life most teenagers have. Instead of sneaking out and dating she was sneaking into digital worlds all alone in the quiet of her bedroom. Making friends with people who used fake names to live hypothetical lives.

GUERRILLA TACTICS

But now that life was real and so was the world she lived in as a way to pretend she wasn't alone.

One earbud popped free. "Do you actually have the music on?" Harlow held the bud close to her own ear. "What in the hell are you listening to?"

Heidi grabbed the tiny speaker back as she shut off the playlist she listened to when life felt more complicated than it should be. "Do you need something?"

"Yeah. I need you to find out why in the hell GHOST is involved in this." Harlow leaned to peek at the screen of her phone. "I knew that was freaking Justin Bieber."

"Suck it, Mowry." Heidi snatched her phone away, tucking in into her lap.

Harlow held her hands up. "No judgment here." She thumbed over one shoulder. "That one listens to New Kids on the Block. At least you're listening to someone from your own generation."

"Don't make me fight you, Harlow." Eva leaned back in her seat. "You find anything else interesting out?"

"Looks like GHOST might be sort of a mystery even to the government." Harlow linked up to the printer and sent her screen shots to the queue. "Lots of people have heard of them, but no one really seems to know where to find more than that." She jumped up and went to get the papers, catching each one as it dropped out. "So far the general consensus is GHOST is an unclaimed division of the Secret Service that no one seems to be able to prove exists or even know where to look to find that proof."

"I know where to look." Mona sat in her seat, both hands resting on her desk. "I can almost guarantee Zeke knows who they are."

"Well get on it then." Heidi motioned to the door. "Go get him, Monster."

"No." Harlow backed to her desk. "She needs to be careful." Harlow sat down. "You already asked Zeke for help. He'll be suspicious if Mona comes sniffing around."

Mona wrinkled her nose. "I didn't say I was going to sniff around."

"You know what I mean." Harlow turned to Heidi. "What did he say when you talked to him?"

"Not really anything." She pursed her lips, twisting them to one side. "We were sort of interrupted."

"So maybe you should go talk to him again. Resolve that instead of Mona coming in and raising his suspicions."

"I don't think that's a good idea." Heidi chewed her lip. Explaining why she didn't want to talk to Zeke again was complicated and possibly presumptuous.

Harlow frowned. "Why not?"

"Because Zeke can't help her with anything." Shawn strode into the room decked out in the white tactical gear she'd seen Rogue and Shadow wear when they went out on a mission.

Her heart skipped a beat, but it was tough to know if it was from the way the tight ribbed fabric clung to Shawn's broad shoulders, or the thought of him being in danger. "Going somewhere?"

His dark eyes rested squarely on her. "I won't be gone long. When I get back I will take you to the range."

"Hopefully I don't need to murder anyone before then."

"Hopefully you keep your ass in that chair and figure out what in the hell's going on." Shawn's lips did that barely twitchy thing for a second before his eyes scanned the room, catching on the women watching him with interest. "I'll see you later, Rucker."

Heidi bit down on her lip, trying to hold back the concern twisting her insides. As Shawn walked through the door she couldn't stand it anymore. "Be careful."

He turned back to face her, out of sight of anyone else in the room. The intensity in his gaze made the air clog in her lungs. It was unlike any way he'd looked at her before.

There was no annoyance. No frustration.

Not even the blind lust she'd seen in his gaze a time or two.

This was different. Very different.

He didn't turn away until Dutch came down the hall behind him, stealing that unnerving gaze away.

Leaving her feeling a little lost without it.

Heidi dropped her head, popping her earbuds back in place, this time without the music she used to distract her from the current state of her life.

Because maybe it wasn't too bad after all.

162

Heidi went through the rest of the boards she frequented, posting short questions from a few random handles she'd established over the years. It would make it significantly more difficult for anyone to find out who she really was, and now that there was the possibility it wasn't just Harlow's ex-husband Tod trying to find a way in, she wanted to be a little more cautious.

Because if GHOST really was who she was beginning to believe they were, it would take everything she had in her arsenal to keep them from following her trail and finding their way to Alaskan Security.

Heidi glanced up about an hour after Shawn left to find Dutch's brows pressed tight together. She popped out the earbud muffling the sounds of the room enough she could successfully ignore them. "What's wrong?"

Dutch's eyes bounced to hers, holding for just a second before he shook his head. "Nothing."

The word came out too late and too tight to be the truth.

Heidi stood, looking to the screens lined across the wall behind Dutch and Harlow's desks. One immediately went black.

In the second before it cut off there had been something there. A cluster of men in a sea of snow and ice, barely discernible in their white gear.

She leveled her gaze at Dutch. "I will do shit you can't even imagine if you don't tell me what's happening right now."

Dutch glanced at Harlow.

"Oh for God's sake." She reached over to plug his computer back into the screen. "Don't freak out."

Heidi took a few steps closer to the screens, her eyes locked onto the movement. It was impossible to tell the men apart. The image was too grainy even if the masks they wore weren't covering their faces.

Her breath caught.

Maybe is wasn't impossible to tell them apart. One of them at least was easily identifiable. His large frame and broad shoulders were as unmistakable as everything else about him was.

Shawn was on the ground, one arm wrapped across his chest, the white of his shirt marred by a splash of dark.

Not dark.

Red.

Harlow stepped around her desk, arms out as she rushed Heidi's way. "Shawn's been shot."

CHAPTER 13

"WHY IN THE hell is he not at a hospital?" Heidi's voice carried down the hall as she laid into whoever was tasked with bringing her to the medical ward. "I swear to God if he needs to go to the hospital I will pick his ass up and drag it there myself."

He smiled in spite of the burning in his shoulder.

"They barely got you didn't they?" Eli was perched on a stool, cutting away the layers of shirt and vest between him and the bullet lodged just under Shawn's skin.

"There's probably some of the vest caught in there." He tipped his head to watch as Eli pulled the blood-stained fabric away from the wound. "It hit me right at the edge."

Heidi's soft gasp seemed to suck all the air from the room.

All the air from his lungs.

She stood in the doorway, eyes wide, skin pale.

"Catch her." Shawn shoved Eli out of the way, sending the team physician scooting across the floor on his wheeled stool. He managed to get a hand on Heidi just as she started to wobble on her feet. She latched onto him, her hands gripping what was left of his vest and shirt as her gaze locked onto the blood oozing from his shoulder.

"There's a hole in you." Her eyes rolled to meet his before dropping back to his shoulder. "There's a hole in your—"

"Stop looking at it." Shawn tipped her chin up, leaning down to catch her hazy gaze. "It's fine."

"But you're blee—" She went down, her body going limp in his arms.

"Damn it." Shawn turned to find Eli just behind him. "Help me get her on the table."

"Who in the hell let her back here?" Eli grabbed the arm and leg closest to him and helped Shawn maneuver Heidi onto the table.

"She was already coming this way." Reed stood in the doorway. "Wasn't any stopping her."

"She's stopped now." Eli frowned down at Heidi.

She suddenly sucked in a sharp breath, her eyes flying open.

Shawn grabbed Eli's stool, scooting it right against the table and sitting down. "How ya doing, Kitten?" He reached up to smooth back the soft wave of blonde hair falling over her forehead. "Take a deep breath." He inhaled long and loud, smiling as she followed along. "Good job."

166

Heidi's eyes slowly moved, aiming toward his shoulder.

"Nope." Shawn gently pressed her cheek, aiming her face to his as he leaned closer. "Just look at me."

"I was looking at you." She blew out a slow breath as he did. "The part with a hole in it."

"You should probably stop doing that. Doesn't seem to agree with you." He tipped his head to Eli, angling so his hit shoulder was as far from Heidi's line of sight as he could get it.

Eli grabbed another stool and went back to work as Shawn kept breathing along with Heidi.

"Why did you hold Lennie's hand on the plane?" The question tumbled out of her mouth so fast Shawn almost didn't catch all the words.

Heidi's lips rolled in, pressing tight together, her eyes locked onto his.

He'd never been on this side of things before. Never had to explain away something that was literally nothing.

That wasn't true actually.

"She was scared. I sat beside her because I didn't want to have to deal with a hysterical passenger ten thousand feet in the air." Shawn continued stroking her hair and breathing deep, the acts soothing him as much as he was hoping they did Heidi. "When we took off she reached over and grabbed my hand."

"So you're saying she held your hand?" Heidi's tone was familiar. One he'd heard coming from his own mouth more than a few times.

"I'm saying she grabbed my hand and I let her hold it until we were in the air."

Heidi's eyes left his to fix on the ceiling. "It doesn't matter. I don't know why I even asked."

"It does matter." Shawn tried not to wince as Eli injected the anesthetic. "Or you wouldn't have asked."

Heidi didn't turn back his way. "It's not like we are a thing."

"A thing?" Shawn gently turned her head his way. "Look at me, Heidi."

She shook her head again. "It's fine. I'm fine." Heidi started to sit up, her skin immediately went white.

Shawn glanced back at Eli. "Are you almost done?"

"It takes more than two minutes to get a bullet out of a body, dick." Eli dug a little deeper, the bite of cold instrument testing the limits of the local anesthetic.

Shawn turned his full attention to Heidi. "Lay back down." He reached for her hand. Heidi immediately pulled it out of his reach.

"I'm fine."

"You're not." Heidi was clearly not fine. All across the board. "Let Eli finish what he's doing, and then we will go somewhere and talk about this."

"You really want to talk about it?"

He studied her face for a few seconds, taking the time to really look at what was there.

What he saw took him by surprise. "I do want to talk about it."

Heidi's blue eyes slowly came to his, the edge of innocence lining them growing a little more. "Okay."

She'd been so forward from the first second. It never occurred to him that anything about Heidi could be inexperienced. Not until just now.

Heidi was quiet while Eli finished cleaning and dressing the wound. As he laid the last strip of tape in place the team physician let out a breath. "Just don't do anything strenuous for the next few days. Keep it dry. I'll find you to check on it tomorrow."

"Fantastic." Shawn didn't wait for the last bit of Eli's instructions. He was up off the chair and hefting Heidi off the table.

Eli threw his hands out at his sides. "What the fuck, Shawn? I just said take it easy."

"I used my good arm." Shawn tucked Heidi into his side and led her down the hall.

She leaned into him, one arm wrapped around his waist.

"I don't feel so good." Heidi's voice was softer than normal.

"I know, Kitten. We're almost there." Shawn led her down the hall connecting the main building to the one where their rooms were. "Just a little longer." Instead of taking her straight to his room he went to the kitchen area, pulling out a stool. "Sit down."

She silently did as he instructed, not giving him even the slightest bit of attitude.

"You're awfully quiet, Rucker. If you don't start giving me shit I'm going to take you back so Eli can check you out." Shawn eyed her as he opened the fridge and pulled out a container of grilled chicken and vegetables.

Heidi chewed her lower lip, eyes fixed on the counter in front of her. "I just feel a little stupid."

Shawn smiled a little. "Lots of people pass out over blood. No reason to feel stupid."

Heidi's brows came together as her eyes lifted to his. "That's not why I feel stupid." Her gaze dropped again. "I shouldn't have been upset about whatever happened with Lennie. Normally that kind of shit doesn't bother me."

"That kind of shit?" Shawn scooped out some vegetables and a chunk of chicken, spreading the food across a plate before sliding it into the microwave.

She shrugged. "I don't usually care what the guys I'm spending time with do when they're not with me."

"Not even if you're in a relationship?" Shawn dished out another, bigger serving as the first heated.

"Um." Heidi picked at the pale pink painted on her nails. "I don't know that I would say I've ever been in a relationship." Her focus lifted to him.

It made sense.

Not complete sense considering the woman was at least twenty-five and fucking gorgeous.

But it explained a lot.

"Never?" Shawn pulled out the first plate, moving the vegetables around to be sure they were hot before setting it in front of Heidi. "Eat so you don't pass out again."

"Pretty sure I'm not going to pass out from hunger, Captain." She poked at the curve of her rear. "In case you haven't noticed I don't miss many meals."

Shawn leaned down against the counter so their eyes were even. "Eating shit all day is not the same thing as being nourished, Kitten." He stood, leaning back to slide his food in the microwave. "And I need you to be fueled up tonight."

Her eyes went wide. She stared at him without blinking.

He pointed to the plate. "Eat."

She tucked her chin and eyed the food he'd given her. "Is this just chicken and vegetables?"

"What's wrong with chicken and vegetables?" Shawn pulled his out of the microwave and immediately forked a bite into his mouth. "It's fine."

Heidi's nose wrinkled on one side. "I don't really eat because food is fine." She poked at a zucchini with her fork. "I eat because it tastes good."

His chewing slowed. "Food is fuel, Kitten. Who cares how it tastes?"

"Um." Heidi eased off the stool. "Apparently everyone but you." She opened the fridge and dug through the contents, pulling out a bag of shredded cheese and a bottle of Italian dressing. She went back to her seat and sprinkled on some of the cheese before drizzling the dressing on top. She took another bite, nodding her head as she chewed. "Much better."

"You didn't even try it the first way." Shawn eyed the stringing cheese as she took another bite."

171

"Didn't have to try it to know I wouldn't like it." She stabbed a broccoli and chunk of chicken and held it out to him.

He looked at the offered food before focusing on the woman tempting him with every breath she took.

"What's wrong, Captain?" Heidi's voice was soft. "Scared of a little bit of change?"

If she only knew.

He leaned down to take the bite.

Heidi smirked as he chewed. She knew damn well what she offered was better than the shit he brought to the table.

"I'm right." She didn't ask. She already knew the answer.

"You're a pain in the ass." Shawn smiled back at her as he went back to his own, less-flavorful dish of food.

"You want me to fix yours for you?" Heidi picked up the bottle of dressing, tipping it from side to side.

"Maybe next time." Shawn leaned against the counter at his back.

Heidi shrugged. "Suit yourself. Eat bland shit."

"This isn't all I plan on eating tonight, Kitten."

Her eyes immediately jumped to his, a flush creeping across her cheeks.

She'd come onto him from almost the first minute. Been as forward and brazen as any woman he'd ever met.

It was intimidating as hell.

But it seemed like the playing field had suddenly leveled out.

"You look a little flushed, Rucker." Shawn rinsed his plate and racked it in the dishwasher. "There a problem?"

"You." She pointed at him. "You're the problem."

He leaned against the counter separating them. "Seems like I just fed you and now I'm about to go take care of any other needs you might have. I'd say that's a good problem to have."

She glanced around the open space. "Shh."

"Shh?" He chuckled. "If I remember correctly you first propositioned me in front of three other people."

"That's different." Heidi's fork hit her empty plate.

Shawn dropped it into the dishwasher next to his before rounding the counter and heading her way. "I'm having a hard time seeing how that's any different, Kitten."

Heidi leaned back in her seat as he closed in on her. "It just is."

"Could that be because what you were offering up meant nothing?" Shawn rested both hands on the seat of the stool just beside her thighs. "And you know what I'm offering does."

She started to choke, coughing as her eyes watered.

"You okay?" Shawn grabbed a bottle of water from the fridge and cracked the cap before handing it over.

She swallowed a bit of it down. "I choked on my spit."

Shawn leaned in close. "I feel like I need to be honest with you right now, Rucker. Can you handle it?"

"Is it going to make me choke on my spit again?"

"Maybe." He studied her face, the softness of her features. The pureness that was there from the first time he saw her.

Not purity in the sexual sense. He didn't want that anyway.

She was pure in an honest way.

Heidi was authentic. Real. No apologies. No excuses. She didn't hide who or what she was.

Except it seemed like Heidi maybe didn't realize all the potential that was out there.

All she might be missing by boxing herself in.

The same way he did.

"I do not do anything but monogamy. Period."

Heidi's eyes moved to one side before coming back to his. "What does that mean?"

"It means from the minute I put my hands on you there was no one else. Not until the minute you say you are done with me."

Her brows came together. "Why would I be done with you?"

The question settled deep in his gut, quieting the broken parts of him, soothing the damage inflicted by a woman he once loved deeply.

A woman he put all his faith in. Believed in the face of overwhelming evidence to the contrary.

"That's not a question I can answer for you, Kitten." He paused, knowing the next words he had to say could change everything. "I'm not an

174

easy man to deal with, Heidi. I do a lot of things that drive the people around me crazy."

"You mean like how you eat dry chicken and vegetables?"

"What?" The comment caught him off guard. "No." He leaned back just a little. "Does that drive you crazy?"

"Not crazy." She tipped her head to one side. "But I need cheese, Shawn."

"Noted." Shawn laughed, shaking his head. "You make it hard to be serious sometimes."

Heidi's lips lifted. "Isn't that a good thing?"

"Maybe." He straightened. "Come on."

She jumped off her seat, not showing any sign she'd fainted less than an hour ago. "So what about you drives some people crazy?"

"Not just some." Shawn paused outside the door to his room. "Most."

Her brows lifted. "What is it that drives most people crazy?"

Shawn swiped his badge across the sensor before unlocking the door. "I like to tell people what to do." He watched as Heidi immediately went inside.

No hesitation.

"I'm also a little uptight."

She snorted as she dropped to his bed. "A little."

He stood at the door, taking in the sight of her sprawled out on his mattress. "I like to keep things organized."

"I caught that when you snuck in and cleaned my desk."

"No one would call that clean." Shawn unhooked the belt around his waist, sliding it free with his uninjured arm before going to hang it on its designated hook in the closet. "The thing was still covered in white dust." He glanced over his shoulder. "If I didn't know better I'd think you were doing lines across it."

"Donuts." Heidi grinned up at him. "They're my drug of choice."

He hadn't had a donut in years. Long enough he could almost pretend not to remember what they tasted like. "Better than cinnamon rolls?"

"Hmmm." Heidi rolled to her side as he unzipped the mangled vest still strapped across his chest. "That's a tough choice."

Shawn winced as he rolled his injured shoulder in the process of working off what was left of his vest.

"Here." Heidi stood up, moving in close. "I can help." She reached out to gently lift the shredded edge away from the bandage Eli stuck to his skin. "Tell me if I hurt you."

Shawn watched as she carefully eased the weight of the body protection over and down, managing not to even come close to touching his wound in the process. Once one arm was free she walked around his back to slide the other side free. Heidi held the vest up, her eyes sticking to the blood-stained area that almost succeeded in serving its purpose. Her gaze moved to his shoulder where the arm of his shirt was cut away. "I think both of these are ruined now."

"I hope you're talking about the gear and not the shoulder." He reached out as she worried her lower lip between her teeth. "It's not a big deal. This kind of thing happens."

Her attention snapped to his. "Do you know who it was?"

Shawn almost took a step back at the venom in her voice. "I do."

Her chin lifted. "Are they still alive?"

He hesitated just a second, unsure how she might handle the truth. "No."

Heidi let out a breath. "Good."

It was one more time this woman managed to surprise him. "I'm not sure what to do with you half the time, Kitten."

"You're doing better than most people. They don't know what to do with me all of the time." Heidi's lip snuck back between her teeth. It was the only indication she'd said something she didn't really mean to.

"Seems to me like there's at least a roomful of people who know exactly what to do with you." Shawn ran one hand up her arm. Seeing how close the rest of Intel was with Heidi from day one dug into that old wound he'd never been able to heal. Reminded him of who he really was and why he should never even consider trying to get close to her.

Because he would never be her one and only. Heidi was so bright, so magnetic, there would always be someone he had to share her with.

But in this moment he was almost grateful for the fact. For her. She deserved to be appreciated and adored by everyone, not just one selfish man.

"They just need me." Heidi brushed off the truth, stuffed it into a box it didn't fit in.

"That's not true, Kitten." He leaned down, trying to catch her eyes as she went to work on his shirt. "You are one of them."

Heidi's head barely shook as she lifted the hem of his shredded shirt. Her skin went a little pale. "There's blood everywhere."

Shawn glanced down to find a few streaks across his skin where the tiny trickle from his wound soaked its way down the knit fabric. "I don't know that I would call that everywhere."

"What would you call it then?" Heidi pushed his shirt higher, her complexion paling with each inch of skin she revealed.

"I would call that a smear." Shawn backed away. "I'll go take a shower."

"No." Heidi moved with him, her palms coming to rest on his bared skin. "Eli said not to get it wet." Her shoulders pushed back a little as her chin lifted. "I should probably help you."

CHAPTER 14

IT WAS JUST a little blood.

A smear.

Heidi stood in front of the sink of warm water, a washcloth in her hand, staring down the massacre covering Shawn's perfect chest.

Almost perfect. It could use a little more hair, but you can't have everything.

"I think this is a bad idea." Shawn reached out to take the washcloth from her.

She smacked at his hand. "No. It's a good idea."

"You look like you're going to pass out again."

Heidi narrowed her eyes as she stared up at him. "I've never passed out in my li—" She paused. "I've only passed out once in my life."

It also happened to be the first time she saw a gunshot wound. That had to be a completely normal reaction to seeing a hole in the man you were dating.

Were they dating?

Shawn tried to take the cloth again, earning another swat. "Stop being difficult."

"You're the one being difficult." He frowned down at her. "Just let me do it." Shawn made another grab for the washcloth.

Heidi reached up and pinched his nipple.

It seemed like a reasonable way to get him to stop.

But the rumble that moved through the chest inches from her face said otherwise.

"I'm not sure that's going to have the reaction you're going for, Kitten."

She stared at the brown blood dried across his skin, suddenly grateful it was there to keep her distracted from the darkly intense way Shawn's eyes settled on her face. "How do you know what reaction I was going for?"

"It's a short distance from what you did to me smacking your ass when you start dishing out that mouth of yours."

Her hand froze over the spot she was trying to wipe clean. Heat collected in her belly and started to drop, pooling between her legs. "I'm always mouthy."

That low rumble from before tickled the tips of her fingers where they rested on Shawn's chest. "You should probably keep that in mind before you start something you don't want to finish."

She'd had her fair share of sex. Usually with men who were just super excited to be having sex in general.

But so far Shawn hadn't even attempted to actually have sex with her. Not in the biblical sense anyway.

And that wasn't all he hadn't done.

"So you want to spank me but you haven't even kissed me yet?" Heidi focused on the task she'd given herself, keeping her eyes straight ahead on the wide wall of chest she was wiping down like her life depended on it.

"*Yet* being the operative word, Kitten."

Heidi forced herself to keep breathing. She'd already collapsed once tonight. It would look bad if it happened again.

And he definitely wouldn't feel right spanking her after that.

Which would be a shame.

"Heidi."

She focused on wiping away the last of the blood staining the skin just beside the bandage.

"Heidi." The second time Shawn's tone was sharp enough her eyes reflexively jumped to his.

"Breathe."

"I am breathing." Now she was. Maybe she'd forgotten for a minute there.

"I think if you scrub at me any harder I'm going to end up with another hole." Shawn gently pulled the rag from her hand, tossing it onto the counter.

Heidi glanced at the cloudy water still filling the sink and the rag dangling off the side of the sink. "I thought you liked things in order."

"Maybe some things need to be put into order before others." Shawn wrapped one arm around her waist, pulling her body tight to his as he turned toward the bed.

Heidi grabbed onto his neck, trying to be careful not to bump his injured shoulder. "You're going to hurt yourself."

"I don't care." Shawn pressed one knee into the bed, dropping her ass to the mattress before pressing against her, taking both of them down. "Eli will fix whatever I fuck up."

"But…" Heidi's eyes moved to the bandage. "But I think you should just be careful."

"I like that you worry about me, Kitten." Shawn leaned in close enough the tip of his nose brushed along the side of hers.

"Maybe I just don't want to end up having to clean up your blood again." She skimmed her fingers down the bare chest she would scrub clean any day.

With her tongue if possible.

"Don't lie to me, Kitten. I always need the truth from you." His voice was different. Missing the edge of control that made her thighs clench and her nipples tight.

But what she heard now affected her just as much.

Heidi trailed her touch to his face, feeling across the thick beard covering his jaw. "Why?"

The question was only one word, but she understood it was asking a lot. Maybe more than he was ready to share with her.

"It's a long story, Kitten." Shawn's dark eyes moved over her face. "One that might make you look at me differently."

"Maybe that's not a bad thing." Life was easier when you knew what you were getting. The honest, unfiltered truth.

It's why she never tried to be something she wasn't, even when no one liked who she was. At least they didn't like some fake shell of a person trying to earn unwarranted affection.

Shawn smiled, a single, soft laugh curving his lips. "You look at things differently than anyone I've ever met, Kitten."

"Thanks." Heidi passed her fingers over the lips she had yet to feel against hers.

She'd felt them on most other places on her body, but somehow the desire to know how they would feel in that one particular spot was more intense than any other desire she had. "You were about to tell me something that will make me look at you differently."

Shawn inhaled long and slow. "I don't even know where to start."

"Start with once upon a time." Heidi moved her hands to his hair, stroking the longer strands at the top of his head. "That's how all long stories start."

Shawn cleared his throat a little. "Once upon a time..." He paused, his eyes closing as she continued to comb her fingers through his hair in slow drags. "Once upon a time I loved a woman."

A pang of emotion that was becoming more familiar than she cared to admit cut into her gut, settling into a dull ache. "You loved a woman?"

It was a normal thing most people did. Find someone they like. Fall in love.

Do things people in love do.

She just never really felt the inclination to put herself out there. Especially considering she wasn't particularly interested in bending to a shape that might fit into someone else's life.

"I loved her very much." The pain in his admission added to the ache deepening in her insides. "She was my whole world."

"That's nice." What was she supposed to say to him? *Super glad some other chick was great enough for you to fall in love with when I can't even get a mouth kiss.*

His eyes opened, meeting hers. "It was not nice. It was a fucking nightmare."

That was better.

Which was worse. Because it made her an asshole.

"What happened?" Part of her wanted to know, hoping it would soothe the foreign pain overtaking her abdomen. Part of her wanted to know what it was like. To experience the sort of things most people her age had already faced. Most of them more than once.

"I was all in with her. From the very beginning. She was all I wanted." Shawn shifted, one hand coming to catch a bit of her hair, twisting it between his fingers as he continued on. "She was all that made me happy."

So far this sounded terribly wonderful. A man desperately in love with a woman. Dedicated and satisfied.

But that beautiful story would not lead to this moment. "Did she love you back?"

Shawn's eyes dropped from hers. "No. She did not."

Ouch.

Heidi winced at the pain in his words, on his face. Was this what all that felt like? This hateful, horrible ache?

She'd done the right thing all these years by avoiding it. It was bullshit.

"She's stupid."

Shawn shook his head. "Not loving me doesn't make someone stupid."

"You're being awfully nice about this." Considering she was already trying to figure out who this woman was that hurt a man as strong and steady as this one, with the intent of causing her some sort of painful but manageable digital damage, it was definitely better she didn't date.

She'd have burned down half the internet by now.

"There's nothing to be mean about. She just found someone she did love."

Wait.

"When did she find this man she did decide to love?" Heidi wrinkled her nose as she waited for the answer, knowing full-well she was not going to like it.

I don't share.
I only do monogamy.

There's no one else until you're done with me.

She was going to kill a bitch.

Blood issues be damned.

Shawn didn't answer her. Honestly he didn't have to. The truth of what happened was written all over his face.

Hidden between the lines of everything he said. Tucked neatly into the folds of all he did.

"Well that just sucked a bag of dicks didn't it?"

The sharp lines of his expressions broke apart, softening as he smiled. "It really did."

She smiled back at him. "You don't smile very much."

Shawn's smile slipped. "I told you there were things about me that—"

Heidi reached up to press one finger across his mouth. "That's not what I was trying to say." She'd sacrificed many things to live an authentic life. One where she could be who she was without fear of rejection.

It was almost impossible to imagine a man as strong and solid as Shawn had done anything different.

"I like that you only smile when you really mean it." She felt across the lips that held so much more back that she realized. "I like that I make it happen sometimes." She traced the corners of his mouth, her breath catching as it eased closer.

The second their lips met she felt it with every part of her body. The fingers touching both his skin and hers. The warmth of Shawn's breath against her cheek. The roughened skin of his palm as it came to cradle her face.

The heat of his body as it soaked into her, warming her from top to bottom, inside and out.

It was like pulling on the coziest clothes you owned after being caught in the rain. The feeling of bone deep comfort after fighting an unexpected chill.

One she didn't know surrounded her until this moment.

Heidi wrapped her arms around his neck, pulling Shawn closer, trying to soak up more of the sensation.

Of what she'd been missing.

His mouth was as focused as everything else about him where it covered hers, claiming something he probably already owned.

Something she never intended to put up for sale, instead holding it close.

Protecting it.

The scent of his skin surrounded her. The barely-there bite of iron still lingering from the blood she washed away.

"Why did you have to go and get shot?" Her mouth struggled to move under the press of his.

Shawn tried to pull away, but it only made her hold him tighter.

Her heart stopped when she saw him on the ground, cold and bleeding. In that moment there was only one thought blanketing her brain, covering it with inescapable fear.

She just wanted to be close to him. To see that he was okay.

This man who was supposed to be nothing more than a provider of physical release.

Heidi wrapped her legs around his waist, hooking her ankles together. It was what made her feel better. Knowing the only way he could go was if she went too.

His mouth eased into one of the rare smiles that made her heart squeeze. "Something wrong, Kitten?"

"What if that bullet went just a little to the left?"

"Then I would have been better off because my vest would have been able to stop it." His smile was still there, lingering on the lips moving against hers.

"Then what if it was higher and to the left?" The possibility sent her stomach rolling.

Shawn fought his way up enough his dark eyes could meet hers. "Then my pretty face would be a little less good-looking."

Heidi reached up, resting her hands against the beard that was just to the point of softness. "You really are pretty."

He chuckled. "Pretty? Really, Rucker?"

She lifted one shoulder. "Why can't you be pretty?"

He looked at her for a long minute, his eyes moving across her face. "I can be whatever you want me to be."

"I think I would like for you to be more careful then." She traced down the line of his neck and around the edges of the bandage covering the evidence of just how dangerous this life she stepped into could be.

It could hurt someone as indestructible as the one holding her now.

"I'm fine. I promise." He leaned down to drag his nose along her neck, breathing deep. "Better than fine actually."

"Because I'm here?" She wasn't needy. It was a word she could honestly say literally never applied to her.

Until this second. With this man.

"Yes, Kitten. Because you're here." His lips traced the jut of her collarbone before working their way back to hers.

She sighed as he kissed her again, sinking deeper into the feelings Shawn's presence brought. The safety. The security.

And something else. Something she never sought.

Never thought she wanted.

His tongue dipped between her lips, strong and sure but not aggressive. Demanding but not taking.

It was exactly how he turned out to be. A man who demanded so much but would only take what was willingly given.

And God help her, she wanted to give him all of it.

Whatever in the hell it even was.

And she wanted to give it to him right now.

Heidi grabbed for the button of his pants, working them open before reaching in. The press of his pelvis to hers stopped her wandering hand, keeping her from getting anywhere interesting.

She grunted out of frustration, yanking at the fabric, trying to get where she wanted to go.

"Something wrong, Heidi?"

"I'm not freaking Heidi right now." She snapped her eyes to him. "I'm Kitten and I want to touch your dick."

Not just want. Need. She needed to touch his dick. Needed to have all of him closer to all of her.

And it had nothing to do with getting off. Which made no sense considering that was the whole point of having a penis near her.

"Get it out. Now."

Shawn lifted a brow at her. "That's an awful big demand, Kitten." He leaned close, keeping his body tight to hers. "What makes you think you get to decide what happens in this room?"

Uh. Because she always decided what happened in a bed. It made things more efficient. Women were not consistent with their needs in the way most men were.

A little bit of thrusting and a man could get off. Women not so much.

So if she wanted to get off, and she did, it was best if she just ran the show.

Shawn's head moved side to side in a slow shake. "Not with me, Kitten. I'm the one in charge here. Always."

Oh hell.

Her thighs clenched tight around him. It was an involuntary response to the man who had never given her what she wanted.

Not fucking once.

But damned if he didn't always give her what she needed.

"You like that, don't you, Kitten?" One wide palm pushed up the fabric of her shirt.

She grabbed the hem, intending to pull it off and get his hands on her faster.

Shawn grabbed her wrists, catching both with one hand before pulling them high above her head. "What did I just say?"

She gulped. An actual, cartoonish gulp. But it wasn't out of fear or concern.

It was pure anticipation that made her throat and thighs spasm.

"I'm waiting for an answer." His hold on her hands tightened.

"You're in charge?"

"You don't sound sure of that." The hand of his injured arm tugged her thigh free of his waist, the other one falling to the mattress along with it. Shawn grabbed the waistband of her pants, yanking them down in jerky movements. "Do you not trust me to give you what you need?"

"I do." She resisted the urge to use her legs to help him work her pants all the way off.

But Shawn wasn't trying to get her pants off completely.

He only bared from her waist to her thighs before rolling her over, his body immediately coming to press into hers. His voice was low and deep in her ear. "Do you think I will leave you wanting, Kitten?"

"No." Her hair was tangled over her face, his weight on her back and his hold on her hands making it impossible to do anything but try to breathe as excitement and arousal squeezed her chest.

His fingers moved over the side of her face with a gentle touch, pushing away the mass of hair keeping her from seeing him. "It seems like you are still worried I can't fulfill you, Heidi." His words were rough and edgy. A little dark. A little strained.

She thought it was hot when he called her Kitten, and it was. To the point that the word alone made heat immediately pool in her pussy.

But now he might have just ruined her name too.

She pushed back, rubbing her ass against him, trying to get some blessed friction on the ache pulsating between her thighs.

The clear line of sight he'd provided a second earlier offered an unobstructed view of his hand as it moved, giving her a second to prepare for the sharp slap on her ass.

It wasn't nearly enough time.

"Holy shit." No one had ever fucking spanked her. Not in her whole life. Not her parents and certainly not any of the men she chose to invite into her bed.

Shawn's hand stroked across the stinging spot. "Don't doubt me, Heidi. Not ever."

"Or else I get spanked?" That might not be as big of a deterrent as he seemed to think it was.

Shawn nosed against her neck, shoving up the shirt she tried to work free earlier, and would be trying to remove again if she could, now that she knew what it would earn her. "Why do you always push me?"

She smiled, wiggling her ass against him. This wasn't a struggle for power.

192

This was a struggle for control.

Not of him over her.

It was of Shawn over himself.

And she was happy to participate in his journey of self-discovery.

"Damn it, Heidi." Another sharp slap made her skin burn and her cunt clench, dragging a whimper of pleasure from her lips.

Shawn growled against her skin as he bit down on her shoulder, the hand holding hers pulling free. His weight left her back suddenly as he moved off the bed.

Heidi lifted her head. "What happened?"

Shawn shoved down his pants, freeing the rigid length of his dick. "You wanted to take your clothes off." His hand went to his cock, stroking down the length as his eyes settled on hers. "Take them off."

Didn't have to tell her twice. Heidi rolled to her back and kicked her legs as she wiggled her way out of her pants while pulling her shirt over her head, managing to take her bra with it. Didn't even have to unhook the thing.

"Spread your legs, Kitten." Shawn slowly walked to the foot of the bed, dark gaze moving down her body. "Show me what is mine."

She pushed her knees apart, happy to oblige.

"Wider." Shawn's growled demand came as he moved to the other side of the bed, opening the drawer to pull out a condom.

Heidi did as he asked as Shawn rested one knee on the bed.

"Not good enough." The hand that just held his dick came to smack against her already swollen labia. "Wider."

Whatever it took to get him where she wanted, she was happy to do. Heidi grabbed her knees, pulling them back and as far apart as she could get them.

Shawn reached out to run his hand along her slit, his chest rumbling as his fingers slid across her soaked flesh. "Who makes you wet, Heidi?"

"You do."

"Who else?"

She shook her head. "No one. Only you, Captain."

His eyes snapped to hers.

He wasn't the only one willing to offer what was needed.

Shawn was on her in a heartbeat, his big body settling into the spot she made just for him as his dick prodded her ready entrance. His hand came to her face, bracing over her chin to hold it tight like he had that first time in his office. "Who fucks you, Heidi?"

"Just you." Her eyes rolled closed as he pushed into her.

"Look at me." Shawn's words were a sharp command. One that spoke of need and a pain she was only beginning to understand.

She immediately did as he asked, locking her eyes onto his.

"You will look at me while I fuck you, understand?"

"Yes." He was definitely nice to look at, but keeping her eyes open as his hips rolled into hers proved more difficult that it seemed. As he ground against her clit with his pelvis her eyes dropped closed again.

"Eyes open, Heidi." His tone was gentler this time. "I want you to see only me."

She grabbed his face with both hands, pulling it closer, forcing her eyes to stay open even as her thighs shook and her nipples pulled tight. "Shawn, I'm—"

"Give it to me, Kitten. Give me what I want."

It wasn't what he wanted. It was what he needed.

To know she was there. With him. Only him.

His eyes locked hers as the swell of his dick sent her over the edge a second before Shawn's whole body went rigid, his own climax following hers almost instantly.

Her vision blurred and her muscles went weak as her eyes finally closed. Shawn's body slipped free of hers and the mattress lifted as he left the bed. Heidi sat straight up. "Where are you going?"

She'd left a bed just as abruptly countless times. Sort of a *thanks for the dick but I've got shit to do* thing.

"I'm coming right back, Kitten. Don't get all upset."

She blinked.

She *was* upset.

Shawn appeared in the doorway to the bathroom a second later. "No one wants a cold rubber stuck to their skin." He pulled the covers back on the bed and climbed in next to her, immediately pulling her close and pressing his lips against hers.

She'd never kissed anyone after sex. Once it was done she was done.

But being done with Shawn didn't seem like a possibility.

She sighed as he stroked her face, his mouth moving against hers. It was soft and gentle.

Sweet enough to lull her to sleep.

****

"KITTEN."

Heidi pried one lid open, peeking out into the dark room. "What?"

"It's time to get up."

She leaned up to stare at the clock sitting on Shawn's nightstand. "It's four in the morning." Heidi squinted at him. "Are you already dressed?"

"Pierce woke me up."

Heidi sat up a little more. "Why did Pierce wake you up?"

"Something happened and we need you to come see what you can do to handle it."

"Me?" Heidi wiped at her eyes. "Why not Harlow?"

"Piece is concerned Harlow might struggle with this particular issue."

"Hell." Heidi tossed the covers back and scooted across the mattress. "What has Tod done now?"

"Tod's not doing anything anymore."

Heidi froze. She straightened, eyes finally focusing. Shawn's expression was grim as he watched her from the other side of the bed. "He's dead?"

Shawn's head tipped in a nod.

"What happened?" She should be happy that Tod was dead. He'd done horrible, terrible things to Harlow. Things no man should ever be forgiven for.

But it was one more death. One more person in the same circle around her who met an early demise.

"How are you feeling this morning?" The question seemed out of place.

"I mean, fine considering you woke me up to tell me someone else is dead." Heidi grabbed her shoes. "How exactly am I supposed to be helpful in this situation?"

"Tod was dropped off at the gate about thirty minutes ago."

"The gate here?" It was so close. Too close. "Is he here?" She glanced over one shoulder as if a dead man could be sneaking up behind her.

"He's in the basement." Shawn slowly stood. "There's something we need you to look at."

Her throat clenched tight as saliva pooled in the back of her mouth. "You want me to look at a dead person?"

Shawn stood, coming close enough to grab her and hold her close. "I will be right beside you the whole time."

"I don't understand why you need me to do it." Heidi buried her face in his shirt, breathing in the smell of his warm body.

"You will." Shawn leaned back, one hand coming to tip her face toward his. "I wish I didn't have to ask you to do this, Kitten."

"Me too." She wrapped both arms around his waist, pulling the comforting heat of his body closer. It was strange to find something like that in another person. She'd always been emotionally self-sufficient.

Met her own needs.

Not that there were many. Her life was pretty easy and uninteresting up to this point.

She sure was freaking making up for it now.

"Okay." Heidi straightened, sucking a breath in through her nose. "Let's get this over with."

Shawn took her into the underground system of tunnels she only knew about because it was where Mona shot Bobby. The air was cool and still as she tucked in close at his side, her heart rate picking up with each step she took.

She was about to look at a dead man. For some reason she would supposedly understand.

Pierce and Zeke stood outside of a heavy metal door, their expressions tight as they watched her come closer.

Pierce was the first to speak. He reached for the door. "Thank you for coming. I'm sorry to start your day under these circumstances." Pierce pushed the door open and stepped in ahead of her. Shawn was close at her back with Zeke coming in last. "The body was dumped not long ago. Rolled out of a black sedan and left lying in the middle of the street." Pierce stepped to where a sheet laid across what was clearly a body.

Without warning he pulled the white covering back, revealing the mottled, slightly grey complexion of a man who might have been attractive if you didn't know what a piece of shit he was.

Heidi pressed back against Shawn. His hands rested on her shoulders, warm and solid.

She leaned a little closer, peeking at an odd mark on the skin showing between the open plackets of the button-down shirt Tod put on not realizing it would be the last thing he wore. "What's on his skin?"

"That is why you are here." Pierce stepped close beside the dead man. "I thought you might be the most likely to know what it was."

Heidi tried to lean a little more, but gravity made it impossible to accomplish. Shawn pressed into her. "Go ahead. I'll be right with you."

She glanced at him before turning back to the body. Heidi took a step forward, inching her way across the floor until the full extent of what was marked on Tod's chest came into view.

Her gasp echoed in the silence of the room. Both her hands went over her mouth as she stared at the letters inked across Tod's skin.

Pierce turned to her. "You know what it means."

She nodded, trying to swallow down the ball of panic and bile fighting its way up her throat.

"Those are people I know."

CHAPTER 15

"WHAT DO YOU mean you know those people?" Shawn stepped closer to Tod's dead body, being careful not to push Heidi any closer. "Those aren't names."

"They're handles." Heidi's blue eyes moved over the list neatly penned on Tod's chest. "We use them in chat rooms to protect our identities."

"Is yours on there?" The thought that Heidi might be on someone's fucking hit list made him consider burning the world down just to be sure he took out whoever thought they had the right to threaten the woman beside him.

She shook her head. "No."

"Why do you think someone would do this, Ms. Rucker?" Pierce stood next to Tod's dead body, his hands tucked into his pockets.

"Can we talk about this somewhere else?" Her eyes avoided one specific person in the room.

And it wasn't the dead one.

"Of course." Pierce turned to Zeke. "Please send the images to me in case Ms. Rucker would like to use them for reference."

Zeke nodded his response, standing in the corner of the room with his arms across his chest.

"Shall we?" Pierce opened the door, holding it for Heidi as she passed.

Shawn stared Zeke down as he left. Having the lead for Shadow so close to her pissed him the hell off, especially considering the possible things Shadow could be involved in.

Shawn pulled the door closed as he left, finding Heidi waiting for him just outside the door. Pierce lifted a brow at him. "Are we ready?"

Heidi grabbed his hand. "I need to go to my computer so I can warn everyone." Her eyes stayed on him as she spoke.

"I'm not sure that is a good idea." Pierce led the way through the tunnels to the staircase leading to his office.

Heidi tucked closer into Shawn's side as they walked, her eyes moving around the space.

He leaned into her ear. "No one is down here. I promise."

She gave him a tiny nod before turning her eyes to where Pierce held the door open. "But they could be in danger."

"They are almost definitely in danger." Pierce's eyes followed Heidi as she moved past him into his

202

office. "However, alerting them to that fact could possibly put them in more danger."

"So I'm just supposed to let them walk around not knowing?" Heidi stood in the center of the room, her frustration at the situation becoming more obvious by the second. "The same way you just let me come here, not knowing what in the hell I was walking into?"

Her anger wasn't surprising. Part of him was angry for her.

Not all of him though. The rest was willing to face down the rage happily.

Whatever it took to keep her here with him.

Pierce's chin dipped. "Are you positive you wouldn't have ended up involved anyway, Ms. Rucker? From my understanding you were quite involved in things you should not have been from a very young age."

She stood straighter. "From your understanding?" Heidi's eyes narrowed on the owner of Alaskan Security. "Exactly how did you come to this understanding?"

"Even in circumstances such as this I run extensive background checks on anyone I bring into this company."

Heidi's eyes slid to Shawn before moving back to Pierce. "And how would you have access to that sort of information?"

Shawn looked to Pierce. He'd been in charge of running the basic background checks for anyone Shadow took on as a client just like all the other team leads had done for their own respective clients. Charles, the company attorney handled the legal side of the search with Shawn using a basic service to execute the civil portion.

But that was before Intel was formed.

And he'd never run a check on Heidi. Or any of the other members of Intel. Even Eva provided all her own information, limited as it was.

For reasons he now understood.

"Who did the check on her, Pierce?" Shawn's blood heated at the prospect of someone else digging into Heidi's private life. Seeing things they had no business seeing.

"That is classified."

Heidi snorted. "It always is." She smirked his way. "Guess that means I'll just never know." She turned to Shawn. "I've got work to do. Would you walk me to my office?"

"Absolutely." He shot Pierce a glare, hoping his friend understood it meant they were nowhere near finished with this conversation.

He opened the door to Pierce's office, wrapping one arm around Heidi as they walked toward the office at the end of the hall.

"The lights are on." Heidi walked a little faster. She hurried through the open door, stopping short as she walked inside. "Why are you here so early?"

Mona's eyes lifted from the pile of work on her desk. "I couldn't sleep." Her clear blue gaze narrowed on Heidi. "Why are you here so early?"

Heidi let out a sigh Shawn could feel. "Tod's dead."

Mona's eyes widened. "What? How do you know?"

"Cause I had to look at his dead ass." She bobbed her head to one side. "Not really his ass, just his dead body."

"Wow." Mona leaned back in her seat. After a couple seconds her expression changed, confusion drawing her brows low. "Why did you have to look at his dead body?"

"It's a long story." Heidi turned his way. "What time is the meeting today?"

"What meeting?"

She frowned up at him. "The one to discuss who in the hell dropped Tod off?"

"Hasn't been scheduled yet." He reached out to tip her chin up. "But you'll know as soon as I know."

Heidi smiled in spite of everything she'd been through in the past twenty-four hours. "Thank you."

"Anything you want." He leaned down to drop a kiss on her lips. "I'll go so you can get to work."

"Okay." Heidi grabbed his shirt as he started to walk away. "You aren't going anywhere today, right?"

He slid one hand along her cheek, the concern in her eyes digging under his skin in a way few things could. "I don't know yet."

She frowned. "But you're hurt." Heidi's hands fisted tighter in his shirt. "You shouldn't be going out if you're hurt."

"This is a war, Heidi." He pulled her close, leaning into her ear. "And I will do whatever it takes to end it before it gets close to you." He took one, self-indulgent breath of her skin before letting her go and walking away.

He needed a little space. A little room to find his way back to a reasonable, rational mindset.

Because she made him want to kill anyone and everyone who might try to get too close.

His office was too quiet when he sat down at his desk. The silence made it impossible to find anything else to focus on.

He grabbed his gym bag and headed to the only place that could ever clear his head.

"Already?" Heidi's voice carried down the hall. She was smiling softly, standing outside the break room, stainless steel cup in her hand.

"Already what?"

She pointed to the bag in his hand. "Better not stress that shoulder, Captain. I might decide to act up later." Heidi gave him a wink before turning away and walking back to her office, lush hips swaying in a way he couldn't look away from.

He had to figure out how to keep her safe. Make absolutely sure no one in this place could put her in any danger.

Shawn went back to his office, tossing the bag back in its spot before firing off an email to each of the leads, as well as Dutch and Roman. Then he went to Pierce's office, barging right in.

Mona stood in the center of the room, her arms crossed tight over her chest as she stared down the owner of Alaskan Security.

"Can I help you with something, Shawn?" Pierce's gaze never left Mona.

Mona's head turned Shawn's way, her eyes holding Pierce's until the very last. When they finally landed on him he almost took a step back at the fire simmering in their cool blue depths.

The woman looked primed and ready to string someone up by their balls.

"I was just leaving." Her back went perfectly straight and her chin lifted as she turned her attention back to Pierce. "Our discussion is finished."

Shawn watched Mona walk out before turning back to Pierce. His old friend's head was in his hands.

He'd known the man for years. Long enough to think he was untouchable.

Unbreakable.

And yet a tiny woman with a growing strength just laid him low without even raising her voice.

"You okay?" Shawn took a slow step toward Pierce.

Pierce sucked in a breath as he straightened. "It's just been a long night." His gaze came to Shawn's. "What is it you need?"

Adding another pile to the one already steaming on Pierce's shoulders didn't feel right, but there were no other options. "I sent an email to the leads and coordinators." He stood tall, knowing Pierce was not going to be a fan of what he had to say next. "We're going to find GHOST."

Pierce's eyes sharpened. "You believe you can find them?"

"Of course." He didn't believe that at all, but it wasn't going to stop him.

Someone threw down a threat he wasn't willing to sit on. One hacker was dead and he'd be damned if he waited to see if there was another on the line.

"Fine." Pierce stood. "Do it."

It wasn't the response Shawn was expecting. Their relationship with the government was touch and go at best, each using the other for anything they could get while trying to give very little in return. Hunting down their most secretive of divisions wouldn't go over well.

But he wasn't going to stand by while Heidi put herself in the line of fire.

The owner of Alaskan Security stood from his chair. "Do whatever it takes to find them and when you do make it clear we are not going to tolerate this disrespect." Pierce rounded his desk. "If you'll excuse me, I have a meeting."

"A meeting?" Shawn hadn't seen any meetings on the books. "With who?"

Pierce turned to face him and for the first time in a long time he saw the side of Pierce no one knew existed.

Wouldn't believe was there even if he told them.

"Zeke."

There weren't many people in this world Shawn wouldn't fuck with.

Pierce was one of them.

He had extreme power and it didn't end with the reach of his money and connections.

The man was capable of things most men made empty boasts about.

"You might want to take a deep breath before you do that." It was a pointless suggestion. Pierce would handle Zeke in any way he wanted.

And God help the lead of Shadow, Shawn had only seen this look in his friend's eyes once before.

And not everyone made it out of the room alive that night.

"I promise you I will not do anything I will regret." Pierce straightened the lapels of his jacket.

"Do you regret anything you've done in your life?"

Pierce's eyes met his. "No."

"Hey." Dutch poked his head out of the conference room Shawn listed in his email. "You dragged my ass out of bed and now you're fucking late."

Shawn turned back to find Pierce was already gone, halfway down the hall.

Dutch watched him disappear before turning to Shawn. "Should we go after him?"

"He's going to find Zeke."

"Oh." Dutch shrugged. "That's fine then."

"It's fine unless he kills him." Shawn stood with his hands on his hips, contemplating the possible ramifications of leaving Pierce alone with Zeke. "Then we've got one whole mess added to another."

Dutch glanced at the way Pierce left. "You don't think he'll really kill him, do you?"

"I've only seen him look like that once."

"Hell." Dutch set his coffee down before taking off down the hall with Shawn following right behind him. As they reached the main entrance Wade and Brock were just coming through the door of the walkway. Without any questions both men took up the chase.

Pierce's suited form disappeared into Zeke's office just as Shawn rounded the corner. By the time he made it to the open door Zeke was out of his chair, facing Pierce down like he didn't realize who the hell he was dealing with.

"She came to me."

Shawn nearly ran into Dutch as they both came to a stop at Zeke's words.

She?

"I think we all just need to take a deep breath." Dutch stepped in between the two men, one hand on each of their chests. "Whatever this is about can be worked out."

"It cannot." Pierce's words were short and clipped.

While Zeke looked like a caged beast ready to pounce, Pierce looked almost exactly like he always did.

Which was part of the problem.

"Then why don't we wait to work it out until all the other bullshit we're dealing with is resolved?" Shawn moved in beside Dutch, adding another body for Pierce to go through.

"I don't think that's a possibility." Pierce's cool gaze held Zeke's. "I'm unwilling to let this slide." His eyes narrowed. "Period."

Zeke snorted. "You're walking a thin line with me, Pierce. All I have to do is walk out and you're fucked."

Pierce's lips lifted. "But I'm not the only one who would be fucked, now am I?"

Zeke's nostrils flared.

The two men stared each other down as Brock and Wade edged closer, ready to step in at any second.

"You're the one who sent her my way in the first place."

"A decision I regret greatly." Pierce slow walked, rounding where Zeke stood, forcing Shawn to move to maintain his position between them.

"Just tell her not to bother me." Zeke wasn't backing down.

"The lady does not appreciate being told what to do." Pierce's jaw set as he eyed Zeke. "And she made it very clear that she will continue to do exactly as she wishes."

Shawn forced his expression to remain blank in spite of the revelations Pierce was throwing out about a very specific woman.

One who was turning out to be just as big of a handful as her teammates.

Zeke's mouth twisted into a smirk. "Sounds like you're fucked then."

Pierce took two quick steps toward the larger man, moving fast enough no one had time to stop him. In the blink of an eye Pierce had Zeke's arm twisted behind his back and his face pressed tight to the wall. Shadow's lead struggled for a second, thinking it was a good idea to attempt to break loose.

Pierce didn't react at all, simply pulled the hold he had on Zeke's arm tighter. "Don't think for a second I won't break it, Zeke. I will."

"You're fucking crazy." Zeke didn't flinch, his skin reddening from rage as Pierce held him tight.

Pierce leaned closer, his voice low. "You have no idea what I will do to protect the people I care about. You should keep that in mind from now on. I will not hesitate to do whatever is required to make absolutely sure no harm comes to them."

Zeke twisted his neck, straining to glare Pierce's way. "Is that what you fuckin' think? That I would hurt her?"

"I think being around you will put her in more danger than she realizes." Pierce's tone was deadly calm. "And that's not going to happen."

"And you think being around you is less fucking dangerous?"

Pierce's expression changed in an instant.

He dropped his hold on Zeke and stepped away, smoothing down the front of his suit before turning to walk toward the door. He paused, giving the lead for Shadow one last glance over his shoulder.

"I expect to see you at the meeting this afternoon."

CHAPTER 16

"WHAT'S WRONG?" HEIDI watched as Mona stormed across the room. "You look like someone just peed in your Cheerios."

Mona glanced around the empty office before stomping her way closer to Heidi's desk. She dropped to a crouch, her eyes scanning the open door. "I just went to talk to Zeke."

Heidi sat up a little straighter in her seat. "Yeah? What happened?"

Mona's lips pressed to a frown. "Nothing. He said he can't help me."

Heidi slumped in her seat. "No shit?" She dropped her head back against her horrible chair. "What the hell?"

Mona fell to her ass on the carpet. "I thought I could do it." She let out a sigh. "I really thought I could help us get somewhere."

"For what's it's worth I'm pretty sure if you couldn't do it no one could." Heidi grabbed for the water on her desk and sucked down some of the icy liquid.

"Maybe you should try talking to him. Maybe I just came on too strong." Mona rested her head against the desk behind Heidi's.

"I definitely can't talk to Zeke." Heidi didn't even think about the words as they came out of her mouth.

Mona sat straight. "Why not?"

Well, shit.

"Um." There had to be some sort or reasonable explanation. Something besides it pisses Shawn off.

Except maybe that was a reasonable explanation.

"It bothers Shawn." Heidi had yet to tell anyone about her entanglement with Shawn. Not because she didn't want to, just because she wasn't sure if that was something adults did.

Mona gave her a slow smile. "Does that mean Captain Uptight finally came around?"

Heidi sipped at her water a little more. "It would seem that way."

"So, is it a serious sort of thing or more of a fun while it lasts kind of thing?"

Heidi sat on the question for a minute. "How can you tell the difference?"

Mona's narrow shoulders lifted and fell. "I don't know. I've only had one of the two."

Heidi bobbed her head in a nod. "Same." She tipped her head toward Mona. "But I think whatever I've had is the opposite of what you've had, so maybe you can help me."

"Well." Mona pursed her lips. "I guess when it's serious the man makes it clear he only wants you to see him and he only wants to see you."

"Oh." Heidi chewed on the end of her reusable straw. "Well, then I think it might be a serious sort of thing." She wrinkled her nose. "Is it bad that it's like that already?"

"I'd say it depends on what you want. Do you want something serious?"

She'd never had anything serious with a guy, let alone a man.

And Shawn definitely fell into the latter category.

"I don't *not* want something serious." Admitting she wanted something more permanent than she'd ever had seemed like a bad idea.

She'd gone her whole life knowing she was a little different than most people, and structured her world accordingly. Her closest friends lived worlds away and used nonsensical names that spoke volumes while also saying very little. She never considered trying to get to know a man in a romantic sense because then he would want to get to know her.

Then probably realize she was odd and back slowly away.

Or he would not realize she was odd and want to spend all his time up her ass. Bothering her with stupid conversations about nothing important.

Which didn't sound particularly appetizing either.

"I just don't really know how that would work." Heidi reached for the pile of files strewn over her desk, stacking them up as she continued. "I have things I like to do." She set the stack off to one side, collecting her pens and plunking them into the glass that appeared on her desk out of nowhere. "I don't really know how to have another person in my life."

Mona was quiet for a little bit. Finally she tucked her knees to her chest, wrapping both arms around them. "For a long time I didn't know how to live without another person in my life." She stared across the room as she spoke. "And made some really stupid choices because of it."

"Are you talking about twat face?"

Mona's lips pressed down on one side. "Among others." She turned to Heidi. "I think if a person should be in your life they will just fit into a spot. You won't have to figure out how to make them room."

Heidi looked down at the woman she was just beginning to really know. "You're really smart."

"You'd think." Mona inhaled and blew it out with a lip-vibrating raspberry. "If he fits then just stick him in there."

Heidi snorted as a laugh snuck out. "That sounds more like how I handled men up until now."

"Why in the hell are you two here already?" Eva walked through the door looking a little worn down. "Do you know what time it is?"

Heidi leaned to one side, checking to be sure no one else was coming. "Tod's dead. Someone dumped his body at the gate."

Eva stumbled a little; the hand clutching her coffee slipped forcing her to scramble to hang onto it as it tried to slide free. "What the fuck?"

"That's what I said." Heidi glanced at the container of yogurt and fruit Shawn brought her an hour ago, but the thought of eating still turned her stomach. "I had to look at him."

"What? Why in the hell would you have to look at him?" Eva fell into the chair behind her desk.

Heidi rubbed her burning eyes and groaned. "It's such a freaking mess." She linked her computer up to the wireless connection she'd set up to the monitors on the wall.

"Holy fuck, Heidi." Eva shoved her chair back, putting as much distance as possible between her and the screen displaying Tod's dead chest. "You need to warn me before you do shit like that."

"Sorry." She stared at the same dead skin she'd stared at for the past hour.

"Who are they?" Eva studied the row of chat room handles listed in neat block letters down the center of Tod's well-sculpted, but very dead chest.

"Some of the people I checked in with yesterday." Heidi went over it more times than she could count.

Only part of the people she reached out to were on that list.

"Some?" Mona stood from where she'd been on the floor next to Heidi's desk. "Not all?"

"No. Not all." There were three names missing. Three people she'd spoken with who were not on the list. "Two of the people listed never got back with me."

217

She'd only actually interacted with four of the people on the screen now.

Which made her wonder who in the hell killed Tod and dumped his body at Alaskan Security?

And why in the hell did they do it?

"So the list is wrong." Mona tapped the tips of her fingers against her chin as she slowly walked between the desks. "They don't actually know who you've been in contact with, but they want you to think they know what you're doing?"

"Maybe." Heidi caught sight of Harlow coming down the hall and quickly minimized the photo so it no longer displayed.

Harlow stepped into the room, her eyes immediately going to Heidi. "Show it to me."

Dutch came in right after Harlow. "Nope. Don't do it."

"I'm not going to be the decider here, Dutch." Heidi shook her head. "If she wants to see it I'm going to show it to her."

"I want to see it." Harlow marched straight to Heidi's desk and crossed her arms. "Come on."

Heidi clicked the window with the photo, watching Harlow as it populated the screen.

Harlow stared at dead Tod for long seconds. "Do you know all of them?"

Heidi nodded.

"I think we need to break the rules." Harlow's blue eyes finally left the screen to lock onto Heidi's. "We've got to figure out who they are."

"I know." It was the only conclusion she'd been able to come to. The only option was to do the one thing she never thought she would do.

Hack a hacker.

And not just one.

"But those are not the only people I've been in contact with." Heidi tapped the screen, pulling up the markup option. She ran her finger across the screen, highlighting the people she hadn't actually been able to contact. "And I haven't actually heard anything from these people."

"If the list is wrong that means whoever made it doesn't know what they think they know." Dutch stood close at Harlow's side, his eyes spending most of their time on Harlow.

"Or it means they know something we don't." Mona still hadn't looked away from the screen. "What if the list we're looking at is right for what it is?"

Harlow's head snapped Mona's way. She pointed a finger at her. "You are so friggin smart." Harlow turned back to the pale skin of her ex-husband's dead chest. "I think we should go on the theory that the list is right. We just have to figure out what it's a list of."

"Are all those people still alive?" Dutch went to his desk. "Maybe those are the people who they've already found."

"Who is *they* in that scenario?" Heidi rolled her neck as tension she didn't usually have tried to crank her shoulders up against her skull. "GHOST, or whoever Chris and Tod and Howard work for."

"Worked for." Eva chewed her lower lip. "They're all dead now."

The room went silent. Heidi looked at the women around her. "There's only one person we know of who's not dead."

Eva's gaze met hers. "They're killing everyone we can identify."

"Chandler's on deck then." Mona's tone was surprisingly flat.

"How are we going to find them if they kill everyone we know to look for?" Eva sounded panicked enough for both her and her best friend. "We're fucked."

"No." Heidi's eyes lifted to the screen. "Not if we can figure out who's on this list. They tie into this somehow and if we can figure it out we'll—"

Her heart stopped.

What if that was the whole goal? To get her to go exactly where they wanted her to be?

"How did Tod die?" Heidi turned back to her computer as the loose ends fraying around her suddenly connected in an unexpected way. "Do we know yet?"

"The coroner just came to get him." Dutch met her gaze. "We should know first thing tomorrow."

"That's too late." Heidi pulled up Alaskan Security's system. "I think we might have a problem if we don't get ahead of this real freaking fast." She immediately disconnected the internet. "If that list is what I think it is we might already be fucked." She pulled out her computer and worked off her hotspot. It wasn't as fast as the company's service, but right now speed was a luxury she would have to do without.

Shawn was out of his office immediately, coming down the hall toward her.

"Damn it." Harlow grabbed her own personal laptop and flipped it open. "I'll make sure we're clear."

Heidi didn't bother responding. There wasn't any time. "Who else has a private computer and a hotspot?"

"I do." Mona pulled her computer from her bag and started to open it.

"Have you logged it onto the company network?" Heidi pulled up the multiple chat rooms she ventured into yesterday.

"It's not logged in anywhere."

"Stop." Heidi turned Mona's way, holding her hand out. "Have you ever logged it onto the company's network?"

Mona's eyes moved from side to side. "I think maybe once or twice."

"Shut it." Heidi went back to her computer. "Don't use anything that's ever been logged into the system through the company's internet."

Mona slowly closed her laptop. "Did they get in?"

"I don't know yet." Heidi glanced up as Shawn came through the door.

"What's wrong?"

"I had to shut the internet down." Heidi moved through the chat rooms on her laptop, checking to see if anyone from the list reached out to her. She opened one of the first rooms she ever found her way into as a teenage girl who never seemed to fit anywhere. Her eyes landed on the handle she was searching for. "There you are."

Eva was up out of her seat and at Heidi's side. "Who is it?"

Heidi shook her head. "I don't know."

The handle was innocuous enough looking.

sunshineandbutterflies

It wasn't the kind she normally saw around the hacking world. Probably why it didn't need a series of numbers after it.

"That handle's on the list." Eva crouched down at her side. "Any idea who that is?

Heidi took a deep breath. "Not yet." She glanced up to Harlow. "I don't want to do this."

Harlow scrunched her face up. "I know. Me either."

But finding these people's true identities was a necessary evil. One that might keep everyone around her from ending up like Chris and Howard and Tod.

"Find her. Hunt her down so we can take these assholes down." Eva glared at the screen.

"It might not be a her." Heidi's fingers hovered over the keyboard as she worked up the balls to make that first move.

Seek out a person she promised never to find.

But this was war. And for the first time in her life she had something on the line.

"Be careful." Shawn's voice was low as he came to her side. "If this will put you in danger then don't—"

"If I don't do it everyone will be in danger." She bobbed her head from side to side. "Even more danger."

Mona hadn't been able to get anything from Zeke.

Chandler was the only known player they had left to investigate.

Something had to be done, and right now she was the only one who could do it.

Shawn stared at the side of her head as she started to type.

"Are you just going to sit there and watch me work?"

"I don't like the possibility that something could happen to you because of this." The scowl on his face was almost comical.

If anything could be even remotely funny right now.

"They can't come through the screen after me, Captain." She gave him a little smile. "They'll have to come get me if they want me."

Shawn leaned closer, his voice low enough so no one else could hear. "They can't have you."

She shivered a little as the heat in his words scrambled over her skin, trying to distract her from what she had to be doing. Heidi leaned his way. "If you're going to talk like than then I'm going to have to kick you out so I can work."

"If you're going to be mouthy then I'll have to remind you who's in charge, Kitten."

Heidi peeked at Shawn out of the corner of her eye. "Let's be honest here." She turned to face him, pressing one finger under his chin. "There's only one place I'm not in charge, and even that's debatable."

She wasn't sure what she expected his reaction to be but it definitely wasn't the slow smile that crept across Shawn's lips. "I'll be happy to debate that with you tonight, Rucker."

"It's a date." She swatted at his chest. "Now go away. I can't work when you're here. You distract me."

Shawn leaned closer to nuzzle her neck. "Maybe I like distracting you."

She swatted at him again. "There is shit happening in case you haven't noticed. Go away."

"Didn't she chase you around this place for days?" Dutch grinned at Shawn.

"You're not helping." Heidi pointed to Harlow. "Get your man in line."

Dutch's head dropped back as he laughed. "I'm leaving." He stood and walked to the door. "We're both leaving actually." He thumbed over one shoulder. "We've got a meeting to get to."

Shawn huffed out a breath before standing, leaning in her ear as he did. "Be careful, Kitten."

"I'm always careful." It was actually her number one priority from day one. Being underage wouldn't protect her from the trouble that could come of being caught in the places she explored as a kid, and the fear of being caught never diminished.

Not everyone felt the same way, which meant some people were less careful than others.

Hopefully *sunshineandbutterflies* was of the less careful variety.

Heidi popped her earbuds in, leaving the music off so she wouldn't miss anything important.

Like someone getting shot.

After a few hours it was clear *sunshineandbutterflies* was not of the less careful variety. Heidi was getting more and more frustrated with every dead end she ran nose-first into.

She stood up, grabbing her cup as she did. "I need some water." She marched out of the room and went straight to the break room where she loaded her cup with ice before switching the dispenser to water, resting her forehead against the stainless-steel fridge door as she waited.

"Still wearing your earbuds so no one will talk to you?"

Heidi looked toward where Alec stood. She was not having a great day and was not in the mood for a chat.

Especially with him.

Heidi stood up straight.

Alec had always been perfectly nice to her. He was pleasant enough, even after they each moved on with their lives.

But talking to him felt uncomfortable.

Wrong.

"I've gotta go." Heidi turned from his surprised face and hauled her ass to Shawn's office, walking straight in. She looked at where Dutch was sitting in one of the chairs. "Get out."

Dutch's brows went up.

"Now." A wiggle of guilt chewed at her belly. "Please."

Dutch turned his high-browed gaze to Shawn as he stood up. "We can finish this conversation later."

Heidi grabbed the knob, closing the door right behind Dutch before turning to face Shawn.

"I used to fuck Alec."

CHAPTER 17

"NOT FOR VERY long. Just a month or two." Heidi pursed her lips, eyes moving from one side to the other. "Maybe three now that I'm thinking about it."

"Does that mean you weren't thinking about it before now?"

Her lip curled, lifting one side of her nose along with it. "Not really."

"Why not?"

"Because it wasn't an interesting thing to think about." She shrugged. "It was sort of irrelevant."

He'd feel bad for Alec if he wasn't currently wishing him pain. "Now it's not irrelevant?"

Heidi's brows came together. "No." She said it like the fact was confusing to her.

Two days ago a revelation like this would have sent him into a downward spiral. One that started and ended with the insecurities and jealousy that ruled his life.

"Why does it matter now?" Keeping his tone even was easier than he anticipated it would be.

"Well." Heidi chewed her lip. "I think because it might matter to you."

"It shouldn't matter to me." It was a truth Shawn wished he could say he felt.

But Heidi was right. It did matter to him. It mattered to him that any other man touched the woman he was beginning to think of as his, let alone a man he had to look at on a daily basis.

"But it does." Heidi's eyes moved over his face. "That's why I'm here." She stepped away from the door. "Because it matters to me that you held Lennie's hand." Her eyes lifted to the ceiling. "Which is bizarre."

"Why is that bizarre?"

"Because I never care what a man does." Her gaze dropped to rest on his face. "But I've struggled not to wish something mildly awful on her. Like maybe a pimple between her butt cheeks." Heidi's words sped up. "Nothing terrible, just uncomfortable enough to make her suffer too."

"You're suffering?" Thinking that Heidi might suffer just a bit of the jealousy that plagued him made him happier than it should.

"You are asking a lot of questions right now, and it's making me nervous." Heidi's expression didn't hide her uncertainty. Her hesitation.

She wasn't an uncertain woman. Definitely not a hesitant one, and he was bringing those things on her.

His issues were creating hers.

It wasn't fair.

Shawn stood from his chair. "I'm asking questions because I want to know what you're thinking. What you're feeling."

"Oh." Heidi clutched her steel cup with both hands. "Then I think I'm probably a little jealous of when you held Lennie's hand."

"I am more than a little jealous of you fucking Alec." She'd given him the truth and he wasn't going to give her anything less back. "I want to find a way to wipe the memories of your body from his brain." Shawn moved closer, sending Heidi a step back. "I want to erase the feel of your skin. The smell of your hair." He kept advancing on her. "The sound you make when you come." He pushed against her, pressing her back against the door.

Heidi sucked in a breath, eyes wide on his. "He doesn't have that last one."

"That's unfortunate for him, because it's a beautiful fucking thing when you come, Kitten." Shawn braced her body with his, shoving one knee between her legs.

She whimpered a little when his hand found one nipple through her shirt. "I have to work, Shawn."

"Then stop wasting time." He pinched just enough to get her attention. "Spread your legs for me."

Heidi's feet immediately moved wide.

She was so accepting of everything he wanted to give her. He loved that unexpectedly open and willing side of her.

Needed it.

Wanted to nurture it to be sure it would grow and bloom.

He pushed his hand into her pants. "I love these pants you wear, Heidi." The fabric was soft and stretchy, making it easy to get where he wanted to go.

Her head dropped back as his fingers found her clit. "I'll wear them forever."

Forever.

The word carried weight when it hit him, driving it deep into his chest, forming an ache he didn't plan to acknowledge.

Shawn worked a finger into her, keeping his thumb against her clit, forcing his focus to the task at hand.

Heidi's cup hit the floor between them and a second later her arms wrapped around his neck, pulling his mouth to hers. The soft sweetness of her lips cut into that ache, making it burn as she clung to him.

He wrapped one arm around her waist, holding her closer, needing to feel as much of her as he could. Her sweet taste in his mouth. Her soft scent in his nose. Her heated flesh pressed into his palm.

He swallowed down her cries as she came, hoping they might ease the pain pressing into his lungs. That her satisfaction would soothe the fear joining that pain.

He gave her what she needed. He always did.

Always would.

Everything would be fine.

She wouldn't have any reason to need anything but him.

****

"SO WHAT IS the plan?"

"Shawn?"

He glanced up from the spot he'd been staring at on his desk. "What?"

Seth lifted his brows. "The plan? Where do we even start on this shit?"

Shawn grabbed his clipboard, hoping the move would rewire his flailing brain. "I think we need to start with the information Intel collected on Shadow's members. See if we can find something that might give us a direction to go in."

"Were they able to find anything interesting?" Gentry took a file as Dutch handed out the stack he brought.

"Some more than others." Dutch passed the last file to Shawn. "Obviously we came up with less on Zeke. He's an information wasteland."

Seth snorted. "Is that what Harlow called him?"

Dutch smiled. "It is."

"She's something else." Seth grinned along with Dutch, the easy discussion adding weight to the pressure taking up residence in Shawn's chest.

Would he ever be capable of something like that? Hearing another man praise the woman he was with?

But Dutch wasn't just with Harlow. He loved her.

Loved the fuck out of her. It was easy to see, but difficult to watch.

Because for Dutch love appeared to be a comfortable place to be.

Shawn forced his attention to the file in front of him. "Looks like Zeke's not the only one they didn't find much on." There were eight other names on the list and three of them were as blank as Zeke. "What's the connection between the four?"

"Heidi thinks they probably all share a similar past." Dutch crossed his bad leg over his good, elevating the injury that still caused him pain to this day.

In some ways Shawn envied him. Dutch's injury was easy to see, to explain. To understand.

It was something most people could empathize with even if they'd never been in combat.

His was not as clear and sympathetic.

A woman cheated on him.

Big fucking deal. It shouldn't have mattered the way it did.

Shouldn't still be mattering.

Seth's gaze lifted to Shawn for a second. He cleared his throat as he turned back to Dutch. "Anything else?"

"What was that look for?"

Seth shook his head. "There was no look."

"There was a look." Shawn's aggravation at his own shortcomings fueled his irritation at the lead of Alpha. "And I want to know what the fuck it means."

"It means everyone knows they've got to tread lightly around you now, dick." Gentry sat back in his seat. "Cause you get your dick in a kink whenever anyone mentions your lady."

"Because there's not a damn reason any of you should even be thinking of her."

Gentry held one hand his way. "And that's why." He didn't bat an eye as Shawn stood up. "What now? You wanna fight us because we know her goddamned name?"

"I want you to keep her name out of your mouth is what I want." The rage came easily. It always did.

"None of us wants Heidi, Shawn." Seth stood up. "But we all have to work with her. You can't expect us to ignore her. It's just not gonna happen."

Is that what he wanted? Everyone in the world to ignore her? Walk past her like she didn't exist?

Just because he was sure one wrong move would send her looking for another option?

A better man?

"Fuck me." Dutch stood up, grabbing Shawn by one arm, his hold tight and unflinching. "We don't have time for this bullshit." He dragged Shawn past Seth and out the door of the conference room. Wade and Brock were just coming out of the break room as they passed. "Come on. It's time for an intervention." Dutch didn't stop until they were inside Pierce's office. He shoved Shawn down into one of the chairs. "You've got to get your shit together."

"My shit is together." Shawn started to stand up but Dutch planted one hand right in the center of his chest, knocking him back into the seat.

"It's not." Dutch turned to Pierce. "Tell him what you know about Cassondra."

Pierce's dark brows lifted.

Dutch waved his hand, trying to speed Pierce up. "Come on. We've got shit to do."

Pierce slowly leaned back in his chair. "She's married now."

"So?" Shawn tried to brush the information off. He'd purposely avoided his ex and anything to do with her in the years since she cheated on him with a man who she found to be better in every way.

He had more money. More friends.

And apparently was significantly more satisfying in bed.

"She's married *again*, Shawn." Dutch stood beside him. "She married the man she left you for then left him for someone else."

"I don't give a shit." He tried to sound just as forceful with that declaration as he had with the first.

But the truth was he did care.

Not only did Cassondra find one man more worthy. She found two.

"I know of both men she married, Shawn." Pierce rested his arms on the chair. "I may not find my way into that world anymore, but that doesn't mean it doesn't occasionally find its way to me." He paused, eyes studying Shawn where he sat. "There are some people who know nothing of loyalty. People who are only loyal to themselves.

People who will hurt anyone to get where they wish to go." Pierce's expression sharpened. "And most of those people are part of that world."

"She didn't leave me because I was broke." He wasn't the richest, but he sure as hell had enough to take care of the family he and Cassondra talked about and planned for.

He planned for anyway.

Pierce stared at him. "Why do you think she left you?"

Shawn shrugged. "I wasn't enough."

No way was he admitting what she told him.

The ways she found him lacking.

"She left you to climb the ladder." Pierce steepled his fingers. "There are people who do that." His expression hardened. "Many of them."

Shawn glanced to where Dutch stood with Brock and Wade.

Brock gave him a nod. "It's the truth, man. She was just working her way up."

Shawn rubbed his eyes. "I don't want to talk about this anymore."

"You have to." Pierce reached for his buzzing phone, checking the screen before silencing it. "Because your issues are about to make everyone's life here very difficult." He set the phone on his desk, screen down. "Especially the woman at the center of it."

"You can't hold what one person did against Heidi and everyone else." Dutch crossed his arms, leaning back against the front edge of Pierce's desk. "She doesn't deserve it and neither do we."

"I'm done with this." Shawn stood up, pushing his way past Wade and Brock to go back into the hall. Instead of going to the conference room he went straight to his office, grabbed his gym bag and turned to the door.

"Something wrong, Captain?" Heidi stood in the doorway, propped against the frame, sipping on her straw.

"No." He tried to move around her but Heidi stepped right into his path.

"Seems like that might not be the whole truth." She lifted a brow at him as he moved to the other side of the door.

Heidi followed along.

"Please move."

She shook her head. "I don't think so. I think you're upset, and I would like to know why."

"Why? Why do you want to know?" Shawn glared down at her, the tightness in his chest squeezing so hard he couldn't breathe. "Because you think you can fix me? Fix the shit that's broken and then I'll be good enough for you?"

Heidi's other brow raised to join the first as she stared at him, poking the straw back between her lips.

Her indifference only made everything worse. The fear. The pain. The crushing doubt.

Shawn pushed past her and this time she let him go.

Didn't even try to stop him.

He went straight to the gym, changing with angry movements before going to the treadmill and setting it to a grueling pace. He stared at the digital display as he ran, punching the speed higher anytime his mind found its way to her. As his lungs burned and his legs ached he took a single glance up at the mirrored wall. He stumbled, nearly falling off the treadmill at the sight of Heidi sitting on one of the weight benches, still sipping at that damn straw, her blue eyes locked on him.

He shut down the machine, jumped off and went straight to his office, abandoning his bag and clothes in the locker room. He shut the door and locked it before dropping down into his chair and catching his head in his hands.

He knew the first time he saw her that woman was going to make him crazy and she'd done it. Driven the demons he buried from their graves to torment him.

Tease him with all the things he tried to fight.

Tried to conquer.

She just made it clear how lacking he still was.

Too lacking to be the kind of man a woman like her would ever want to keep.

CHAPTER 18

"WHAT ARE YOU doing here?"

Heidi sat in the center of Shawn's bed, her computer perched on her lap. "Working." She picked up her cup and took a sip of water. The chill of it helped soothe the fear clawing through her belly.

This might be a bad idea. She'd never put herself out there, and this might not be how it was supposed to be done.

Shawn stood in the door to his room, holding the damn door open. "Get out."

"No thanks." Heidi pretended to be focused on the screen as she watched him out of her peripheral vision.

All he had to do was step inside. Let the door close behind him.

Then they could discuss this.

That's what people did when they were more than fuck buddies, right? They talked about things when they were upset.

It's all she'd been trying to do earlier after seeing him race out of Pierce's office.

Shawn was clearly upset and she wanted to be there for him. Help him not be so upset.

But then the twat had to go and throw a temper tantrum, making all this more difficult than it had to be.

"I said get out." Shawn's voice sounded rough and ragged.

But it also sounded something else.

Broken.

And that meant she was sticking this out. Whatever it took to figure out why he was so upset, that's what she was going to do.

"And I said *no thanks*." Heidi snapped her eyes to his, glaring in a way that hopefully made it look like she meant business.

"I swear to God, Heidi." Shawn took a tiny step into the room but still held the door. "Now is not the time to—"

"To what, Shawn? To attempt to have an adult conversation about what's bothering you?" She lifted her shoulders and looked from side to side. "Because it seems like it might be the perfect time for that."

"I need you to get out." The desperation in his tone was growing.

Hopefully that meant he was almost ready to tackle this.

She smiled at him. "Then come make me."

240

His hand released the door.

Heidi held her breath as he came for her, watching the steel panel swing closer to the frame. Just as it clicked into place Shawn reached for her.

She tapped the pad of her laptop.

Shawn froze at the sound of the lock clicking into place. He swung around to stare at the locked door.

Heidi closed her computer, sliding it off her lap and onto the nightstand before standing on the mattress and launching her body at his, latching onto his back with her arms and legs. "Tell me what's wrong."

Shawn lurched forward and for a second she thought they might be going down.

Oh freaking well. She'd take injury over whatever the heck this mess was.

"Why won't you ever leave me alone?" Shawn grabbed at her arms, trying to work them loose from the hold they had around his neck.

"Because I don't want to." She wrapped her legs tighter and tried to loosen her arms just a little.

She wasn't trying to choke him out.

But maybe she should have been, because the minute she gave him a little slack Shawn pulled her arms loose, knocking her off balance. She hadn't done the squats she intended and her legs alone weren't strong enough to keep her upright, which meant she went tipping backwards, her top half falling straight toward the mattress.

Luckily her immediate fall caught Shawn by surprise and he went down with her. Heidi grunted as his weight bounced against her. She grabbed hold of him before he could scramble away, gripping the fabric of his shirt and pulling it toward her. "Stop being a pain in the ass." She locked her ankles, trying her best to hang onto him. "I know you like me so just quit."

Heidi blinked up at the ceiling. "Shit." She let Shawn go.

He stood up right away, panting a little as he glared down at her. "What is wrong with you?"

"The same damn thing that's wrong with you." She pushed up to stand on the mattress.

Shawn took a quick step back.

"I'm not jumping at you again." Heidi dropped her hands to her hips as she tried to catch her breath. "I think that's a once a day move."

Shawn backed to the wall, his own chest lifting at a faster pace than normal.

She pointed at him. "You know what? You're frustrating." She threw her hands out. "You said I was frustrating, but I'm not" She shoved the finger at him again. "You are."

"I—"

"Zip." Heidi clamped the fingers of one hand together. "Just shut it. I'm not done with you."

Shawn's mouth dropped open a little but he didn't say a word.

It was close enough.

"You—" She wiggled the finger pointed at him then added in the whole arm just to be sure he understood what she was talking about. "You have all this baggage, which is fine." Heidi jumped off the bed, getting as right up in his face as she could. "I don't mind the baggage, but you're sure as hell going to let me help you unpack that shit."

"It's not going anywhere, Heidi. I tried—"

"I said shut it." She glanced down at his junk. Smacking his probably wouldn't have the same result so she settled for pinching his nipple. "I didn't say it had to go anywhere, I just said you had to unpack it."

Shawn's palm came to rub across the nipple she pinched.

"Everyone has baggage." She pressed both palms to the side of her face. "And I was honest with you about mine. I put it out there because I know you have this shit," she wiggled her hands around his head, "going on in your brain, and I thought that's what I should do. Tell you upfront about something that would mess with your head."

Shawn was quiet, his lips pressed tight together as he watched her continue ranting.

"And I thought we worked through it. I thought we figured shit out." She poked him right between the eyes. "But then you went and had a whole freak-out and acted like you thought I would just be like 'okay, never mind then' and walk away." She'd been stewing on this for hours. Thinking of all she would say when he finally came to his room, and now it was pouring out.

She'd never had an emotional relationship with a man.

Never wanted one.

And now that she had it, there was no way she was letting him pretend it wasn't there.

"But I'm not walking away from you, Shawn." She grabbed the front of his shirt, yanking as hard as she could, managing to get him to lean just a little her way. "I like you. I like that you are sneaky sweet and stupid clean. I even like the weird food you eat as long as I can put cheese on it." She put her weight behind the hand holding his shirt, getting his eyes almost in line with hers. "And I like that you are sensitive enough that one bad relationship almost broke you."

His eyes barely widened on hers.

She smirked. "You might fool everyone else into thinking you're this tough guy with big muscles and a grumpy attitude, but I know the truth." She touched the tip of her nose to his. "You're the kitten, Shawn. Not me."

He held her gaze for a heartbeat longer.

And then he tackled her to the bed.

Heidi grabbed at his clothes. They were the same shirt and shorts he'd been wearing on the treadmill. His skin was still a little sticky from the workout and she didn't give a flying shit.

She wanted him however she could get him. Happy. Pissy. Fresh out of the shower or right from a workout.

It didn't matter to her.

"You make me fucking nuts, Heidi." Shawn's hands were as fevered as hers, grabbing at her shirt and yanking it over her head. "I feel like I'm losing my mind."

"Stop being dramatic." Heidi shoved down the shorts she'd watched bounce around as he ran, knowing damn well what was under them. "You're just having a bad day."

Shawn shoved up the cup of her bra, dropping the swell of her breast free for his mouth to latch onto. He growled against her skin as his hand worked the clasp open, snapping it free before shoving up the other side for his fingers to find the nipple and work it.

Heidi reached between them to fist his dick. "I missed you while you were being mad at me."

"I wasn't fucking mad at you." Shawn wrapped his hand in her hair, pulling her head back tight until her eyes met his. His lips skimmed over hers. "I missed you too."

She smiled against his kiss. "I know." Heidi reached lower to cradle his balls, lightly trailing the tips of her fingers over the skin. "Next time maybe you should talk to me instead of throwing a fit like a giant man baby."

Shawn's hold on her tightened. "Man baby?"

"That's what I said." She grabbed his beard with both hands, holding his face close to hers. "You acted like a man baby."

That growl she couldn't get enough of vibrated from his body to hers. She'd aggravate him every day just to hear it.

"I'll show you fucking man baby." Shawn pulled her pants down as he pushed her legs up, the fabric bunching up around her knees as he reached for a condom, ripping it open and rolling it down his length as he used the binding of her pants to pull her legs into the air between them, holding them in place as he pressed into her in one long, swift push of his hips. He ducked his head under where her pants hooked her ankles together, gripping her thighs as he fucked her relentlessly.

There was no teasing. No working up to the main event. Just pure need feeding into a frenzy she was just as caught up in.

No man ever took her the way he did.

No man ever took her full stop. They might have had her, but never once had one taken her because she was what they wanted.

Needed.

Not like this man did.

And she might need him too. In a way that she didn't fully understand.

But she would.

Heidi reached up, grabbing the short hairs of his beard with both hands. "Come here."

Shawn fell toward her, his shoulders pulling her legs with him until she could literally bend no farther.

"Next time I probably need to do some stretching beforehand."

Shawn laughed low and quiet. "Damn it, Heidi." He worked his shoulders through her still connected legs, the ankles tangled in her pants falling against his back as his front blanketed hers. His smile held as his eyes met hers. "Don't make me laugh right now."

"Why not?" She wiggled her hips a little, trying to remind him what they were supposed to be doing. "Sex is supposed to be fun, I think."

"You think?" Shawn picked up on her thinly-veiled clue, thrusting into her, the tip of his dick rubbing against a spot that made her eyeballs roll back into her head.

"Not when you do that I can't." Her pussy clenched when he repeated the move.

Shawn pulled her close, nuzzling her neck as he continued fucking her at whatever angle it was that might wreck her whole existence. "So you can distract me but I can't distract you?"

"Didn't say that." Getting all three words out was almost impossible as his pelvis started to grind against her clit with each thrust of his hips.

"That's what it sounded like you were saying." His mouth trailed along her jaw. "I think I like distracting you. Makes you significantly less dangerous."

Heidi grabbed onto his shoulders, holding on for dear life as everything started to fall apart around her.

Shawn was the only constant.

All that grounded her. Kept her from spinning away with the rest of the world.

So she held him tight, clinging to the only thing there was, closing her eyes as she came in a completely foreign way, calling for him by name.

Hoping he could save her from whatever this was.

Because while it was amazingly perfect and overwhelmingly pleasurable, it was also terrifying.

She didn't realize he came until his body became heavier on hers, his head sagging into the crook of her shoulder.

Heidi stared at the ceiling with wide eyes.

Something just happened.

Something big.

Something new.

Something that drained everything she had.

"I'm hungry."

Shawn laughed. The sound was lighter than anything she'd heard come through his lips before. "I can fix that." He eased away, the loss of his closeness making her almost uncomfortable.

Lonely.

She was never lonely.

"Where are you going?" Heidi sat up as Shawn walked toward the bathroom.

He glanced over one shoulder. "Right now I'm getting rid of this thing." He pulled the spent condom off his still half-erect dick before disappearing into the bathroom. "Then I'm going to go get you something to eat."

Her breath caught as he reappeared in the doorway.

The man was fucking magnificent. Long limbs. Lean, wide frame.

And maybe the amount of chest hair was better than she remembered. Just enough.

Shawn continued coming toward her, the weight of his cock catching her eyes where it fell against his thigh. He crawled onto the bed. "And after you eat I'm going to fuck you again." His lips found a nipple, teeth gently raking over the tip before releasing it. "And then maybe one more time just to be sure."

Heidi fell back against the bed as he settled over her. "To be sure what?"

His expression changed for the blink of an eye. The confident, commanding man she knew giving way to the uncertainty she'd caught glimpses of. "Just to be sure."

Heidi swallowed. Today sucked. She didn't like Shawn being upset.

But she also didn't want to pretend everything was already fine. "You know when people cheat it's a them issue, not a you issue, right?"

This was clearly a sore spot for him. Possibly an infected, seeping wound of a sore spot.

And she knew what happened to infections that weren't addressed.

They spread. Like a virus they would touch everything around them to varying degrees.

She didn't want to suffer for what some other chick did.

And Shawn shouldn't have to either.

"I don't want to talk about this." His tone wasn't hard or sharpened with the edge it usually carried when he was upset.

"I know." Heidi reached up to stroke the perfect amount of dark hair scattered across his chest. "But it has to be done."

"It doesn't." Shawn pressed his face into her hair, breathing deep.

"It won't go away all by itself, Shawn."

He was quiet, his body still.

So she kept going. "If it could have, it would have already." Heidi wrapped her arms around his wide body, trailing her fingers down his back. She

249

wanted to comfort him. Soothe the pain he seemed to sometimes wallow in. "I don't deserve for what happened with her to poison your relationship with me."

"Is that what this is, Kitten? A relationship?"

"I'm not Kitten. You're Kitten." She shoved at him, pushing Shawn's body up until his eyes met hers. "And you know that's what this is so don't pretend you don't."

"Maybe I wanted to hear what you thought."

"Then ask me." Heidi tipped her head as she studied Shawn's face. "I'll tell you the truth."

Shawn's hands rested on each side of her face. One thumb slowly stroked over her skin. "I don't know how to do this, Heidi."

"Neither do I. I've never tried to do it before." She assumed never having been in a relationship would put her at a disadvantage, but based on what she was seeing right now, having been in a bad relationship could do more harm than good. "All we can do is try, right?"

"It's not that simple."

"I didn't say it was simple, Kitten." Heidi smiled. "I said we can just try."

"You can't call me Kitten in front of other people."

"I can do whatever I want." Heidi lifted one brow. "I'm grown."

Shawn's gaze turned dark. "There's consequences for everything, Heidi."

"I should hope so." If he thought the threat of a spanking would deter her, then Shawn was about to find out it was anything but. "And I thought you were going to get snacks."

His lips twitched before easing into a smile. "You might want to brace yourself while I'm gone." He pushed his big body off hers, grabbing a pair of shorts from a drawer before pulling them on. "Because I feel a second wind coming on."

CHAPTER 19

"HOW'S IT GOING?" Dutch stood in the kitchen of the rooming house, assembling a peanut butter and jelly sandwich at the counter.

"Fine." Shawn glanced toward the hall leading to his room. The thought of the kitchen being occupied hadn't even occurred to him. "How about you?"

"Just trying to get Harlow to eat something before she passes out." Dutch picked up a jar of strawberry jam in one hand and a jar of grape jelly in the other, holding them Shawn's way. "Which one?"

"Strawberry. Definitely."

Dutch put the grape back in the fridge and twisted the lid off the strawberry. "Girls got the internet back up."

He figured as much when Heidi was able to lock him in his room. "That's not surprising." Shawn opened the fridge, scanning the shelves, trying to decide what in the hell Heidi would want to eat.

"I've been thinking."

Shawn's hand clenched where it held the door. He'd had enough of his friends thinking to last him a lifetime. He was done talking about Cassondra. He was done thinking about what happened.

Trying to figure out why.

Maybe she was trying to climb the ladder like his friends thought. Maybe she wasn't.

At the end of the day it didn't really matter.

"Didn't Shadow clear one of the warehouses?"

The unexpected direction of Dutch's thoughts was welcome as hell. For more reasons than one.

Shawn turned to look Dutch's way. "They did."

"So, what if it's not as clear as they claimed it was?" Dutch stacked a second piece of bread on the first and cut it from corner to corner. "There's no cameras anywhere near that one, so there's no way for me to check from here."

Shawn let the fridge door swing closed. They'd been systematically checking locations since discovering whoever they were dealing with had taken up rotating residence in a few. "Did you check to see who's listed as the property owner?"

"Harlow did." Dutch went digging around the fridge Shawn just abandoned, pulling out a carton of chocolate almond milk and pouring it into a glass. "It's an LLC. She and Heidi couldn't connect it to our guys in any way, but it just had me thinking."

"I don't blame you." It had Shawn thinking too. "I think it's worth checking out. See if it really is clear."

Dutch turned to face him as he screwed the cap back on the milk. "What if it's not?"

"I don't know what would be worse." If it was vacant then it would be one more dead end to add to the pile they were drowning in.

But if it wasn't...

"We'll just have to deal with it as it comes." Shawn crossed his arms, trying to look the way he always did.

Calm. In control. Focused. It's what the men around him deserved to see.

Not the man they witnessed this afternoon.

Dutch gave him a nod. "Good enough." He grabbed the sandwich plate with one hand and the milk in the other. "See you in the morning."

Shawn waited until Dutch was well down the hall before going back to the fridge. He pulled out any cheese he could find and stacked slices across a plate before adding in some crackers. He stared down at the lackluster snack.

She couldn't just freaking eat cheese and carbs. There was no fucking value to it.

He went back to the refrigerator and dug around the vegetable drawer, coming up with a cucumber and a pepper. After adding some chunks of vegetables he went into the fridge one last time, coming out with a pack of sliced turkey.

He held the stack of slices in one hand, intending to slap them onto the plate.

Which was already too full for that.

He rolled them up and shoved them at one side, managing to fit them in. There was one more little vacant spot so he dropped on some nuts from a container in the pantry.

It looked a hell of a lot better than fucking cheese and crackers and it would do more than just fill her up.

Heidi was propped up against the pillows when he went back to the room. She wore one of his shirts and her computer was back on her lap.

"You gonna lock me in again?" Shawn walked toward the table beside her.

"Depends on what you have on that plate?" She grinned, her deep dimples on full display. "I might have to send you back out."

"If there's not something for you to eat on this then I'm not sure what in the hell you want from me." He set the plate down on the nightstand.

Heidi's eyes went wide. "Holy crap." She leaned closer. "I did not expect you to be a charcuterie master."

"What in the hell is a charcuterie?"

Heidi snorted out a little laugh. "I'll show you sometime." She stacked a cracker with a slice of cheese and a roll of turkey. "So about this warehouse that Shadow supposedly cleared."

Shawn eased down onto the bed beside her. "What about it?"

Heidi's brows came together as she typed with one hand and held her cracker stack in the other.

"The company name it's under sounds weird." Her chewing slowed down as she stared at the screen. "I just can't figure out why."

"What's the name?" Shawn eased in a little closer, the comfortable weight of companionship settling around him.

"Subhex Solar." She wrinkled her nose. "Are there really any solar companies up here?"

"Solar is actually big up here." He wrapped one arm across her belly. "There are days where the sun never sets." Shawn studied her profile. "You'll get to see it happen soon."

"I don't know that I would call months from now *soon*." She lifted her brows. "And the way things are going it will feel like freaking years."

"I'm sorry you were dragged into this. We shouldn't have brought you here." It wasn't as much of a lie as he expected it to be. Knowing Heidi might be in extreme danger was almost worse than the thought of not having her here with him.

Heidi's head tipped his direction. "If you hadn't come to get me I might have been on Tod's dead stomach."

He hadn't considered that.

Heidi's blue eyes widened. "You just got really pale." Her face split into a wide smile. She reached out to poke at his chest. "You like me."

Her sing-songy words and poking made him want to smile even though his guts were twisting into knots. "Stop." He tried to catch her hand as she moved it around, stabbing her finger at him.

He finally caught it and used the hold to tug her close enough he could press a kiss to her lips.

It was the easy playfulness he'd seen between Brock and Eva. Even between Dutch and Harlow.

He'd never had it. Never thought he was capable of it.

But somehow Heidi found it in him and dragged it free, kicking and screaming.

She stayed close, her eyes moving over his. "You're pretty."

"Thank you." He'd let her call him pretty or Kitten or Captain or whatever made her happy. As long as she was right here on his bed at night, eating char-whatever in the hell it was and wearing his shirt.

And making this seem easier than he remembered.

"So." Heidi turned back to her computer. "Subhex Solar might be a real company then."

"Might be." Shawn watched as she worked her way through the plate, including the veggies and nuts.

After a few minutes her computer pinged.

Heidi's brows went up. "Oh, hell no." She turned to him, her eyes wide. "You have a hurt shoulder."

"What?" Shawn leaned to get a better look at her screen.

Damn Dutch.

"You can't go." Heidi shook her head. "No freaking way."

"We have to go check it out and Alpha and Beta aren't even close to being ready to do it." He

258

scanned the email from Harlow letting Heidi know of their plans to investigate the warehouse Shadow cleared. "And it's probably just a solar company, remember?"

Heidi glared at him. "You can't be serious."

"I'm their team lead. I have to be with them."

"Then stay in the van or something."

Or something. It was a tiny loophole she'd given him without realizing it. "I can do that."

Heidi's blue eyes lifted to one side, her head tipping as she considered it. "Fine." Her gaze came right back to him. "Can I have an earpiece like Dutch gave Harlow?"

"No." Shawn smiled as she scoffed. "There is no way I could concentrate knowing I could be talking to you instead."

Her expression went soft. "You like talking to me?" The question was hushed and a little hesitant, stirring up the guilt in his gut.

He'd made her hesitant. Uncertain.

"I love talking to you." Shawn reached up to cradle her face in his hand. "I'm sorry for being such an ass to you, Kitten."

She lifted one shoulder. "It's okay."

It was an attempt to brush off something that did more damage than he ever could have expected.

She seemed invincible to him. So much stronger than he ever was.

But that was a mistake. One he was happy to pay for in whatever way she required.

****

"TIME TO GET up, Kitten."

"Ugh." Heidi rolled to her belly. "I'm not going to keep sleeping here if you're just going to wake me up all the time." She snapped her head up. "No one's dead again, are they?"

"No one's dead." Shawn held out one of the iced coffees Dutch brought in the day after Harlow's incident.

She reached for it, grabbing the cold cup. "There aren't donuts to go with this, are there?"

"No donuts this morning." Shawn was crouched beside the bed. "I know how to scramble eggs, though."

She wrapped her lips around the straw, sucking down some of the sweet, frosty goodness. "With cheese?"

He smiled. It wasn't wide and open. Shawn's smiles never were. But it was real, and she would take that any day.

"With cheese." He stood and started toward the door.

"And toast?"

Shawn glanced over his shoulder. "And toast."

"And bacon?"

He laughed. "And bacon."

Heidi wiggled up to a sit. "Fine. I'll get up then."

"Get ready. I'll be back."

She sat on the bed a minute longer, drinking her coffee. Who'd have thought Captain Uptight was so attentive? He was a sneaky sweet pile of mush.

And she was the only one who knew.

Heidi tossed back the covers and climbed out of bed, bringing her cup into the bathroom and setting it on the counter before pulling off Shawn's shirt and turning to twist on the shower.

She caught sight of herself in the mirror. "Holy shit." Heidi twisted, trying to get a better view of the blotchy red mark right in the center of her butt cheek.

That twerp gave her a butt hickey.

She grabbed her hair and twisted it up and out of the way since hair washing was not on the morning schedule.

"Son of a bitch." There was another mark on her shoulder and one at the base of her neck. None of them could be seen while she was clothed, but they were unmissable when she was naked and paying attention.

"Giant man baby." Heidi climbed into the shower, using Shawn's soap to scrub down before toweling off and going out to get dressed. She was in her panties and bra when the door opened and Shawn came in, a plate balanced on each upturned palm.

Heidi glared at him as she twisted, yanking down one side of her underpants to expose her marked butt cheek. "What is this?" She snapped the garment back into place before pointing to her neck and shoulder area. "And these?" She turned to face him. "One wasn't enough?"

He looked like a deer in the headlights. A little surprised. A little scared.

A little worried this might be the moment he died.

She took a deep breath.

It made sense. He was clearly affected by what his ex did, but come on.

Heidi dropped her hands to her hips. "From now on if you give me one, I give you one."

"Deal." He didn't hesitate. "Here." Shawn passed her a plate. "Eat. We've got to get moving."

Well shit.

Now she had to hickey him.

Heidi eyed his body and almost started laughing.

Now she got to suck on some random part of his body.

Maybe this was a win.

She glanced down at the plate in her hands. "What the fuck is that?"

"What?" Shawn had a piece of the offending food item already stuffed in his mouth.

"This." Heidi pointed to the very flat, not at all pig-filled, liar of a bacon strip on her plate. "Did you bring me turkey bacon?"

"It's better than regular bacon." Shawn had a second piece in his mouth, crunching through the Elvis impersonator of pork products. "Try it."

She stared at him as she picked it up and crunched off a bite. It was like smoky, salty, cardboard.

Not the worst thing she'd ever had in her mouth.

"See?" Shawn grinned, obviously feeling like he'd introduced her to something amazing.

"Mmmmm." She swallowed down the bits of crumbled fako baco. "Yup."

He looked so damn proud she couldn't make herself pee on his parade. It was cute how he wanted to share what he liked with her—

Oh hell.

This was what she'd always been avoiding.

Making concessions for someone else. Doing what they wanted instead of what she wanted. Pretending to be interested in what they were interested in.

Eating turkey masquerading as bacon instead of the gloriously amazing real thing.

But real bacon didn't matter as much as the expression on Shawn's face did.

If he fits, just stick him in there.

Mona was a smart chick, but she was a little wrong on that one.

Shawn didn't fit perfectly into her life, but making room for all of him didn't feel like a sacrifice.

"Come on, Rucker. Put a wiggle in that ass." Shawn was making the bed, pulling the blankets and sheets perfectly tight as he smoothed out any sign it was ever slept in.

Among other things.

She alternated taking bites of eggs, toast, fruit, and weird turkey cardboard as she pulled on a pair of blush pink joggers and a long-sleeved white t-shirt. By the time she was dressed and fed, Shawn was stacking her plate on his.

"Ready to go?"

"I guess." She eyed his white shirt and pants.

"It will be fine, Kitten." He moved in close. "The faster we find out what's going on, the faster we can live a normal life."

"I don't think we are normal life kind of people." She looked up at him. "You kill people. I break into government systems. Those aren't normal people activities."

His lips lifted at one side. "Normal for us, then."

"What does that look like?" She kept her eyes on his.

Shawn walked around the bed, coming to stand close enough she had to tip her head back to look at him. He rested one finger under her chin. His expression was still relaxed and the line of his mouth was still in an almost smile. "I guess we'll have to figure that out as we go."

CHAPTER 20

SHAWN DUCKED DOWN, tucking deeper into the branches of the scrappy trees surrounding one of the warehouses scattered around Fairbanks that Alaskan Security identified as possibly being connected to what was happening.

The same warehouse Shadow claimed was vacant.

Unused by the men they were hunting.

But this warehouse looked to be anything but deserted. A line of sleek SUVs sat in front of the building. Footprints dotted the snow around the lot and the walks were cleared and salted.

"You think Pierce knows this place is active?" Brock voiced Shawn's own thoughts through the earpiece.

"I hope to hell he doesn't." Shawn eased down to the ground, peering through his binoculars at the huge warehouse. "How we lookin' Dutch?"

"Clear as far as I can tell." Dutch's voice was muffled for a second before it came back through the line. "Heidi says if you're not careful she'll kick your ass."

"Tell Heidi if I'm not careful I'll let her kick my ass." The ache in his shoulder was a constant reminder of what could happen if he made a misstep. "I'm not planning to get shot again."

Shawn squinted through the brush, counting the number of vehicles sitting near the door to the massive building. "Looks like we've got five parked."

"Can you get the plates?" Dutch's voice was calm and cool. Relaxed even.

"Working on it." Reed was the closest to the lot, working his way in inch by inch as Wade and Brock watched his back.

Shawn was stationed near the back edge of the treeline, keeping an eye on the road leading to the supposedly empty building. He hated being so far from everyone else, but right now his shoulder made him a liability. One they wouldn't be smart enough to leave behind.

Plus he promised Heidi he wouldn't be in the middle of any shit that might go down.

"We've got someone coming in." Dutch's tone was tighter now. A little more like the way he'd been the past year as the weight of too much to do pushed down on his shoulders. "Just caught a glimpse of a black vehicle about two minutes out."

266

"We're not leaving without something." Reed had to be almost to the front of the trees by this time. Too close.

"Pull back." Shawn barked out the order, knowing it was going to be ignored.

"Not happening." Reed's voice was low and even. "I'm taking the shots now."

The line went quiet. They needed this information. Something to go off of now that they'd lost almost all the connections they knew. Chandler was the last direct link they could chase.

They needed more.

Not that he expected them to be around long. It seemed like joining whoever this was ended up being the last thing most people involved did.

"You should see the new arrival in thirty seconds." Dutch's voice was hushed but his fingers were loud as they moved over the keys of his keyboard.

Shawn eased his frame around, angling himself so he could see both the road and the patches of warehouse peeking through the trees. It was quiet as hell, nothing but the frigid breeze breaking up the silence.

The sound of tires on messy asphalt carried across the ground. "He's coming."

Shawn went silent and still, knowing one wrong move could be the end of all of them.

As the car came closer he held his breath.

Except it wasn't a car. It was an SUV.

A familiar one.

"We've got an Alaskan Security vehicle pulling in." Shawn watched as the Rover turned down the lane leading back to the warehouse. "Coming your way now."

"Are you shitting me?" Brock's broken words said he was moving and moving fast. "Pull back."

"I'm getting what we need." Reed wasn't giving in.

It's the same thing any of them would do.

"If it's who I think it is you better be fucking invisible." Shawn strained to hear anything as the line went silent again. Not knowing what was going on might kill him.

Shawn held his position, fighting the urge to move in with the rest of his men. But if they needed to leave in a hurry he had to be here, ready to move the team out and away from whatever shit show might be starting.

The seconds dragged on as he waited, listening for any sign of the rest of the team.

Reed's voice in his ear almost made him jump. "Time to move."

Brock was the first through the trees, breaking the line a few seconds before Wade and Tyson. Jamison and Reed were the last out of the woods, both moving fast as they rushed to the pickup spot. Rico pulled in, the door swinging open as he came to a quick stop. In under ten seconds they were all in and the van was moving, hooking a fast u-turn before going in the opposite direction the SUV from Alaskan Security came in.

Reed pulled off the mask covering his face with one hand. His eyes immediately came to Shawn's. "It was Zeke."

It was one of the worst-case scenarios. For more reasons than one. "Did he know you were there?"

"I don't think so." Reed pulled out the digital camera they used to take photos. "I'm sending these your way now, Dutch. Have Intel get started on them."

"Did you get all the plates?" Shawn leaned in close to peek at the small screen.

"I did one better." Reed grinned as he linked the camera up to the hotspot on the van's wireless and sent the photos over. "I got faces."

"You're kidding me." A little of the weight in his chest eased.

They could figure this out. All Heidi and the rest of Intel had to do was identify the men in the photos and—

"Shit." Dutch swore under his breath.

"What?" Shawn looked to Reed.

Dutch sighed into the line. "Just get your asses back here."

"We're taking the long way. Make sure no one follows us."

"It doesn't matter." Dutch let out a frustrated sounding groan. "They already know you were there."

"How in the hell can they know we were there?" They were the best at what they fucking did. No one knew Rogue was there unless they wanted them to.

"It's GHOST in that warehouse, Shawn, and I can promise you they one hundred percent knew you were out there."

Shawn looked to Brock and Wade. "Is he right?"

He was the only one who didn't get eyes on the place. Didn't get to see firsthand what they were investigating.

Brock gave him a nod. "That's what it looked like."

Shawn stared at the camera in Reed's hands. "So you got pictures of members of GHOST?"

Why in the hell would GHOST just let them take photos? If that was GHOST back there, then Dutch was right. The only way they got as close as they did was because GHOST allowed them to get that close.

"Why are they helping us?" He asked the question out loud, but not because he expected an answer.

Not that they had one.

"Maybe they don't want to get their hands dirty with this one." Wade leaned in as Rico drove into Fairbanks, headed straight back to headquarters.

"Then wouldn't the government just pass it on to Shadow? That's what they've done before." Shawn raked one hand through his hair. This would be frustrating enough if it was just him and the men around him involved.

But now Heidi was a part of it. She was ass deep in this whole thing and there was no way to extract her from it.

He thought finding the answers would shift the focus from her and the rest of Intel, but there was no way around it.

No way of getting her out of the middle.

And that was unacceptable.

"All I know is Zeke's up to something, and I don't fucking like it." Brock's expression was hard, lines of frustration and anger etched into the angles.

The rest of the ride passed in silence. They unloaded and went straight to Intel's office, filing through the door. Everyone was circled around Dutch and Harlow's desks, eyes on the monitors lined across the front wall.

Everyone except Heidi. She sat at her desk, earbuds visible through the blonde drape of her hair. He went toward her, expecting to make it to her side before she noticed him.

"I found one of them already." Heidi didn't glance his way as she pulled one speaker from her ear. "The picture was really good and the facial recognition software immediately had a hit."

"Who is it?"

"That's where things get tricky." Heidi pushed her laptop onto her desk, moving it so Shawn could see.

He looked from the screen to the monitors on the wall. The same monitors everyone was silently staring at. "Are they just watching you work?"

"What?" Heidi glanced up at where Dutch, Harlow, Bess, and the rest of the room stood. "Oh. Looks like." She turned her attention back to her screen. "So I only know it hit because it stopped working almost immediately." She flopped back in her chair, rocking a little. "It said no match, but it takes longer than that to run through the whole process."

"Which means?"

"Which means the government is protecting whoever that is." Heidi met his gaze. "Which means we definitely found GHOST."

It was the best worst news he could have hoped for.

They now had information on one of the most secretive of government agencies.

And one of their own was working with them.

"Why was Zeke there?"

"That is the million dollar question, Kitten." Heidi grabbed her water and sucked down a few gulps. "Especially considering he clearly does not want anyone to know about it."

"Maybe they're trying to play us against whoever we're dealing with." Wade stood in the doorway with Brock at his side. "Maybe they're trying to get both of us out of their hair."

"Why would they do that?" Shawn shook his head. "Shadow cleans up too many messes the government doesn't want to touch. No way would they give that up."

"That only leaves one option then." Heidi let out a sigh as she smiled up at him. "They're helping us."

****

"HE CAN'T PLAY both fucking sides." Pierce's tone was unusually emotional. "He is either with us, or with them. That's it."

"That's not it." Heidi leaned back in her chair, kicking both feet up on the one across from her.

"Maybe Zeke isn't as bad of a guy as everyone thinks."

"He kills people even the government won't kill, Heidi. He's a mercenary. Period." Shawn forced himself to relax through the bite of jealousy trying to clench his teeth.

Heidi rolled her eyes. "I didn't say he was a saint. I said maybe he's not as bad as ya'll think he is." She shrugged her shoulders. "I mean, he taught Mona to shoot. He trained Alpha, and his team has stepped in to help Rogue carry the covert ops. I'm sure their workload hasn't reduced the same as everyone else's has."

Shawn turned to pierce. "Is she right? Is Shadow still working?"

Pierce worked his jaw from side to side. "As we have discussed before, I allowed Shadow certain liberties I should not have entertained."

"So what you're saying is you have no idea what in the hell Shadow has going on." Shawn bobbed his head in a nod. "That's just fuckin' great, Pierce."

"Shadow is a priceless asset that I could not afford to lose."

"But the question now is," Mona met Pierce's gaze, her ice blue eyes a perfect counter to the midnight of his, "can you afford to keep them?"

She sat straight as an arrow in her seat, a completely different woman than the one Shawn met such a short while ago. The one who could have ended up on the wrong side of this war just as easily as she ended up here.

Pierce's focus was only on her, sharp and unwavering. "Shadow is essential to our existence, Ms. Ayers. Without them there will be no Alaskan Security."

"You mean without them Alaskan Security will only be able to handle legitimate jobs." Mona wasn't backing down.

Wasn't caving to Pierce.

"Are you saying what we offered Ms. Hines wasn't legitimate?" Pierce's expression was unyielding, but his tone was even and calm. "What about Ms. Tatum? Do you feel our protection of her wasn't legitimate?"

"Neither of those cases involved Shadow or their," Mona barely paused, "connections."

"They did." Pierce folded his hands on his lap. "What do you think happened to the men who attempted to abduct the three of you? Do you think dead men simply disappear, Ms. Ayers?"

Mona didn't move for a few seconds. Finally her eyes dipped to her lap.

"Shadow gives Alaskan Security the ability to do what society doesn't." Pierce's voice took on the edge most people never witnessed. "With Shadow we are able to rid the world of people who don't deserve to exist."

Heidi's head shot up. "Holy shit." She jumped up from her chair and bolted from the room.

Pierce looked to Shawn. "What's going on?"

"I'd say she just figured something important out." Eva slowly stood from her seat. "She sort of gets tunnel vision."

Shawn pushed out of his chair and chased after Heidi, finding her at her desk, already on her computer. "What's going on?"

"It was GHOST." Heidi scanned the screen, eyes moving as fast as her fingers flew over the keyboard.

"I know. We established GHOST is at the warehouse."

"No." Heidi didn't even glance toward him as he kneeled beside her. "GHOST is who dropped Tod on our doorstep." She pulled up the photo of Tod's dead chest and pointed to the perfectly written names across his chest. "That handwriting is neat as hell. Perfectly legible."

"So?"

"I thought it was a threat at first, maybe a trick to get me to log into a chat room on the company server, but if it was that then they would have just scribbled it out. Who cares if I could read them all, right?"

"Maybe." Heidi was reaching. Stretching this farther than she probably should.

"Not maybe." She wasn't deterred at all by his skepticism. "I'm telling you. This is why those letters were all so clear. They wanted to be sure we could read them all."

"What for? So you would know who to avoid? Who not to talk to?"

"Partly." Heidi glanced at the door before leaning in close and lowering her voice. "Or maybe it was a note they didn't want to risk passing digitally."

Shawn still wasn't following with her theory. Not entirely anyway. "They sent you the message on a dead body to avoid someone finding it online?"

"They definitely wanted to avoid the list being found," Heidi's head shook slow as her lips curved into a smile, "but that message wasn't just for me."

CHAPTER 21

HEIDI WAS ALMOST giddy.

This was why she did what she did. The rush of adrenaline when things finally started to line up.

She got it from hacking. Sometimes from her job at Investigative Resources.

But this was almost euphoric.

"I don't know, Kitten." Shawn still didn't look convinced.

Didn't matter.

"I'm not Kitten." She grabbed his shirt with both hands, pulling his lips to hers. "Today you're Kitten and I'm Captain."

"I'm glad you're happy about this theory you have—"

"It's not a theory." She was still smiling. "It's what's happening. I promise you Shadow is out finding those people and," she used one finger to slice across her neck, "dead-ing them."

"You're saying you think Shadow is working with GHOST to eliminate the people named on that list?" He lifted his shoulders and dropped them back down. "Why wouldn't they just throw the list through the gate?" His brows lifted. "Or better yet, just tell Zeke. Obviously he's in contact with them."

"Zeke doesn't know who any of the people are, and there's no way he could figure it out." This was the part that added everything together. Tied up all the loose ends trying to fly free. "Harlow and I can."

Shawn's eyes paused, hanging on hers. "They killed Tod to get Harlow to help them?"

"No." Heidi snorted. "They killed Tod for the same reason they killed Howard." She picked up a chocolate-covered raisin and popped it into her mouth. "Because he sucked."

It was how she figured it out, what connected all the dots in a way that finally made sense. Pierce saying Alaskan Security wanted to rid the world of people who didn't deserve to exist.

It made her think maybe Alaskan Security and GHOST had similar goals. Certainly not identical, but right now maybe they had a common enemy.

One they had to fight together.

Heidi chewed her lower lip as she looked at Shawn. What she was about to suggest was going to go over like a fart in an elevator, but it had to be done. "I think we should go talk to Zeke."

"No." Shawn's response was sharp and immediate. "No fucking way are you going near him."

"I didn't say *I* should go talk to Zeke." She pointed to his chest and then back at her own. "I think *we* should go talk to him."

It was a risk, letting Shawn near Zeke, but going alone was a bigger risk. Not because she was scared of Shadow's lead.

She was scared of how a private meeting with him would affect Shawn, and his feelings mattered to her.

Weird.

Shawn's jaw set tight.

"I think if I just tell him the truth, then it will make all of this so much easier. We can all work together to find these guys and kill them and then hide the bodies." Talk about things she never expected to hear herself say.

Shawn scrubbed one hand down his face, digging the tips of his fingers into his eyes. "I didn't want you any deeper in this shit, Heidi."

"There's only one way out of it, and that's through." Heidi rested her hands on his shoulders. "We're so fucking close to figuring out who these guys are. If we can get GHOST and Shadow to just freaking work with us we can finish it." She let out a little breath. "Be done. Move on."

Whatever their version of moving on was.

Shawn raked the hand on his face through his hair, messing up the dark waves, leaving one bit sticking up.

Heidi reached out to work it down with her fingers. "I just don't want this hanging over my head anymore."

It was already wearing on her, and she'd only been wrapped up in it for a hot minute. She couldn't imagine how Harlow felt.

How Shawn felt.

"Don't *you* want to be done with it?" She smoothed down the neckline of his shirt, evening out the knit band.

"I want you to be safe." He leaned into her. "And instead you want to take one step closer." Shawn rested his forehead against hers, closing his eyes. "I don't want to have to kick Zeke's ass, Heidi. My shoulder is still sore."

She smiled. "I literally never wanted him, you do realize that, right?" She wrapped both arms around Shawn's neck. "I fully planned to continue driving you crazy until you gave in just so I would leave you alone."

"You don't think that's what I did?" His lids lifted.

Heidi's mouth dropped open. "Did you just tease me?" She pressed her lips to his. "That was fantastic." She jumped up from her chair, grabbing Shawn's hand as she went. "Come on. Let's get this over with so we can go have fun." She dragged him down the hall to Zeke's office. The room was dark.

And locked.

"He's probably in the training area. I think tomorrow Alpha has another session scheduled." Shawn took the lead, holding her hand tight with his as they walked quickly to the next building over. The training room lights were on and the setup had been altered since her last visit. There were more webbed nettings draped around the space, making it impossible to tell if Zeke was even in the room.

"Zeke." Shawn's voice carried through the quiet. His brows lowered. Slowly he put one foot out, taking a step toward one of the many cardboard 'buildings' filling the space.

But she never saw his foot hit the ground.

Because everything went black.

****

"CALM DOWN." ZEKE'S voice was flat. "If you kick me in the nuts again, Rucker, I swear to God—"

"She can kick your nuts as many times as she fucking wants."

The black bag covering her head whipped away, sending her hair into her face. She shook her head, clearing her view of Shawn's scowling face. There was a dark spot on his shoulder where she'd watched Eli bandage him two days ago. "You hurt your shoulder."

"I'm fine." Shawn glared at Zeke. "What in the fuck are you thinking?"

Zeke stepped behind her. "Hold still."

Heidi jumped as the zip ties binding her wrists snapped free. She pulled her hands in front of her body and rubbed her left wrist. Zeke limped a little as he walked around the back of the chair where Shawn sat.

Shawn's eyes moved around the room, locking onto the men surrounding them.

"Come on, Shawn. I can't cut you free if you're going to be a pain in the ass." Zeke looked to Heidi. "Tell him to calm down so he doesn't hurt himself any more."

She was definitely not telling him that. It wouldn't do any good. "Why are we here, Zeke?"

"You're here because you are too loose of a cannon to leave on your own." A lean man who looked to be her dad's age strode into the empty room. He wore the same gear Shawn and the rest of the teams put on when they went out, only his was all black, just like the other men in the room with them. He tipped his head to Zeke.

Zeke cut through the tie on Shawn's wrist. The man immediately held his right hand out. "I assume you're Shawn."

Shawn eyed the man's offered hand but didn't take it. "Who the fuck are you?"

"That is irrelevant information." He turned to Heidi, his hand still outstretched. "And you must be Heidi Rucker."

She glanced Shawn's way before taking the man's hand in a shake. "Why are we here?"

The man chuckled. "You are here because as we anticipated, you got yourself caught up in something that could have ended up with you dead."

"What do you mean 'as you anticipated'?"

The man's smile was soft and his eyes were surprisingly warm for a kidnapper. "We've been keeping an eye on you for years, Heidi. You were too smart for your own good." He pointed at her. "And too focused." He turned his eyes toward

Shawn. "This one didn't even go to her prom. Stayed home lurking around the internet, trying to get into places she shouldn't."

Why did he have to come for her like that? "I didn't just *try*." Heidi lifted her brows. "I succeeded."

"And that is exactly what landed you here." The man crossed his arms. "I always figured we'd meet at some point." He sized Shawn up. "I'm glad to see you made wise choices in who you associate with."

That was an interesting statement. "You are on Alaskan Security's side then."

"There's no sides in this, Heidi." The man started walking away, headed back toward the door he entered the room through. "Only manageable and unmanageable." He glanced her way over one shoulder. "Come on."

Heidi was up and out of her seat before her next heartbeat, ready to follow this man to whatever discovery he had for her.

Shawn caught her arm, pulling her close. "You can't just follow him, Kitten."

She tipped her head back to meet Shawn's eyes. "But he knows what's going on."

"Or, he's luring you someplace he can murder you."

Heidi scanned the room. "This seems like a convenient enough spot and he didn't kill me here."

"Yet." Shawn wrapped one arm around her back, like he would be able to fight off a roomful of men who appeared to be just as well-trained as he was.

It was sweet.

"So you are worried they took us from one location, drove us all the way to this location, and now they're dragging out our murders when they could have killed us a hundred times already?"

"No one's getting killed today." Zeke moved in behind them. "None of us anyway." He tipped his head toward the door where the unknown man was still waiting.

Shawn turned his glare to Zeke. Heidi almost took a step back, would have if Shawn wasn't holding her so tight. She peeked at Zeke over Shawn's shoulder. "*You* might die."

Zeke shook his head. "Not a smart choice, man. I could have left you there and taken just her. Would that have made you any happier?"

Shawn's arm pulled her closer. "I'd have killed you for that."

"You might have tried." Zeke pointed to the open doors. "They need her. Take her in there."

Heidi's eyes followed Zeke's pointed finger, leaning as much as she could, trying to get a glimpse of what laid in the room beyond. "Who are they?"

"You know who they are, Rucker. That's why you're here."

Heidi lifted her eyes to Shawn as she pushed against him, forcing her feet forward.

"I don't like this." His dark gaze moved to the open door.

"I know." She kept dragging him along. "We should do it anyway."

Finally Shawn's feet moved. His arm stayed clamped around her and his eyes narrowed on the men around them, but he walked toward the door, shoulders back, gaze sharp.

Heidi leaned back to where Zeke followed behind them. "You could have told me it was you. I wouldn't have kept trying to kick you in the dick."

"You better have kept trying." Shawn stepped through the door first, holding her back with his arm as he looked around the darkened space. After a few sweeps of his eyes he went all the way in and she finally got her first real look at what GHOST was.

"Holy shit." Heidi couldn't stop craning her neck as she took in the huge space around them. "Who are all these people?"

"That is classified." The man walked along the aisle way that circled the large room. "Information even you can't find."

Desks lined the space, each with a huge monitor anchored to the wall in front of it. At least twenty people sat at the desks. Most wore headsets as they worked, staring at screens filled with windows of coded information. A large u-shaped desk sat in the center of the room. Small monitors inlaid into the desk mirrored the screens filling the walls.

The man guiding them went to the desk and scanned the monitors. "You created quite the mess for us, Heidi."

"I did?"

He pressed his lips together and gave a single nod. "You exposed a whole list of hackers when you sent them our way." He straightened and turned to her. "And not all of them made the same choice you did."

"The same choice about what?" It was hard to pay complete attention to the conversation with so much happening around her. She wanted to run from screen to screen. See what they were doing. Where they were.

What they were finding.

The man's expression became serious. "About who to align with."

Heidi's attention snapped to him. "The list of handles. They made the wrong choice."

"That's correct." He crossed his arms. "We were hoping you could be left on your own, but it quickly became apparent your connections spanned farther than we realized."

Heidi straightened. "Thank you."

"We need you to call off the dogs." The man turned the chair at the desk, spinning it until the seat faced her way.

"What about the list of people you sent me? Are they still," she paused, trying to find a good way to ask a question she wasn't sure she wanted the answer to, "an issue?"

"A few of them are." He pushed the chair closer to her. "The rest will be dealt with."

"You're going to kill them?" Heidi eyed the chair.

She wanted to sit in it. Be a part of something like this, even if it was only for a minute.

But Shawn was right. She had to be careful.

"Our job is to eliminate issues, Heidi." He moved the chair from side to side. "And if you don't do this we will have more issues to deal with."

Heidi eased back against the solid wall of Shawn's chest. "Am I an issue?"

"If you were an issue you would have already been dealt with." The man held her gaze. "We would prefer to establish a working relationship with you. Your skills are considerable, and having an additional contact within a partner company will benefit us both."

"Alaskan Security is a partner company?"

"That is our plan. If you do this it will take us one step closer to making that a possibility."

She tipped her head to look to Shawn.

He gave her an almost imperceptible nod.

She let out a slow breath, a bite of nervous excitement twinging in her belly. "Okay." Heidi walked straight to the chair and sat down. "How secure is your server?"

"You haven't been in it."

She smiled. "Yet." Heidi's hands hovered over the keyboard. "That's why I'm really here, isn't it?"

The man snorted. "You should be careful, Heidi. You might be too smart for your own good."

"Or too smart for your own good." She rested her fingertips along the keys, savoring the moment.

She was in a secret government location, getting ready to do secret government work. She almost laughed.

Almost bounced in her seat.

Heidi shifted a little in the chair. She leaned back. Then sat up.

"Is something wrong?"

"Can you write down what kind of chair this is? I like it." Heidi grinned at the man. "I need a new office chair."

"You could always come work here. With us."

Her breath caught at the offer. A month ago she would have taken him up on it. Snapped up the opportunity to be one of them.

The people who chased hackers.

And it would have been a terrible thing. "I'm really happy where I am." She smiled. "Thanks for the offer, though."

"I imagine we'll be working together one way or another." The man pointed to the main screen in the center of the desk. "That is the monitor connected to your computer."

"I got it." Heidi waved him off as she opened a window and navigated to one of the chat rooms.

"This needs to be handled in a way that won't raise suspicions or interest."

Heidi turned to the man, opening her eyes wide. "What? You don't just want me to go in and say 'Never mind. I found them.'?"

The man's gaze lifted to Zeke.

Zeke crossed his arms over his broad chest. "Told you."

Heidi went back to the computer wiggling her fingers in the air over the keyboard, ready to find everyone she'd contacted and ease them away.

Her gaze lifted to stare at the space in front of her.

sunshineandbutterflies

"It's you." She turned to the man. "Sunshineandbutterflies is you."

The man's mouth eased into an almost smile.

She looked around the room. "We're in the warehouse Zeke was at." Heidi rubbed her lips together as the last bit of the puzzle came together. "Subhex Solar. Butterflies are in the Subphylum Hexapoda classification of insects. Sunshine and butterflies."

The man let out a low chuckle as his eyes dropped to the ground between them. "I've got to say I'm glad you're not against us, Heidi."

She shrugged. "Just hope there aren't any more bored girls with nothing better to do than research literally anything they can find on the internet." Heidi spun her seat back toward the computer. "Can I get some ice water?"

She smiled as the whole room turned to stare at the man behind her.

He cleared his throat. "Sure."

CHAPTER 22

HE WAS GOING to kill Zeke.

Bury the bastard in a hole—

No.

He was going to string him up from—

No.

He was going to dump his carcass in the frozen water of Lake—

"I need you to stop being so pissed off." Heidi spun in her chair to look at him. "It's distracting." She immediately turned back to the computer in front of her.

A computer located in a warehouse outside Fairbanks, Alaska that was currently occupied by one of the government's most secretive of divisions.

Shawn wiped one hand down his face, the ache in his shoulder a reminder that at least he fought for her. Did everything in his power to protect her from—

From fucking Zeke.

Who he was going to kill.

"We can clean that up for you." The man who was clearly in charge eyed him from where he stood on the other side of Heidi, watching her every move, occasionally nodding in approval.

Shawn stared him down. "I'm fine."

"Suit yourself." The man turned back to watch what Heidi was doing. "But suffering is only for men out to prove something."

"I am out to prove something." He didn't give two shits what this man thought of him.

Zeke stood on the other side of Heidi. "She's safer here than she is at Alaskan Security."

Shawn's blood ran cold. "What the fuck does that mean?"

"Means someone's out to take down your company." The man shoved a toothpick in between his teeth. "They've been dicking around with you guys for months, watching you scramble." The man moved the pick to his cheek with a swipe of his tongue. He thumbed Heidi's way. "But then you stumbled onto this one and it pissed them the hell off."

Heidi's head jumped up. "Why?"

The man turned, leaning back against the desk. "Cause they wanted you." He pointed to Shawn. "Instead this guy got you, and we had to get involved so the whole thing didn't go to shit."

"You mean you got involved to make sure we were still there to do your dirty work." This guy could paint it however he wanted, but GHOST was just worried about their own best interests.

"You think your back doesn't get scratched in return?" He lifted his brows at Shawn. "Because it does."

Zeke sighed. "Come on." He tipped his head toward a set of doors. "I'll take you to the clinic for a new bandage."

"I don't want a new bandage. I want Heidi to finish so we can get the fuck out of here."

"This is going to take a while." Heidi turned in her chair. "I have to wait until everyone responds to me and then make it seem like it's not a big deal after all." Her eyes rested on his shoulder. "I'll be fine." She gave him a smile. "I promise."

Shawn glared around the room.

No one was paying any attention to Heidi.

Maybe getting Zeke alone wouldn't be such a bad thing.

"If you need me—"

"If I need you I will start screaming at the top of my lungs and I won't stop until you get here." She smiled at him again. "Go."

Shawn leaned down, holding her chin in one hand as he pressed a kiss to her lips. Her mouth smiled against his. "I'll be fine. I promise."

He walked out of the room, checking back over his shoulder every few steps. He was almost at the door when she finally turned his way, her dimpled smile joined by a wink.

"If she's not fine you can shoot me." Zeke led him down a long hall.

"I'm planning to shoot you anyway." Shawn followed Zeke into a brightly-lit room where a man sat on a stool. The setup was remarkably similar to Eli's.

"He needs his shoulder rebandaged." Zeke leaned against the wall while Shawn shucked his shirt and let the doctor bandage him up.

"You could have just said she needed to come here." He winced as the doctor flushed out the seeping wound.

"And you would have let that happen?" Zeke snorted. "No fucking way. Then I never would have gotten her out of there."

"You didn't need to get her out of there." All this just pulled Heidi deeper than he thought possible into a war he still didn't fully understand. "She didn't need to be a part of this."

"She's already a part of this." Zeke pulled out his phone, glancing at the screen before tucking it into his pocket. "And if she didn't do this she was going to be their number one target."

"They couldn't have gotten her."

"Why? Because she was at headquarters? They've managed to get in at least twice. You think it won't happen again?" Zeke lifted his brows. "Because it will. We need to finish this before one of the girls gets hurt."

"Is that what you're trying to do? Finish this?" Shawn barely waited for the tape to be in place before he stood up. "Is that why you're buddy-buddy with these people?"

Zeke didn't move as Shawn came closer. "Why I do what I do is none of your business."

"It is when you drag her into it." Shawn shoved one finger right in the center of Zeke's chest. "She's my business."

"Watch yourself, Shawn. I've had a rough fucking week and I'm not in the mood to put up with your caveman bullshit."

A week ago the comment would have hit home. Stung as it stabbed the sore spot he'd wrestled with for too long.

But this wasn't about that. "She didn't deserve for you to drag her here the way you did, and she sure as shit doesn't deserve to be used like she is right now."

"She's getting something out of it." Zeke was still leaned against the wall, cool and calm as ever. "She's getting to live her dream. Do what she never thought she would." He held Shawn's gaze. "She could do it every day."

"She said no." He tugged his shirt over his head, pulling it into place. "You heard her."

"She said no because of you." Zeke tipped his head back. "Is that what you want? To hold her back from her dreams?"

The possibility of Heidi leaving Alaskan Security sat heavy in his gut. "Fuck you, Zeke."

He walked out of the room and back down the hall, pushing through the doors and into the darkened room where over a dozen hackers sat at their computers, keeping tabs on the Heidi's of the world.

Heidi turned in her chair as he walked up behind her. She lifted a brow at him. "What's wrong, Kitten?"

"Nothing." He glanced at the screen of her computer. "Are you done?"

"For now." The man was still at her side. "She's all yours."

Shawn's eyes rested on the woman in front of him.

All yours.

It was a dangerous thought. One that would drive him to make the same mistakes he always did.

Being to overbearing. Too controlling.

To domineering.

Heidi rolled her eyes at him. "Stop freaking out." She stood up from the chair, grabbed his hand, locking their fingers together. "Come on, tough guy." She dragged him across the space toward the door to the room they started in.

She stopped just in front of the door, slowly turning. "Is this the way out?"

Zeke barked out a laugh. "Not even close, Rucker." He thumbed over one shoulder. "This way."

She lifted her brows at him. "So now I get to know the lay of the land?"

"You tryin' to convince me you don't already?"

She grinned at him. "I was willing to pretend if I had to." She pointed to where the man in charge was watching. "Thanks for the invite. You can just send me a text or something next time instead of the kidnapping thing."

The man just stared at her.

At least he wasn't the only one she never stopped surprising.

Zeke led them through the building, walking down the same hall Shawn was in earlier, to a heavy door. The lead for Shadow pushed through, heading straight for one of Alaskan Security's Rovers. "Get in."

"Please." Heidi lifted her brows at him.

Zeke paused at the driver's door. "What?"

"You've got to stop acting like such a dick. It makes everyone assume you're doing shit you shouldn't be."

"He is doing shit he shouldn't be." Just because they were walking out of that place in one piece didn't mean what happened was okay or even acceptable. "He fucking abducted two members of his own team and took them to an undisclosed location to work with a government agency he's been secretly conspiring with."

Zeke snorted. "You have no fucking clue what you're talking about." He clicked the button on the fob. "Get in the fucking car."

"No." Heidi crossed her arms over her chest. "Not until you say please."

Zeke scoffed. "Are you kidding me right now?"

"Do I look like I'm kidding?" Heidi had one hip jutted out to the side as she shot Zeke a glare.

Zeke shrugged. "Fine. You can walk back to headquarters."

Heidi continued staring him down.

The head of Shadow pointed to the Rover. "Just get in the goddamned car."

Heidi didn't respond. Just kept glaring his way.

"Fuck my life." Zeke yanked open the door. "Please get in the goddamned car."

Heidi's face split into a smile. "I'd be happy to." She opened the back door and climbed across to sit behind Zeke, leaving the door open.

Shawn got in beside her, slamming the door behind him.

Heidi snapped on her seatbelt, the smile still on her face. "What do you want to do when we get back?" She reached across to grab his hand with hers. The tone of her voice was light and easy.

As if they hadn't just discovered Zeke was as involved with GHOST as he was with Alaskan Security.

"You can't play both sides, you know that right?" He was completely focused on Zeke. "You can't pretend to have Alaskan Security's best interests and go behind our back with GHOST."

"We're not in a fucking relationship, dick." Zeke had one hand slung over the wheel, eyes on the road in front of him. "Stop acting like the jealous bastard you are."

Heidi leaned forward, shoving her head between the seats, blocking Shawn from doing the same thing. "Why do you have to say shit like that?" She reached out and flicked Zeke in the ear. "Stop being an asshole."

Zeke's hand shot up to cover the assaulted ear. "What the fuck is wrong with you? I'm trying to drive."

"You're what's wrong with me." She flicked him on the end of the nose. "You're being a dick for no reason."

"Questioning my integrity is no reason?" Zeke jerked his head away as Heidi reached for him again. "Shawn, get your woman under control."

Shawn settled back in his seat, draping one arm across the back as he watched Heidi stick up for him. "If you think that one is controllable then you haven't been paying attention."

He thought control was the key to finding security with a woman. That if he could just keep her close, keep her satisfied, then he wouldn't worry she'd find something better.

But he was wrong.

The key to finding security with a woman was finding one who was secure herself. One who saw him for what he was and wasn't afraid to stand up to him.

And this woman wasn't afraid to stand up to anyone. Present company included.

"You think just because you used to be a part of GHOST I'm going to put up with your shit?" Heidi licked her finger and wiped it down the side of Zeke's face. "You don't scare me, Zeke."

"What the fuck is wrong with you?" Zeke's hand on the wheel jerked to one side as he fought off Heidi's attack. "Every woman Pierce finds is crazier than the last."

"Maybe you make us crazy." Heidi flicked him right in the Adam's apple. "Why couldn't you just tell us what was going on? I've wasted so much damn time because of you."

The vehicle lurched to one side.

Shawn reached for Heidi. "That's enough. You're going to make him wreck."

Heidi's whole body suddenly slammed back.

"Get her down." Zeke's palm was planted in the center of her face as he pushed her into the back seat.

The edge to Zeke's voice was unmistakable. Shawn lunged at her, wrapping her body with his as the first ping of gunfire hit the back windshield. He fought with the buckle of her belt as the sound continued. "Call Dutch. Get someone out here to help us."

Zeke hesitated.

"Are you fucking kidding me?" Shawn reached for the gun in his waistband, pulling it free. "Do it now."

Zeke punched the dash console, switching on the communication unit before hitting Dutch's name. The tech coordinator for Rogue answered immediately. "Shawn?"

"We need anyone you can get at," he risked a peek over the edge of the door, looking through the heavily tinted glass, "the east end of Fairbanks on Birch Hill Road. Headed toward Steese Highway." He dropped down as a dark Charger pulled up alongside, curling around Heidi's still body as a bullet came through the side window.

"What the fuck is going on?" Harlow was less calm than Dutch was as her voice filled the interior. "Where's Heidi?"

"Just get someone out here." Zeke yanked the wheel hard, knocking against the Charger.

"Zeke?" Harlow's voice got louder. "What in the hell—"

Dutch came back through the speakers. "Rogue is moving as fast as they can. I've got a location on your GPS." The sound of his typing was barely audible over the wind whipping through the busted out windows. "ETA is fifteen minutes."

"Call GHOST." Heidi's voice was loud and strong from where he held her in place, his body blanketing hers. "Have Zeke call GHOST."

Zeke flipped out his phone, thumbing across the screen as he pressed the gas harder. "I need you two to brace yourselves." He took a sharp turn at a speed that forced Shawn to brace against both doors to avoid flying across the vehicle. "Yeah. It's Reaper. I need a team out to the open lead on Chena at the Steese bridge. Now."

"What?" Heidi tried to lift her head but Shawn pressed his hand to the back of her skull, holding it down. "Did he say the Chena River?" The pitch of her voice went higher. "What is he going to do?"

"Everything will be just fine, Kitten. I will take care of you. I promise." He leaned up to catch Zeke's eyes in the rear view mirror.

Zeke held his gaze for a second before taking another sharp turn, this one onto the Steese Highway onramp.

Shawn lifted his body from hers, hovering over her as Zeke raced down the highway, moving in and out of the sparse traffic. "Turn over, Heidi. Hang onto me and don't let go, understand?"

She immediately rolled, her body bumping against his in the small amount of space he gave her. Her blue eyes were wide and watery as they met his. "I can't swim, Shawn."

Swimming was the least of their worries, but telling her she'd freeze to death before she drowned wouldn't do any good. All he could give her was the truth. "I won't let anything happen to you."

One way or another Heidi would walk away from this.

Even if he didn't.

She sniffed but nodded.

The engine revved as Zeke floored the accelerator.

"Grab on, Kitten. It's go time." Shawn gripped the door handle near their heads and braced his foot against the other door before wrapping his free arm under the seat and holding on with everything he had as the front of the Rover jumped the barrier, sending the nose high enough into the air to clear the cement wall of the bridge, sending them over the side, falling down into the icy waters of the Chena River.

CHAPTER 23

HER STOMACH ROLLED as the SUV came to a sudden stop.

No. Not a stop.

A slow down. It was still moving.

Sinking.

"Come on, Heidi." Shawn was trying to wrestle her across the seat with one arm as the other fought the side door open against the chunks of ice and water pouring through the broken glass of the window. "I need you to move, Kitten."

She blinked at the tears clouding her vision.

"Rucker." Zeke's voice was loud and sharp, catching her attention to where his hard eyes were on her. "Move it."

She sniffed up the snot running out of her nose and nodded her head as she started working her way toward the door and the water that was rising at a rapid pace.

Not rising.

They were still sinking.

She almost couldn't feel the cold of the water, which was odd since it had to be freezing.

Shawn wrapped one arm around her body. "Time to go." He put his back against the door, grunting as he fought the weight of the river. "Just hold on and don't fight me. That's all I need you to do."

Her eyes stayed on him as they squeezed out of the small space Shawn managed to make and into the black water.

Her teeth chattered and her body shook even though she wasn't cold.

Just tired.

So very tired.

"She's going into shock." Shawn's head bobbed along the water as he fought the current moving under the sheets of ice around them.

"Rucker." Zeke moved in at her back, his hands coming to support some of her weight, lifting her higher in the water. "Keep your eyes open so this motherfucker doesn't kill me."

"I can't swim, Zeke." She met the lead of Shadow's eyes. "Am I going to drown?"

"No, but I think after this you should definitely have this asshole teach you to swim."

"Maybe we can do it at a beach." She closed her eyes at the thought of warm sand and bright sun.

"Nope." Zeke's hand pressed to her cheek. "Eyes open, Heidi."

She blinked a few times, trying to focus on his face. "You called me Heidi. That was nice." She turned to Shawn. "See. I told you he wasn't as bad as you thought."

"I'm not sure I'm ready to take it that far, Kitten." He shifted his hold on her as his head dipped a little lower in the water. "We're in a fucking frozen river."

Zeke's head snapped to one side as something fell over the side of the bridge, dangling into the water beside them. "Swim time's over, boys and girls." He grabbed the rope and held it out to Shawn. "Get her the fuck out of here."

Zeke's arm wrapped around her middle as Shawn shoved the looped edge of the rope under the water then grabbed the length of it just above his head. "Pass her over."

"Hang onto him, Heidi. Hold as tight as you can." Zeke reached out to yank the rope twice.

Heidi wrapped her arms around Shawn's neck just as they began to move, their bodies lifting from the water.

She pressed her face to Shawn's chest.

"I got you, Kitten. I promise I won't let you go."

They started to swing, making her suck in a breath.

"Breathe. We're almost there." Shawn's voice was calm and even.

"You're really good at this."

He chuckled. "Not too good considering I've been shot and almost frozen in less than seventy-two hours."

Her body was suddenly being pulled from his. Heidi held tighter, trying not to lose her grip. "I'm falling."

"Relax." Shawn was still just as calm as ever, in spite of the fact that she was sliding away from him.

A warm wall slammed into her body from behind.

"You can let go now." Shawn's freezing hands pulled at her arms, unwinding them from his neck. He grabbed the wall of heat and pulled it tighter around her before pulling her close, dragging Heidi along until she collapsed into a seat. Warm air blew around her as the cold biting her skin finally registered.

Her whole body shook. Chunks of ice were stuck in her hair and clinging to her skin. Shawn stood in front of her rubbing her arms through the blanket wrapped around her body. Someone tossed a blanket on Shawn's back but he didn't make any move to pull it around him.

"You okay?"

She blinked, squeezing her eyes shut hard, trying to clear her vision.

Men milled around the van she sat in, all of them geared up like the ones from GHOST. A line of them stood along the damaged cement barricade at the edge of the bridge, leaning to look over the side.

"Reaper's down."

306

Shawn straightened, his head turning toward the men. "What did you say?" He rushed to the edge, his towel falling to the ground as he went. He leaned over the edge for a second before turning back to face Heidi.

He held her gaze for a heartbeat.

If her heart could beat at a time like this.

"No." She stood up as Shawn grabbed the rope that pulled them to safety. "No!"

A man in black came to block her as Shawn gave her one more glance.

Then disappeared over the edge.

****

"SHE THREATENED TO burn the place down if we didn't get you here in five minutes."

Shawn ran down the hall, his legs finally working again after being nearly paralyzed from the freezing water of the Chena. "She doesn't actually have the shit to make that happen, does she?"

The member of GHOST running along with him glanced his way.

"You might want to grab a fire extinguisher." Being away from her the past hour was painful as hell, but she needed to get dry and warm and neither of those could happen in a van on a bridge.

He rushed through the door held open by another member of GHOST.

Heidi stood in the middle of the room, arms crossed over her chest. "I should kill you."

"Or," he held one hand up between them, "you could be happy to see me."

"Or," she gave him the middle finger, "you could apologize for potentially dying after you finally let me like you."

"Someone had to go in after Zeke, Kitten."

"There were ten other men there who could have gone in after him." The mask of anger on her face began to slip. "Why did you have to be the one?"

"I'd already been in the water, Heidi. He's part of my team. I can't let him go down."

Not long ago he would never have admitted he and Zeke were on the same team.

Because he didn't think they were.

"Does that mean you're not mad at him anymore?" She eyed him as he came a little closer.

"I'm definitely still mad at him." He reached out to grab a bit of her blonde hair. "You don't look too bad all geared up, Rucker."

She glanced down at the black ribbed shirt and pants that were too long. "It's all they had." Heidi's lower lip pushed out in a pout. "These pants are awful. I don't know why you wear them."

He smiled. "They definitely aren't as accessible as the ones you wear."

"Your things are all dry." The man in charge of GHOST strode in, a neatly-folded stack of clothes in his hands. He passed the pile to Heidi before turning to Shawn. He slapped him on his good shoulder. "You did well, son."

"Where's Zeke?" Shadow's lead was whisked away as soon as he got him onto the bridge, shoved into a waiting van and Shawn hadn't seen him since.

"He's being taken care of." The man looked from Shawn to Heidi. "You two successfully eliminated any doubts I had about Alaskan Security." He pointed a finger Shawn's way, wagging it. "Zeke has been pushing for this alliance for a long time and I held out." He dropped his hands to his hips. "Maybe I shouldn't have."

"I thought you already had an alliance?" It was no secret that Shadow was involved in government-connected ops. "Shadow's been doing your dirty work for years."

"Is that what you think?" The man smirked. "Shows what you know, son." He turned to Heidi. "You should fill him in on the ride home."

Her skin paled a little. "Is it safe to go back now?" Her big blue eyes darted to Shawn. "What if—"

The man rested his hands on Heidi's shoulders. "I can guarantee what happened won't happen again." He gave her a smile. "Things are about to start changing real fast, Heidi, and I'm counting on you and your team to keep up." He straightened, eyeing Shawn. "It's time to do what needs to be done."

The man turned without another word and walked from the room, leaving them alone.

"What the fuck is he talking about?"

Heidi stared at the open doorway.

"Heidi."

He waited, expecting her to answer.

"Kitten."

Her eyes were fixed, focused on nothing.

"Rucker."

She jumped a little, head snapping his way. "What?"

"What just happened?" He looked to the spot she'd been staring at before pressing one hand to her head. "Are you okay?"

She might still be in shock. Reeling from her first taste of the normal he lived.

"Oh." She pushed his hand away. "No. I'm fine. I was just thinking."

"What did he want you to fill me in on?" It had been so long since anything made sense. So long since he'd felt like things were under control.

Maybe it was almost over.

"Can you close the door so I can change?" She was already grabbing the waistband of the black pants covering her lower half.

Shawn hurried to shut them off to the hall. "You're killing me with this, Kitten."

"Shadow doesn't work for Alaskan Security. Not really." She dug through the stack of clothes, retrieving her panties before stepping into them. "They're part of GHOST." She pulled on the pale pink pants she wore when they went into the river, sighing as she situated them. "That's so much better."

Shawn stared at her. "You think Shadow is a part of GHOST?"

One side of her nose lifted. "No. They definitely are." She shucked the shapeless black shirt that did nothing to hide the perfect form beneath it. "Some of them."

"Not all?" This was like pulling freaking teeth. Painfully drawn out.

"No. Just like," Heidi's eyes lifted toward the ceiling as she strapped into her bra, "five maybe." She pulled on her shirt and socks before grabbing her shoes, holding them up. "They're still wet."

"You'll be fine." Shawn grabbed her hand. "Come on. I'm ready to get out of here."

She trailed along behind him as he practically dragged her to the door leading to the back of the lot. The man stationed there opened the door. "We've got a car waiting to take you back."

"Thanks." Shawn turned and grabbed her, one arm at her back and one at her knees, hefting her against his chest as he stepped out into the cold and snow.

Another man held the back door of a black SUV open and Shawn slid her inside before climbing in after her.

"Hello." Heidi leaned between the seats. "I'm Heidi and this is Shawn."

The man driving gave her a nod.

Heidi scoffed. "Are you serious? I'm still not allowed to know your name?"

He lifted a brow at her. "No one uses names here."

"That's weird." She eyed him.

"Says the woman who goes by *beiberlover530*."

Heidi's eyes went wide. "You know what—" Her lips curved as her gaze narrowed. "Fine. What do you go by?"

"Kraken."

She snorted, her smile flattening out almost immediately. "You're serious."

The driver continued his lifted-brow stare.

"Did they give that to you or did you choose it yourself?"

"Again," the driver shifted the SUV into reverse, "says the woman who goes by *beiberlover530*."

"I was fourteen when I picked that." Heidi leaned back against the seat. "So don't get all judgy."

Shawn wrapped one arm around her shoulders, pulling her closer. But not because he was worried about the man in the front seat and the possible thoughts running through his mind.

He just wanted to be closer to her. To take a deep breath and relax after a rough day.

Month.

And there was still more to come.

CHAPTER 24

"WHAT IN THE hell is going on?" Eva ran down the main hall, her arms stretched out. She grabbed Heidi in a full-contact hug. "I've been ready to throw up for over an hour."

Mona was the next down the hall with Harlow and Bess hot on her heels. The three women added to the hug, forming a giant clog in the main entryway.

"Can we move this somewhere else?" Shawn still sounded irritated.

Made sense considering he was still trying to wrap his brain around what was going on.

"I need to talk to Pierce." Heidi tried to get free of her team's embrace.

"Not yet." Eva held her tight. "We thought you were dead."

"I really need to talk to Pierce." She tried again to worm her way loose.

"Pierce can wait." Harlow held onto her from the back.

"But I need to tell him some things about Shadow."

Mona straightened. "What about Shadow?"

Heidi met her friend's gaze. "Some of them are also GHOST."

"Oh shit." Harlow shoved free. "Let her go." Her eyes were wide. "Are you sure?"

"Oh yeah." Heidi turned to Shawn. "Get the team leads together."

His mouth twitched like it did when he wanted to smile. "Sure thing, Captain."

She gave him a grin and a wink. "Thanks, Kitten."

Heidi turned and marched toward Pierce's office, the rest of Intel at her side. The owner of Alaskan Security stood at the large window, staring out into the snow, his hands clasped behind his back.

He turned as they walked in and the expression on his face stopped her short. She scanned him from head to toe. "Are you okay?"

"Considering I spent the past hour concerned for the safety of multiple members of my team, no. I am most certainly okay."

"Why were you worried? Rogue was there."

Pierce's dark brows lifted. "Were they."

Rogue showed up just as she was driven away from the scene, and since GHOST buckled her in around the blanket pinning her arms in place, she couldn't even put up a fight. Just had to watch in the mirror, praying she'd see Shawn come back over the side of the bridge.

"Yeah. I saw them."

"Is that so." Pierce's dark blue gaze snapped to the door as Shawn walked through. "Unfortunately, they did not update me with that information."

Heidi felt a little bad for Pierce. He was clearly losing control of his company and the men and women employed there. Hopefully what she had to tell him wouldn't make that worse. "Zeke is a member of GHOST." She kept talking as all eyes in the room fixed on her. "So are some of the other members of Shadow. It's why they always worked independently. They weren't really working for you."

Pierce's dark brows came together. "That's impossible. There were contracts and payments for services."

"They were all just so you wouldn't realize what was really going on." She tried not to smile as she spoke. No one else would find this as gratifying and exciting as she did. Definitely not Pierce. "GHOST infiltrated Shadow because they wanted to keep an eye on the company." She shrugged. "And occasionally use it to their benefit."

Pierce was quiet as he listened, one hand tucked in the pocket of his pants.

"But now they want to work together." She glanced at the women around her. "Work with us."

"Why would they want to do that?" Pierce was understandably skeptical.

"Because they need us to get rid of whoever is causing problems." She couldn't stop the smile easing onto her lips. "We can't do it without them and it seems like they can't do it without us."

Pierce's head barely turned to one side. "Do they know who is responsible for what's happening?"

Heidi dipped her head in a nod. "They do."

The whole room was silent.

Pierce took a step away from the window. "Did they share that information with you?"

"No." Heidi tried her best to get it out of the man in charge of GHOST, but he was adamant there was only one person he was willing to discuss that information with. "The man in charge of GHOST wants to meet with you."

Pierce's spine went a little straighter, his shoulders set, and the hand in his pocket came to smooth down the front of his suit. "Excellent." His head tipped to where Shawn stood right behind her. "Any ideas how we can make that happen?"

"Sounds like you should probably ask Zeke." Harlow crossed her arms over her chest, lips turning into a tight frown.

"Zeke's not here." Heidi's stomach twisted a little. The lead of Shadow was rough and abrasive, sneaky and possibly underhanded, but he made sure she went up that rope first. Stayed in the freezing water so she could get out.

"Where is he?" Mona's concern was a little unexpected.

"I don't know. He was in the water a long time. GHOST took him somewhere." Heidi turned to Shawn. "Was he okay when you got him out?"

Shawn's lips pressed tight together. "He wasn't dead."

That didn't sound promising.

"So what you're saying is at least five of my men were never my men, the lead of Shadow actually works for GHOST, and his current status is unknown." Pierce turned back to the window. "Fucking spectacular."

****

"SO WHAT DO we do now?" Eva sat at her desk staring straight ahead. "Do we just sit here and wait?"

"Nope." Heidi linked her computer up with the largest screen on the front wall. "These are the names Harlow and I tracked down to go with the handles from Tod's chest." She scanned the sheet. "Minus the one that was GHOST."

"They put their own handle down?" Mona's brows came together as she looked from the list to the paper where she was copying the names down.

"It was a test." Heidi moved around the items scattered across her desk, organizing them into piles and dropping her pens and pencils into place. "They wanted to see if I could figure it out."

"Thank God you did or we'd be screwed." Harlow was still clearly pissed at the way this was all unfolding. Probably because if GHOST had stepped in a little sooner she wouldn't have ended up almost dead.

Again.

"I don't think so." Heidi opened her personal computer, pulling up the login screen for the chat rooms she now had to monitor like her life depended on it.

Maybe not hers, but someone's.

"I think they were hoping we would figure it out on our own and they wouldn't have to get involved since that's a risky move for them." Heidi yawned, the events of the day catching up with her at a record pace. "They realized we simply didn't have enough pieces to do that." Heidi scanned the lines of text. "And honestly I'm not sure they had enough pieces either."

Harlow pushed both hands into her hair, fingers pressing into her skull.

"You okay?" Heidi didn't want to stress Harlow out anymore than she already was, but they were so close to finishing this.

"Headache." Harlow rolled her head, stretching her neck from side to side before sitting straight in her seat, jaw set, expression focused. "Let's get this shit handled."

"How do we feel about integrating the rest of the team?" Mona looked around the room. "I think at this point it's a necessary evil."

"I agree." Harlow turned to her personal computer. "I say bring them in as soon as possible. We need all hands on deck."

Heidi glanced up as Dutch came through the door, pushing an office chair in front of him. "What in the hell is that?"

"Seems like you made friends in high places, Rucker." He brought the chair straight to her. "They sent you a present."

Heidi jumped out of her old chair, shoving it across the room before plopping down into the new one and relaxing back, letting out a long sigh. "This is so much better."

"I hate you a little right now." Eva stuck her lip out in a mock pout. "I mean, I know you almost froze to death to get it, but it might be worth it."

"There's more in the entryway." Dutch backed toward the door. "They sent enough for everyone."

Heidi reached under the seat, working the lever to get the seat adjusted to the right height. "It's a peace offering."

Eva was already out of her seat and rushing to the door. "They should probably send us cookies or something too. Especially since they know who's behind all this bullshit and just let it keep happening."

"That's the government way." Heidi finally found the perfect setting for her chair. "Stand back and watch the shit storm until it hits too close."

"I'd say someone hiring a whole bunch of hackers and joining them together would definitely affect them." She turned to Heidi. "You think these people would all be willing to do things against the government?"

"Maybe." These were people she'd known for years. People who got off on proving what they were capable of. "Some of them would do it just for fun."

"So we've got someone hiring people and causing problems for the government." Bess looked from the list of names to the white board on the wall. "Someone who wants Alaskan Security to fold." She tapped her pen against the top of her desk, turning it end over end. "Someone with lots of money and lots of connections."

"Someone like Pierce." Mona's brows came together. "But not like Pierce."

Eva came rushing back in, hauling two chairs as she did. She pushed one Mona's way and the other Bessie's before disappearing again.

"She is really excited about those chairs." Heidi watched as Eva sprinted down the hall, running right past a familiar face. "Oh shit. He's here." Heidi lifted one hand in a wave as the head of GHOST caught her stare.

Mona, Bess, and Harlow all jumped up and rushed to stand around her.

"He looks important, doesn't he?" Bess whispered it as if the man could hear them.

"He is, I think." Heidi watched as Pierce led the man to his office just as Eva sprinted past him with two more chairs, not even giving him a second glance.

"At least she didn't run him over." Harlow snorted. "Not that I wouldn't have paid to see that happen."

Eva slowed down as she came through the door, turning to look back over her shoulder. "What are you looking at?"

"You ran right past the guy from GHOST." Heidi pointed as he disappeared into Pierce's office.

"Harlow was hoping you'd take him out by accident."

"I would have done it on purpose." Eva huffed out a breath as Pierce's door shut. "Maybe I'll try when he comes back out."

"I'm guessing he won't help us if we assault him." Mona crossed her arms over her chest. "How long do you think that meeting will take?"

"Hopefully not too long. I'm ready to get this freaking show on the road." Heidi's heart skipped a beat as Pierce's door opened again. "That was quick."

Pierce walked along with the man as they headed toward the front entryway. She craned her body as they turned the corner and moved out of sight. "Pull up the camera."

"On it." Harlow hurried back to her desk and a minute later the feeds from the cameras at the front of the building displayed on the screens.

"Is he leaving with them?" Heidi stood up as Pierce stepped into an SUV similar to the one that brought her and Shawn back a short time ago. "Shit."

"Where are they taking him?" Mona walked toward the screens. "You don't think…" She spun to face Heidi. "You don't think they will hurt him, do you?"

"I mean, they didn't hurt me and Shawn." She watched the SUV pull away, her hopes of a speedy resolution scattering with each passing second. "I thought we were about to find out who was behind all this." Heidi fell into her chair. "What the hell, Pierce?"

Harlow rubbed her eyes. "I'm so tired of this."

Dutch walked into the room, Wade, Brock and Shawn behind him. "Come on, Darling. I think you need some sleep."

Harlow pointed to the screens. "The guy from GHOST just took Pierce."

"He didn't take Pierce. Pierce asked to go." Dutch held his hand out. "Come on. You need to be rested and ready because tomorrow is a big day."

Heidi glanced at Shawn as he came toward her. "Is that right?"

His lips barely twitched. "Seems like."

Heidi turned to the women of Intel. Women who accepted her just as she was.

Maybe even liked her better for it.

And tomorrow they would end this. Together.

****

"HE WANTED TO see Zeke." Shawn laid across the bed, watching as she paced. "That's all, Kitten. He wanted proof Zeke was still alive and being properly taken care of."

Heidi had been through a lot today. More than most people go through in a lifetime, crammed into a few, traumatizing hours. He expected her to collapse of exhaustion, but instead she was going in the opposite direction.

The woman was wound up.

"Oh." She stopped to look his way. "I guess that makes sense." She frowned. "Is he going to let us know as soon as he finds out?"

"Sounds like you're worried about Zeke."

She gave him a tight smile. "Maybe a little."

Something like that would have sent him over the edge not long ago. Make him want to prove how much more worthy he was of her worry than Zeke could ever be.

How much more he could give her.

And it still did that, but for some reason the urge was easier not to act on. He could breathe through it a little. Long enough to remember who he was dealing with.

How different the woman in front of him was than the one who broke him.

"The vein in your head is throbbing." Heidi's chin tucked in. "Are you going to stroke out?"

"No." He took a deep breath. "I'm fine."

"You don't look fine." Heidi finally stood still, her blue eyes fixed on him.

"Come here."

Her lips tipped up on one side. "You didn't say please."

"I don't have to say please." He lifted one finger, crooking it her way. "Come here now."

She immediately walked his way. When Heidi was close enough he grabbed her tight, pulling her down and rolling her soft body under his. "Thank you."

She knew what he needed, when he needed it.

He ran his nose along the side of hers. "I want you to move in here, with me."

"Are you going to make me roll all my clothes up when I put them away?"

"I won't ever make you do anything, Kitten." He inhaled against her skin, relaxing as her

323

closeness calmed him, satiated the beast he fought.

And she tamed.

Heidi smiled up at him. "Okay."

****

Printed in Great Britain
by Amazon